In His
Secret Life

Praise for Mel Bossa

Split

"This amazing first novel was one of the best new romances of 2011."—*Lambda Literary*

"If you only read one romance this year, make sure this is the one. Its ambition is only exceeded by its flawless execution." —*Out in Print*

Franky Gets Real

"Blending the melodrama of the 1983 movie *The Big Chill* with the unsettling drunken confessions of a high school reunion, Bossa has crafted a textured novel that captures the drama of complex, realistic characters confronting the secrets and lies that threaten to fracture their friendship."—*Book Marks*

"We're crazy for young author Mel Bossa. She's got a distinctive voice and a terrific story-telling gift."—*TLA GAY.com*

Into the Flames

"Bossa has created a masterpiece of romance writing."—*Lambda Literary*

"Absolutely riveting in its pacing and focus. Much recommended. Five stars out of five."—*Echo* Magazine

By the Author

Split

Suite Nineteen

Franky Gets Real

Into the Flames

In His Secret Life

Visit us at www.boldstrokesbooks.com

IN HIS SECRET LIFE

by

Mel Bossa

A Division of Bold Strokes Books

2013

Credits
Editor: Greg Herren and Stacia Seaman
Production Design: Stacia Seaman
Cover Art by Daniel Zmigrodzki (trachenberg@gmail.com)
Cover Design by Sheri (graphicartist2020@hotmail.com)

Acknowledgments

Thank you to Stacia Seaman and Greg Herren for their editorial expertise. Thank you to everyone at Bold Strokes Books for continuing to strive for the best. I am very grateful to those who support my work. I extend a very special thanks to those who still read books—in whatever form the books may come.

This story was inspired by a Leonard Cohen song.

PART ONE

CHAPTER ONE

S unday morning, and I sat in my living room, watching Montreal's local news on mute. I'd woken up with a parched mouth an hour ago and crept to the kitchen for a tall glass of water. Since then, I hadn't been able to go back to sleep. After two years of being single, sharing my bed with another warm body made me self-conscious. I never knew how to position my limbs. I'd end up on my back, with my hands tucked under my armpits, listening to the unfamiliar sounds the stranger at my side made in his sleep.

I heard a thump and looked over at my bedroom door. Maxime, the guy I'd taken home last night, was still asleep in my bed.

Last night, on the dance floor, he'd caught my wandering eye. In his terrible, but trendy Jean-Paul Gaultier navy striped shirt, he looked a little pathetic yet cute as a lamb in a room full of wolves. The night had been wearing thin by then, and I'd been in a rut in the last weeks, so I'd gulped down the rest of my drink for courage and pulled him close. By some miracle, he hadn't refused me. Just smiled and held me tight. He was much cuter than me. Younger, too. I was turning thirty soon, so anyone under the age of twenty-five was *much* younger.

"Bonjour."

I turned to see him standing in my bedroom doorway. "Hello," I said, moving to get up. He barely looked eighteen. I needed to start asking for these guys' ID pretty soon or I'd get myself into some trouble. "How do you feel?"

He was dressed already, clearly uncomfortable. *"Ça va?"* he asked, not looking at me, but at the front door. His blond hair stood up and his face bore an imprint of the sheets. I remembered our secret touches in the cab's backseat last night, the way we'd stumbled through my apartment, both of us too drunk for good sex, and now wanted to give it another try. Last night, we'd rolled around in my sheets, trying to make something out of nothing. Trying to chase the loneliness away.

"I have to go," Maxime said in a thick French accent. I'd forgotten how sexy he sounded. "My grandmother likes to brunch me."

"You mean you're having brunch with your grandmother."

"Oui." He made a move for the door.

So this was it, then. I rose. "Would you like some coffee before I call you a—"

"Non, non." He waved away my offer, springing for his running shoes. *"Merci."*

Thank you? Had I been *that* bad a lover last night?

"I will message you in the phone," he said, his cheeks darkening through his wispy blond stubble. He was taller than I remembered. Bonier, too—but more handsome than I'd been able to tell. He had an intelligent face. Beautiful blue eyes.

Yes, and sadly, he was leaving…unless I turned this thing around. It was Sunday, and God, I hated being alone on Sundays. Gave me the jitters. "Hello," I said, holding out my hand to him. "I'm Allan Waterhouse, and I think we've met before." I winked playfully.

His handshake was limp, but he did smile a little. "Hello, yes," he muttered, sticking his hand under his arm, dodging every one of my looks. "I have a memory."

"I think you mean that you remember. Stay a little while." I touched his arm, but he turned around, shaking his head. "But it's so early for brunch." I was steadily going from charming to *needy*. "Have a cup of coffee at least."

He finally met my eyes. His were phenomenal. What was it about blue eyes? "I have an apology." He raised his eyebrows and opened his hands, offering me only emptiness.

I still had a few crumbs of my pride left. "Okay then, good-bye." I opened the door for him and we both looked outside. It was a crisp, clean blue morning. A perfect May day beckoning us. So many things to do, and why should we have to do any of them alone? "Can I have your number?" I spotted my phone next to my keys on the entrance table. "Maybe later, when you're done with—"

"My grandmother, no." Maxime shook his head, looking at me with a mixture of pity and remorse. "I eat my boyfriend."

Ah, of course. The infamous boyfriend excuse.

"You're having brunch *with* your boyfriend," I corrected him, looking down at my cell phone. How many numbers had I punched into this thing in the last two years, since Anthony and I had split up? So many. Too many.

"You're good and nice," Maxime whispered into my ear. "Very nice."

I decided he meant nice as in *crazy sexy*. "I'll see you soon, then," I said, knowing that was a lie as well.

❖

Upstairs, Fay was running up and down the hall, making my ceiling thump.

Good, she was awake. I finally had something to keep me busy.

Maxime had left an hour ago. I'd tried taking a nap in front of the TV, bored out of my mind but too tired to sleep.

Not bothering with my slippers or shoes, I sauntered up the wrought iron staircase connecting my sister's apartment to mine. Six years ago, Anthony and I had bought this duplex in hopes of drawing in a third income. When he'd left me for Lucas the man slut, I'd emotionally blackmailed Anthony into signing the property over to me. That done, I'd moved my sister and my niece Fay upstairs. I charged my sister ridiculously cheap rent, which allowed her to actually live instead of survive. She was a single mom, but she had me to count on. I was Fay's godfather, and not a day went by when the three of us didn't see or speak to each other.

At their door, I looked through the glass pane and saw my niece run up.

"Uncle Allan, look at this," she said, pulling me in. "I can hit her straight in the head." She ran back to the end of the hall where she picked up her favorite doll—the one I'd given her at her seventh birthday, in February—and propped the blond baby girl up against a pillow. She ran back to me and nodded seriously. "Ready?"

I shut the door behind us and returned her serious look. "Go."

She rolled a rubber ball between her little fingers and crouched down. "Right between the eyes, you'll see."

"I'm watching."

Fay threw the rubber ball with striking precision and hit the doll in the face, knocking it flat on its back. She jumped up and clapped her hands. "It's ten times now. That's my record."

"Impressive."

Fay wasn't a violent child. She just liked aiming at things. She wanted to be a cop. And my sister was a vegetarian florist who couldn't even kill a spider in her shower. Go figure.

I tousled her hair. "Your mom still asleep?"

Fay ran to the kitchen. "I want the Nutella pancakes."

"Want?" I followed her into the messy kitchen. Last night's dishes were in the sink and bills were scattered all over the table. I stuffed the utility bill in my hooded sweater pocket. I'd take care of it this week. "Let's clean up first, okay?"

Fay looked at me as if I'd spoken to her in a foreign tongue.

"Come on, your mom needs a little help."

"Hell yes, I do." Elsie yawned, dragging her bare feet into the kitchen. "And I need a cup of coffee, too." She walked in and dropped a kiss on my cheek. "How was your night?"

I pulled a face. "David and Kaliq fought all night and I had to play mediator. Then Kaliq disappeared and David had a breakdown on the curb." I poured some water into the coffee machine. "When David finally left, I went back up to the shooter bar…and, you know." I shot Fay a look, but she was engrossed in her morning cartoons.

Elsie gave me the coffee can. "Cute?"

"So, so cute."

"It was nice?"

"I think so."

"He's gone?"

"Yep."

She squeezed my arm. "His loss."

My sister was my biggest fan. And of course, that was the problem with my love life. I didn't want my fan club to consist of two women I was genetically related to. "He was French anyway," I said, turning the machine on. "And kind of skinny."

"You're so picky."

"And you're not?"

"Well, I think those days are over, my dear boy. I met someone yesterday. A *guy*. At the store. He just waltzed in looking for chrysanthemums for his boss's birthday and…oh my God, we hit it off like crazy—".

"Really?" Elsie's bad luck with men was legendary.

She got some cups out of the cupboard and moved in closer, careful lest Fay hear. In hurried words, she told me his name was Dayton and he was a math teacher. But he wasn't one of *those* math teachers. No, he was built like an athlete and had piercing gray-blue eyes. Wonderful teeth. Good hair. Blondish. Tall. Very, *very* tall. With this voice. Oh, a voice made for movies. And he had broad shoulders and such a wicked sense of humor. He smiled like he was on drugs all the time, but he really wasn't, see, because he was a teacher and he *loved* kids. He didn't have any himself, though he wanted to…well, eventually. Not like they'd *actually* mentioned kids. Or maybe they had, but—

"Whoa, slow down." I laughed.

Elsie didn't date much. When she did, she always ended up hurt or disappointed. Fay's father had run off during her pregnancy, but she'd never been bitter about it. She was a wonderful woman, and I couldn't understand why she'd been single all these years.

"You know," she said, "we just talked. Eye to eye. Just talked and laughed for thirty minutes." She glanced over at Fay and her face grew serious. "I'm seeing him tonight. Can you take her out to dinner?"

"This *her* here?" I pulled out a chair and fell back into it. "I don't know." I pretended to weigh my options. But soon, Elsie came up behind me and wrapped her arms around my neck, trapping me in her famous chokehold. Ever since we were kids, she'd gotten what she wanted by strangulation. "Go for his belly," she egged Fay on, and I knew I was done for. Fay's little fingers scratched and pulled at my sides and no matter how much I howled, they did not let me go.

Chapter Two

Elsie crept out of my bedroom, tiptoeing to the couch. "Sure you don't mind keeping her here for the night?" It was eleven p.m. and my sister had just returned from her date. She sat next to me now, turning her cup of ginger tea in her hands. "Your futon is so uncomfortable. You won't sleep well."

"It's late. Fay has school tomorrow. Don't wanna wake her up." I knocked my cup on Elsie's. "So, come on, I'm dying here. How did it go?" I was ready to deliver the pep talk I'd prepared in case the date had been rotten. She'd had many of those. As a matter of fact, so had I. We'd laugh about it, her and I. Called it the *Waterhouse curse*. Nice people always finished last, we liked to tell each other. Maybe that was true. Doing the right thing sure didn't seem to pay off these days.

"Allan, there wasn't one awkward moment during the whole night. It was like magic. He told me I was beautiful seven times throughout the evening. *Seven*. I counted them."

I sipped my tea. "I see… rundown time."

"Go for it."

I set my cup down and faced her. "Smoker?"

"No."

"Criminal record?"

"Can't be a teacher if you have one."

"Car?"

"Not electric, but hybrid."

"Bad breath?"

"He was chewing mint gum when I showed up."

"Cologne?"

"Not sure, but it might be Davidoff's Adventure."

"Hmm, one of my favorites. Apartment or house?"

"Condo."

"Cleanliness of the premises? On a scale of one to ten."

"Nine." She bit her lip. "Okay, *five*, but the bathroom was spotless."

"We now come to the final question."

"Hit me."

"He's beautiful, athletic, childless, smells great, owns a hybrid car and a condo. *And* he doesn't smoke." I cocked a brow. "Sounds gay to me."

"I knew you'd say that. No, Allan, he's straight. Look, women know about these things. Trust me, he's straight. *But* his brother, on the other hand, *is* gay. And check this out. His name is Dali. Like the painter. Their mom is quite the character, Dayton says. He and his siblings all have unique kind of names."

"I see."

"Anyway, I saw a picture of Dali. He's like Gael Garcia's spitting image. You know, the guy from *Mal Education*. That movie you loved."

"The brother."

"Yes, and he's *single*."

"The gay brother who looks like Gael Garcia and whose name is Dali."

"I know it sounds a little out there."

"A little?"

She stared at me from over the brim of her cup. "Can you imagine how cool that would be? You and me, dating brothers?"

I grimaced, blinking the very thought away. "No, thank you."

"I'm seeing him again tomorrow."

"What about Fay?"

"It's okay. We're just having lunch. She'll be in school."

"You won't rush into this?"

"What do you take me for?"

She was right. She'd never put her needs in front of her daughter's. Ever. "I've just never seen you like this, that's all."

"Well, you haven't seen *him*. Believe me, when you do, then you'll understand."

CHAPTER THREE

Saturday night all over again.

I was at the main bar, trying not to watch David and Kaliq make out on the dance floor. It was nearing one a.m., and I was well on my way to being drunk again. It had been a hectic week at work. Not that being a legal clerk was anything close to exciting, but some weeks were tougher than others.

On nights like these, I missed Anthony. Or maybe I missed being in a relationship. More and more of my friends were pairing up, leaving me with David and Kaliq, who I suspected felt obliged to take me out on Saturdays. Yes, they'd become my Big Gay Brother mentors.

Was I feeling gloomy because my sister had met someone? Elsie had become completely engrossed with this new affair. That's all she could talk about, and of course, I understood.

Of course I did.

But part of me couldn't help wondering if I was going to end up the old queer uncle Fay would visit every Sunday. The old man who spends his time thinking about his youth with regret.

"Jeez, Allan, cheer up." David bumped my shoulder with his and faked a smile. He was just as depressed as I was, but he'd popped a pill or two to perk up. "You look like you're shopping for a noose."

"Aren't you sick of this club?" I said as a guy shouldering himself to the bar pushed me without even a slight apology.

"Oh, come on, let's not have this conversation." Tonight, David wore his tight Prada jeans and it looked like he might split the seams. He'd gained weight because he and Kaliq had been having problems.

While Kaliq turned to music and long walks to work it out, David turned to Häagen-Dazs triple fudge ice cream. The two of them were quite the pair on a good day, but on a bad day they were worse than Sid and Nancy. There was too much possession and aggression in their relationship. One of them would eventually throw the other out the window if they didn't tone it down in the coming years.

"Allan, you have to learn to let go—"

"Fine. All right. Let's just stand here and watch a whole generation's soul be eaten alive by phoniness and cowardice."

David hung his head, smiling thinly.

"I'm gonna go walk around," I continued, "until I find some random guy whose despair matches my own."

"What are you doing here, anyway?" David stopped me. "I mean, why do you come here every weekend? You obviously hate it. This isn't your scene."

I just looked at him.

"Allan, go home. Go online. Find a nice man and marry him."

I glanced around the club, seeing the same faces I'd seen last week. And the week before. There was Patrick. I'd slept with him in March. And Kevin. We'd gone up north for a weekend this summer. He was bipolar. And over there was Julian. I'd chased him all winter only to find out he was in love with the barman and didn't even know I existed.

All these men. Chests. Asses. Names. Cocks. My lovers were a never-ending string of bodies with an interchangeable face.

"Here." I pushed my drink in David's hand. "I'll call you tomorrow."

He saluted me and bowed. "That's my boy."

I skipped down the steps and walked through the mess of couples on the dance floor and right out the front door.

The night was warm, so I decided to walk home.

❖

My phone had run out of power half an hour ago, so I walked in silence, my headphones hanging around my neck. I was tired but sober, and somehow, the sounds of the street didn't reach me. I felt alone, yet was surrounded. Although the sidewalks were still bustling with people, I was detached from them all, completely unseen and unimportant. An average man with ordinary features, that's what I was, and until you got to know me, saw me smile, or heard my thoughts, you would never know what I had to offer. People were so busy looking down into their phone that I could have been Jason Lewis wearing nothing but a bottle of vodka and still go unnoticed.

As I walked back from the club, I turned an inner eye to my soul. Was I truly done with clubbing? Finished with the meat market? And what would I do now if I wanted to meet men? Go online? No, that wasn't for me. What, would I randomly bump into the man of my life at the grocery store? Might as well believe in the Easter Bunny.

I was going to be single for the rest of my life.

I turned the corner of my street and walked through the park I usually took Fay to on Friday evenings. The swing set was empty. The night was still.

As I came up to my home, I heard my sister calling down to me.

She sat on the second-floor balcony with a man I presumed was Dayton. They had a single candle burning, its flame flickering on the table between them. "What are you doing home so early?" She leaned over the railing. "Is everything okay?"

I stood below, looking up at them, trying to see his face. He looked handsome from down here, but I was dying to see him up close. "I'm fine. Didn't feel like staying all night."

"You walked here?" She laughed. "From downtown? You're crazy. Come up here and meet Dayton."

All right, here we go. "Okay." I climbed up the stairs and stopped on the last step. "Hello."

He stood, and she was right, he was *tall*. "Hi there," he said in a cool, even voice. "I've heard so much about you." He laughed and his laugh was quite dorky but absolutely endearing. "I feel like I know you or something." He grabbed my hand, pumping it vigorously. "I'm Dayton."

I liked him. Just like that. I liked this guy a lot. He had one of those open, trusting faces. He wasn't the type of man I'd notice on the street, but he was wholesome-looking. *Safe* is what he was. "Nice to meet you," I returned, shaking his hand.

"Sit down, hon." Elsie unfolded a chair for me and quietly slid the patio door open. "I'll get you a glass."

I wondered if I was intruding, but Dayton insisted. "Join us." He sat down again and the chair creaked under his weight. He looked more like a gym teacher than a math professor. "So the night didn't turn out the way you wanted?" he asked, winking.

Something about him put me at ease. "Not exactly, no."

"Yeah, it happens. The club scene is pretty brutal." He looked over at the door and leaned in. "I'm glad I'm out of it."

I supposed he meant meeting my sister, and that won points with me. "Elsie tells me you're a teacher. What grade?"

"Nine."

"That's tough."

He laughed again. "You said it."

"Here you go." Elsie returned with my glass, filling it up with red wine. "Cheers."

Dayton clinked his glass to mine and held my stare, but his look was direct and clear of any malice. "To beginnings," he said.

We spoke quietly, with great ease, and after fifteen minutes in their company, I felt like I was sitting with an old couple.

Could this be *it* for Elsie? Dayton cleared his throat, stealing a look at his watch. "I should get going," he said. It sounded more like a question than an affirmation. "It's late. Fay's gonna be up early tomorrow. You need your sleep."

My sister was obviously debating. I couldn't blame her. She wanted him to stay. "You could come by tomorrow," she finally said. "For dinner. I mean, if you'd like to meet Fay."

This was very quick. Yet I knew it was also… *right.*

"I heard you're quite the cook," Dayton said, looking at me. Was he inviting me?

"Oh, Allan, it would be great if you were there, too. For Fay, I mean."

"Absolutely," Dayton said, getting up. "She'll feel much more at ease with her uncle around the first time she meets me."

Was this guy for real?

Chapter Four

Months passed. Dayton and Elsie became inseparable. Dayton was indeed *for real*.

And Fay simply adored him. All three of them spent most of their free weekends together, getting to know each other.

I was also included in this budding family, and instead of feeling like Dayton had taken the girls away from me, I felt quite the opposite. These days, I found myself with much more free time on my hands. I didn't need to worry so much about my big sister anymore. One afternoon, I'd walked into her kitchen to find the table had been cleared of all bills. Dayton had picked them up. He was taking over. I'd have to start finding other things to do with all those long, lonely hours.

"Allan?" Elsie flicked a crumb at me. "What are you thinking about?"

We sat around her dining room table, contemplating the last of our traditional Sunday night lasagna. Dayton was in the kitchen washing dishes with Fay. "I was just thinking about you and Dayton. And Fay. And how amazing it's turned out to be."

"I never thought it would happen to me."

"But it has." I raised my glass. "You deserve it. Every moment of it."

"So do you, Allan." She wasn't smiling anymore. "It's your turn now. Remember how we said we led parallel lives? That what happens to one, usually happens to the other? So, maybe love is just around the corner for you."

"Yeah?" I got up and looked around in jest.

"Stop it! Listen, I have something to tell you. I wanted to tell you when we were alone—"

"We are."

"You know what I mean…Allan, Dayton asked me to marry him."

I had to sit down. "I see."

"I love him, you know that, right?"

My sister, getting married? Fay having an actual father? This was too big for me to take in with grace and poise. "It's really fast."

My sister's face turned white. I'd hurt her. We were orphans. We'd been on our own for eleven years. This was our family. She and I. And Fay.

Yes, and Dayton, of course.

"It's fast," I said, reaching for her hand. "But it's real…And it's time." She wasn't a child and I trusted her on this. "Congratulations, then." She burst into tears and I pulled her into my arms. "You'll be happy," I whispered to her, squeezing her against me.

"Hey," Dayton said, hunkering down, nudging my arm. "What's going on?"

"Mommy?" Fay stood nearby, stricken with fear. "Mommy?"

"She's fine," Dayton said. "I think she's just happy." He looked into my eyes and I knew he'd be good to them.

❖

"I love this neighborhood." Dayton leaned up against the railing, facing me. "It's surprisingly quiet at night."

We were on the balcony, drinking our coffee while Elsie put Fay to bed. Fay hadn't reacted very well to the news of the wedding, but Elsie had reassured her it would be a *very long* engagement. There would be lots of time to ease into the idea. For everyone. Fay needed not be afraid—they'd take their time.

"Yeah, it's a nice place to live." I didn't know what to say exactly.

"Allan, listen, you've been amazing, I wanted to tell you that. You could have made it really hard for me, but you didn't, and it makes being part of this family even greater."

"My sister loves you."

"And I love her with all my heart."

"I know. You guys have something amazing."

"Something on your mind? I want things to be on the level between us," Dayton said. "Always."

God, I was actually going to ask him? How lonely was I? I'd been thinking about mentioning this to him for days now. "I don't know what you'll think of this," I said, not making eye contact. "But your brother, I mean—"

"What about my brother?" Dayton tensed defensively.

Why, I couldn't know.

"Is he single?"

"Oh, you mean Dali?" He seemed to relax and lolled his head, looking at me intently, the moonlight dancing in his eyes. "You wanna meet him or something?"

"It's not a good idea. Never mind."

"No, no, on the contrary, I think it's a great idea. Matter of fact, I think he'd like you. He'd like you a lot."

"Yeah?" I sounded pretty desperate. But I was. If I didn't start opening up to people and finding new ways of meeting them, I'd be single forever. I couldn't stand it anymore. I hadn't shared my life with another man in over two years. I wasn't the type to be alone.

"Absolutely." Dayton seemed to be planning a double wedding in his mind. "You're totally his type. Well, I think."

"And what's he like? Is he anything like you?"

"No, not at all. We're very different."

Bummer.

"But Dali's more interesting than I am. He's more fun, I guess."

"What's he do?"

"Right now…Um, well, Dali's sort of in between jobs, but he's actively looking. You know what? I want to throw a little get-together to celebrate the engagement. Make it official." He slapped his thigh. "Yeah, let's do that. Let's get my family and your family together. My brothers will love Elsie."

"Brothers?"

"Yeah, I have an older brother, too."

"Oh, I didn't know that. Elsie never mentioned him."

"He's got a family…Come to think of it, his two boys are just about Fay's age. They'll love her to pieces. It'll be great."

CHAPTER FIVE

Here we were, standing outside Dayton's front door.

"I'm very nervous," I said to Elsie, catching sight of her pale cheeks. "You okay?"

"I feel like puking." She brushed her hair back and looked over at Fay. "How do you feel?"

"Why aren't we going inside?"

"She's right," I said, holding my finger up to the bell. "What if they come out and see us standing here?"

Fay knocked on the door and jiggled the handle. "Dayton said everyone has gifts for me."

The door opened and Dayton stood in its frame. He looked even more nervous than we did. "Hey, there you are." He kissed my sister quickly and rubbed Fay's head, but meanwhile, his eyes were on my face, speaking volumes. This was huge for him.

"Okay, let's go in and meet everyone," I said with false confidence.

We stepped into Dayton's home and were greeted by his mother, Ingrid. She reminded me of Bette Midler with her golden sandals and heavy jewelry. I knew I'd like her. We were ushered into the living room where we were greeted by a younger woman—she was lovely, with very high cheekbones and a small, pouting mouth. Her smile was tense and her hand was cold in mine. There was a general unhappiness about her—something melancholic in her blue eyes. "I'm Eileen," she said. "Dayton's sister-in-law." She grabbed a boy as he ran past us. "And this is Jude, my son." The boy was exceptionally good-looking with striking dark eyes. Eileen was fair-skinned and blond. The boy must have been his father's image.

Another child was introduced to us, this one younger and fairer, then a few other women I was told were friends and cousins, and soon my head was spinning. I couldn't remember anyone's name.

My sister was surrounded. I looked around at Dayton's home and tried to get my bearings back. His house was very cozy. There was sports memorabilia everywhere. Trophies overloaded bookshelves.

"Oh, Allan, this is Dali." Dayton touched my arm and I turned around to find him standing next to a young guy dressed in a flashy baby-blue shirt.

"Well, hello," the guy said, his eyes moving all over me.

Gael Garcia? No, I didn't think so. Not my type.

Not my type at all.

I held my hand out him. "Nice to meet you," I said, trying to be nice.

As Dayton and Dali struck up a conversation, I looked around, losing track of what they were saying. I felt a little out of place here. But Elsie and Dayton had insisted I come.

"So, you're a legal clerk," Dali said, his voice grinding my ears. "What does that mean exactly?"

Didn't the title pretty much explain it?

"I file paperwork for—" But I stopped, my face getting hot. "Lawyers," I muttered. A man was walking up to us... and this man was absolutely *stunning*. He was Dayton's height, but leaner, with dark brown hair and very penetrating equally dark eyes. He was in his late thirties or maybe even early forties. This guy had an air of a man who'd been around the block a few times, but wasn't impressed with what he'd seen. Maybe it was in the way he looked at his brothers—looked at them like they still hadn't figured out what he already knew.

"This must be the little brother," he said, meeting us, offering his hand to me. "Allan, right?"

"Yes, that's me," I said, mastering my wits. This man was not like any other man I'd ever met. It was in the way he watched me just now. There was so much humor and intelligence in his stare. He seemed to be amused with the world yet fighting it with all of his strength. He reminded me of the guys I'd known in college—the quiet troublemakers, the political activists. Yes, this man had that same edge about him.

He looked at me with great interest. "I'm Davinder. Nice to meet you," he said before walking over to his wife, who was fussing over the younger boy, his son.

So, Davinder was the married brother. Just my luck.

"Well, you've met everyone." Dayton wrapped his arm around my shoulder. "Let's get you a drink. You look a little shell-shocked."

❖

I was in Dayton's washroom, leaning up against the door. Elsie was right, it *was* fairly clean.

I needed a little breather. Some time to organize my mind.

I did enjoy this family's company—especially Ingrid, Dayton's mother. She was an intriguing woman. A bit of an eccentric, but so much fun. She was very vocal, and loved to play devil's advocate on any given topic. Her husband had died of prostate cancer five years ago, and by the way they all quickly changed the subject, the wound was still fresh. They were still grieving. Ingrid had spent her life working as an executive assistant for Molson, and during dinner she'd explained how the very day she'd retired, she'd thrown all of her skirt suits into a garbage bag and given them away. She'd never been seen in anything but long colorful tunics and flip-flops since then. We'd shared our horror stories about office politics, and all through our talks, I'd tried to be interesting, but had barely managed coherent.

Every time Davinder moved in his seat, I ended up muttering my words. He hadn't noticed, I was sure of it. I didn't think Davinder even knew what the people around him were saying. He was distracted. Always on his cell phone. He hadn't eaten much and drank one cup of coffee after the other. I'd seen him sneaking away for a smoke a few times—I could smell it on him. His wife, Eileen, the striking blond with the sad face, was clearly upset with him. Maybe they'd had a fight before coming here? At any rate, they were constantly hissing words at each other under their breath, or fussing over the two boys. Jude, the older one, was sullen and an observer. He'd sat in the living room most of the evening, playing video games. The younger boy, whose name I couldn't remember, was very clingy and always crying about something or another. Eileen was agitated, rarely sitting, constantly moving. She made me dizzy.

From what I'd witnessed, Ingrid and she weren't very close. There were definitely some unresolved issues between the two women. Davinder and his mother, on the other hand, appeared to have a wonderful, almost privileged relationship. Ingrid was the only one who could get his attention and keep it for more than a minute. Yes, his mother was the only one who could draw a smile out of him all night. And what a smile he had. There was something about Davinder that kept my attention. But he seemed so preoccupied. I hadn't seen him interacting with his sons much, but there wasn't any room for him to maneuver. Eileen controlled everything and often chased him away when he tried to. I'd watched them throughout the evening, observing their behavior and analyzing their words as I often did with people. Overall, our first get-together as a new family had gone perfectly fine. Yet here I was, hiding in the bathroom.

I looked up and watched my face in the mirror. "Okay?" I said. "Don't be an idiot."

Davinder was married. Married, as in *straight*. And what was my first and only rule?

Never, *ever* fall for a straight man.

❖

I'd gotten my senses back, and thankfully my mind was on the right track again. This was due to Davinder stepping out to make an important phone call. I was now able to carry on a normal conversation.

Dali and my sister were in the dining room just behind me, talking, and I knew Dali was trying to sell himself to Elsie in hopes of seducing me. I pretended not to hear him. He wasn't a terrible person, but he tried too hard. He was still in that angry "in your face" period of coming out, and I was way past that. Dali was still struggling to find his identity and I needed a man in my life, not an angst-ridden teenager. In a few years, perhaps Dali would probably become a wonderful man, but I didn't have it in me to see him get there.

"Well," Ingrid said, getting out of her chair, "I'm going to go wash some dishes before everything sticks." She kissed Jude on the head. "You should take a break from that or you'll hurt your eyes."

"He's fine," Eileen snapped. "He hasn't been playing that long." She looked around. "And where's Davin anyway?"

I looked from Ingrid's face to Eileen's. They were staring at each other.

I coughed. "I'll help you," I offered, getting up as well. "With the dishes."

In the kitchen, Ingrid handed me a towel. "You dry."

"Yes, ma'am." We washed, dried, and stacked without exchanging but a few words here and there. I liked the peaceful sound of the water running, her hands moving over the dishes, her red fingernails shining through the soap suds, the smell of her perfume. I wanted her to be mine for a moment. I remembered what it felt like to be someone's son.

"You and Elsie seem to have such a strong bond." Ingrid handed me a plate. "And you've both raised Fay wonderfully."

"I didn't really raise her. I have to give my sister all the credit—"

"Of course you did. Elsie tells me you live in the same building and not a day goes by—"

"Yes, that's true."

She shot me a sidelong glance. "Dayton's always wanted kids, but his last girlfriend had a change of heart after five years of living together. She left him and took a job in England. He fell to pieces that year and—"

"Mom, is there any of that beef and broccoli left?" Davinder walked into the kitchen. "I think I need to eat something." He dumped the rest of his black coffee into the empty sink. "Am I interrupting?" He gave his mother an uneasy look. "What are you telling him?"

She grabbed his chin. "You're white as a ghost."

He pulled away from her and went to the fridge. "I'm fine." He popped open a jar of something that looked like hummus. He found a piece of bread.

Ingrid snatched the bread out of his hand. "This is not a meal." She turned away and started pulling things out of containers before he had a chance to reply.

Davinder took his phone out of his pocket, and while he fiddled with it, I tried not to analyze his face. Of course, I failed. He looked up at me. I quickly looked down at the paper lying around the counter, flipping a page.

"You live near the Atwater market, huh?"

Could he see how flushed I was? "Yeah, just a few blocks away."

"I rent an office near there."

Davinder worked minutes from where I lived? I'd never seen him. Oh, I would have remembered that face. That walk. Those eyes. "You're a multimedia artist, right?"

"Not anymore. Now I spend my time on this phone." He sighed.

"Davinder runs his own business." Ingrid brushed a strand of his hair off his forehead. "And he needs to be patient. He needs to know that these things take time."

"Yes, and my mother needs to know that an *artist* needs to create or an *artist* loses his mind bit by bit." He looked down at the plate of steamed vegetables Ingrid had set before him and picked up his fork. "But thank you," he said before taking a small bite.

"You're welcome." She laughed and walked out of the kitchen. "Eat up."

We were alone and I was sweating. I was glad for dark clothes. I wanted to talk to him. Wanted this moment to last. "How long have you had the business?" I asked, my voice not quite steady.

"A year next month." He moved his fork around the plate, but he wasn't eating. "She's right, you know…I can't expect to have the time I used to have to draw. Or even think, for that matter. Just *think*. Sit there and daydream. Or stir images around in my head."

I hung on his every word. "What kind of art are you into? What is it that you draw exactly?"

"You're being very gracious asking me about my art, but you really don't have to pretend to be interested." He fiddled with his phone again. "And what is it that you do?"

"I'm a clerk."

"Okay…sounds like a stress-free sort of job." There was a trace of humor in his words.

"Oh, now *you're* the one being gracious by pretending to think being a clerk is anything but *lame*." I smiled. And he laughed. I leaned in a little, feeling more confident. "So tell me, what kind of artist are you?"

He was skeptical. "You're really interested? Yeah?"

"Absolutely."

"All right, well, I'm fascinated by the futility of the body, and that's my main theme. Finding life in the opposites. You know, blue is blue only because it isn't red. That sort of thinking."

This line of thought had always fascinated me. And I'd just finished reading Plato this week.

"You've read Plato's *Phédon* or maybe—"

"You're into Greek philosophers?" Davinder gave me a puzzled look.

"Not only Greek, but American and Russian as well." I was a big geek. In the last decade, I'd steadily read two books a week. My bookcase was about to fall over. Philosophy was my favorite subject.

Davinder touched a finger to his lips. "Interesting. I was a philosophy major until I switched over to fine arts, and finally multimedia."

"Really? You mean, you actually *chose* to read and study philosophy?"

"Philosophy is where it's at."

In that moment, I saw something in Davinder's stare. Something I shouldn't have been seeing in a married man's eyes. He was feeling it, too. This thing between us. This thing that had us both by the throat. What was it exactly? I'd never been this interested in another man's thoughts.

"So that's it," he finally said. His voice was strained as if he'd actually been choking. "That's what I like to draw." He looked at his phone and slid his thumb along its screen.

I wanted him to look at me that way again. "I'd love to see your drawings. I like the theory of opposites, and it's something I've spent a lot of time thinking about."

"Sure. I'll show you sometime." Obviously, he'd gotten his wits about him. The moment was gone.

As he walked out, I felt like a man who'd sipped a fatal dose of poison.

"What are you doing?" Elsie tapped my shoulder. "You okay?"

How long had I been staring out into space? "Yeah, I'm fine."

Dayton walked in, carrying Fay on his hip. "What do you guys say we hit the road? I'll drive you all home while they clean my house." He laughed at his own joke and turned to me. "Wasn't too bad, huh?"

"No, it was great," I said, not recognizing my own voice.

Davinder. What was it about him?

Elsie agreed. "We should do this again soon."

We made our way to the entrance and said our good-byes. All the while, I tried not to look at Davinder. He was busy with his older son—the dark-haired child I'd been introduced to—both of them whispering.

"I'll get in touch with you this week," Dali said near my ear. "If you like."

I couldn't help pulling away from him. "Okay."

"We'll get together." He gave me an insisting look. "You know."

I didn't want to hurt his feelings, so I nodded and gently moved my hand out of his. I looked at the floor, eager for Elsie to finish putting Fay's shoes on. I didn't know how to part with Davinder. Didn't know how to act normal anymore.

Eileen shook my hand and dropped a quick kiss on my cheek. "Take care." She pushed Jude my way. "Say good-bye to your future uncle," she told him.

"Good-bye," the boy mumbled.

I just stood there, waiting. But for what? What did I expect?

"Good night," Davinder said and picked up his younger son.

"Good night," I muttered before walking out. At the end of the hall, I saw Dayton and my sister swinging Fay between the two of them. I was relieved things were going well for the three of them.

"Come by this week if you want." Davinder had stepped out and stood in the hall, frowning seriously. "If you wanna see my drawings, I mean."

"Okay." I hesitated, wanting to walk back to him, but froze instead. "Sure, yeah."

"Okay," he echoed the word back to me softly.

"I'll ask Dayton where your place is and—"

"Wednesday is good." He backed away, not looking at me. "Seven?" he asked in a shaky voice.

What were we doing here? This was a dangerous game.

"I'll be there," I said, against good reason.

When he'd walked back into Dayton's home, my sister called out to me. "What was that all about?"

"Nothing." I held the door open for them. "He wants to show me his drawings, that's all."

My first lie to my sister.

There would be many more.

"Really?" Dayton was shocked. "Wow, that's a first."

CHAPTER SIX

Elsie threw her sandals in the corner of the entrance and shut the front door, setting down a brown bag. "They were out of the hot sauce you like."

It was Tuesday evening, three days since the get-together, and we'd planned to have dinner—just the two of us. Fay was at a birthday party, and tomorrow being a day off school, she was staying the night at her friend's home.

Dayton had thirty-five papers to grade by Monday morning. He'd be cooped up all night.

"It's okay, we'll use the Jamaican one."

"That thing? It's been sitting on your shelf for a year. It'll kill us." She picked up the bag and headed for the kitchen. "Coming?"

I lay on the couch, listless. "Yep." Maybe I was coming down with something. Yes, the need to get laid.

"What's up?" She set the bag down by the wall and came to me. She touched my forehead. "You're hot. You feeling okay?"

"Yep." Tomorrow was the day I was supposed to meet Davinder. "Maybe I caught something," I said. "A virus." The malady of lust.

"No, no, I know you, and this is you tormenting yourself over a decision you don't want to make." She sat by me. "Come on, cough it up."

"No." I tried not to smile. "I can't."

"You're thinking about quitting your job again."

I'd quit a job every year for the last six years. I'd been with this particular law firm for eleven months. They were still oblivious to the fact I spent most of my time trying hard not to work too hard. "Soon, but I'll stick it out until Christmas. I might get a bonus." Being a clerk was not what I'd planned on being when I was growing up. No, I'd dreamed much bigger dreams then. And since I'd met Davinder, I'd found myself dreaming again. He was much more accomplished than I was. It was inspiring.

And a huge turn-on.

"You got another drunken e-mail from Anthony and you're wondering why you don't just go for it instead of being miserable and single."

I looked at her from under my forearm. "No. And the prick hasn't written me in weeks."

"Okay, you wish you'd married that girl in high school…what was her name? Lea-Rose, that's right. You regret not keeping her barefoot and pregnant for ten years."

I couldn't help laughing.

She pinched me. "Oh, come on, what is it?"

I'd known I was going to tell her from the moment we'd left Dayton's home three days ago. I'd never kept anything from my sister. Even in my moments of deep shame, I'd let her in. She'd been there when I'd messed up big-time and had to get tested for HIV. She was there when I'd found Lucas's love letters in Anthony's tennis shoe box and threatened to kill myself. She was there when I'd been bullied by our uncle at our father's funeral, pushed in a corner, until I'd broken down and wept. She'd always stood by me.

I sat up. "I'm thinking of a guy all the time."

She waited.

"I'm finished," I said.

"Can I offer you a word of caution? I don't know, but he seems a little into himself."

"It's more complicated than that, don't you think?"

"No, I mean, he's clearly smitten with you."

"You noticed something? Did you?"

"Everyone did." She got up. "Why don't you call him? He's been telling Dayton he's hoping you will."

"He told Dayton what, now?"

"Yeah, he's been driving Dayton crazy the last few days." She smiled and pulled me up. "Come on, call Dali and I'll find something else to do."

"I wasn't talking about Dali."

"What? Then who?" Now she was having trouble containing her excitement. "Tell me!"

"Davinder," I said in a breath.

She screamed and shoved me into the couch.

❖

Elsie poured another finger of whiskey in her cup. The color was back in her face. "It's easy," she said, wiping her mouth. "You never see him again. You erase all temptation." She drank again.

We hadn't eaten anything. We sat at the kitchen table with a bottle of Jameson between us and two Bugs Bunny cups.

"I can't. I have to see him. *Have to*."

This wasn't like me. I'd never been one to play with fire.

"You could go under hypnosis. Have the whole thing wiped clear off your brain."

"I don't want it wiped clean." I turned my empty cup between my fingers.

"Allan, for Christ's sake, he's married with a family."

"Did I say I was going to do anything?" Talking with her, I realized I wasn't going to *pursue* Davinder. Of course I wasn't. But I wanted to sit here and talk about him all night. "He majored in philosophy."

"So did that fat guy we used to know."

"Did you see his eyes?" I poured another shot, ignoring her last remark.

"Yes, I saw his eyes. And they're striking." She sighed. "He's very sexy, I'll give you that."

"If he was single and gay, we'd make an amazing pair, right?" I drank and felt the bitterness of what I'd just said wash down my throat along with the whiskey.

"I admit it, if he was not, I repeat, *not* married, then yes, you'd make a fantastic couple." She looked at me seriously. "But he's not available."

"Did you see his lips?"

She laughed and slapped my hand. "Shut up."

CHAPTER SEVEN

Wednesday evening, nearing six p.m., and I was still at work. *Wednesday.*

But it wasn't important that it was Wednesday. Not important at all. It was hump day and the weekend was coming up. I'd probably spend Friday with Elsie and Dayton—they wanted to take Fay out to dinner to celebrate the end of the school year—and Saturday, I'd go dancing with David and Kaliq.

There. I had plans.

I stifled a yawn and looked at my computer screen. I had a headache and the air in here was terrible. The cubicle: man's cruelest invention. I stretched and looked around. Maybe I should quit today instead of waiting another six months. Not like I'd make a career here anyway. I had money. Money wasn't a problem. And now that Dayton was in my sister's life, I didn't need to hoard my every penny.

But what would I do with my time?

The answer came to me as it did always, but I pushed it out of my mind. No, I wasn't a *writer*. I was an avid reader who fantasized about writing. But reading a hundred books a year didn't a writer make. Besides, I wouldn't have the stamina for it. I'd give up before the first draft was written. And if I did manage to write a novel, I'd shoot myself when it came down to the edits. I'd crack.

This job was safe. This job was steady pay. What did writers live off anyway? They probably boiled their rejection slips and ate them with gravy.

My phone rang and I jumped. "Hello." It was my sister. "What's up?"

"You're okay, right?"

"Yes, why wouldn't I be?"

"Because it's Wednesday."

"I'm aware of it." I loosened my tie. My throat felt tight all of a sudden. "I'm not going to see him. And I wasn't even thinking about him until you called."

"Liar. Well anyway, for what it's worth, I think you're being remarkably sensible and mature."

I shut my computer off. "I know, and thank you for being so levelheaded and supportive." I threw the rest of my bottled water in the plant on my desk.

"You're welcome."

"I feel better. I'm glad we talked last night." I slipped my tie off and shoved it in my bag. "Still at work?"

"I'm leaving now."

"Yes, so am I." I waved to a few nameless faces and exited the office. "Well, good night."

"You're going there right now, aren't you?"

I stopped, looking around. My God, she was good.

"Allan, you'll regret it."

I got into the elevator. "I'm just gonna look at his drawings."

The doors slid shut and I leaned up against the wall, too excited to stand.

❖

Davinder's office was three blocks away from my house.

It was a two-story building—brand new. I could smell the sawdust around the staircase. The paint was still fresh. I saw the jazzy sign on the door.

Lamontagne Inc.

That was his last name. I knocked. Moments later, I heard Davinder call out, "It's open."

"Hi," I said, stepping inside. I stayed by the door. "You haven't been here long, have you?"

Davinder didn't meet me at the door. He stood by a desk, shuffling papers. "Been here all day."

"I meant the building."

"No. Moved in last month."

"Really?" I tried to make conversation. What was I doing here? This was awkward. He didn't seem happy to see me. He appeared to be deeply engrossed in his work. "Did I come at a bad time? I should have called."

He didn't say a word. Kept fiddling with his papers.

"I'll come back some other time—"

"Wanna go for a drink?" Davinder looked up at me for the first time since I'd walked in. And I saw how tired he was.

"I'd love to," I said. "And no offense, but you look like you need it."

"Okay then, let me make a phone call and I'll meet you outside."

He was going to call his wife. Because he was married. Why couldn't I get that through my thick skull? MARRIED.

"Take your time." I stepped out.

He needed a friend. Someone to talk to. And I'd be that guy. There would be nothing to it. I'd keep my eyes above his neckline all night. I'd drink slowly and have plenty of water between drinks.

"All right, let's go." Davinder came out, and as he walked by me, I watched his ass move in his jeans. I'd have to be a damn *saint* tonight. We walked side by side on the sidewalk, past the antique shops, and every time I saw our reflection in a window, I was startled at how good we looked together. I imagined he was my partner and I could reach out and hold his hand. Davinder wasn't saying much and I searched for something safe to talk about. "So what do you think of Karl Marx?" I asked him, hoping to get a conversation going. It was a quiet night. Shops were closed.

"Marx? I think he's a pompous paternalist."

"Isn't he?" I laughed. "So, if you'd have to take sides during the power struggles of the International—"

"My loyalty would have been to Bakunin." Davinder watched me out of the corner of his eye. Bakunin was one of my favorite historical and political figures of all time. I'd read all of his papers and speeches. He was a romantic, a utopian, a bourgeois turned revolutionary anarchist. His work always fueled me with passion, and every time I read him, I had a burning desire to join some underground movement and write anti-government propaganda for them. I told Davinder this, and we both began speaking faster, with more passion and confidence. Soon we were interrupting each other and having a heated debate about God and the free mind.

"Yes," Davinder said, walking briskly, "but if you believe in the soul, then you can't be a true anarchist. A soul means a god and a god means authority on our—"

"That's only one theory."

At every turn, we were butting heads, but I was enjoying it greatly. Davinder was argumentative, quite stubborn, but he also had a unique way of thinking—an original line of thought that captivated me. I listened to him with pointed interest, forgetting where we were or how long we'd walked.

"Wait a second." Davinder stopped and looked around. "Where are we going anyway?"

We hadn't even decided on that. We'd been walking east for blocks and blocks. With no direction in mind. "I don't know." I laughed and watched the moon catch in his eyes.

"Well," he said, "where do you usually go?"

I *usually* went to gay bars, but I wasn't going to suggest any of them. Hell no. "I don't go out much," I lied.

"Come on, let's get a cab. I know somewhere you'll like."

❖

The place was called Le Réservoir, and I knew it quite well. I'd been here many times. They brewed their own black beer and the ambience was casual. Its usual clientele was trendy and hip—typical of the le Plateau Mont-Royal neighborhood. Davinder and his family lived just three streets away. Their sons went to FACE, a very coveted art school downtown. That's all I knew so far.

We'd had two pints of beer and a few shots of Davinder's favorite drink, a shooter called *liquid cocaine* that tasted like mouthwash and candy canes. I was pleasantly relaxed, but if I wasn't careful, I'd get drunk.

So I was glad to be outside, the air clearing my head a little.

Davinder flicked his cigarette ashes in the ashtray by the pub's door. He'd been good all evening, trying not to give into temptation. He was working on quitting. He said he'd been eating banana peppers and drinking way too much water. Chewing gum all day until his jaw hurt. "What time is it?" he asked, taking a final drag before putting the cigarette out. He looked at his phone. He hadn't looked at it as much as I'd expected tonight. "It's almost midnight."

I didn't want to go home. "Yeah, it's late."

"Yeah." He put the phone back in his pocket. He looked around as if buying time. "Eileen's gonna be expecting—"

"Of course." I didn't move. He hadn't mentioned his wife all night. When I'd tried asking about her or his sons, Davinder had always changed the subject, and I'd understood. He needed a breather. So we'd talked about everything else instead. Art. Our favorite books. Movies. Society in general and our disgust with it. We were both deeply disturbed by today's obsession with consumerism, the steady decline of morals, political corruption…We'd jumped from one thing to another, but somehow, through the noise and chaotic conversation, we'd always found a way back to each other. Then we'd grow quiet again and simply enjoy our beer without a word.

I could have talked all night.

"I'm gonna walk home," he said. "You can still catch the metro, right?"

All night, I'd wanted to touch him. Just a slight meeting of the knees or a brush of our hands, but he'd been keeping his distance. "I can walk with you a little."

He agreed and we walked up Saint-Denis together, not a word passing between us. He seemed closed off to me. Was he feeling like he'd done something wrong tonight? I'd gathered Davinder wasn't one to go out much. Was he going to get the third degree when he got home? "Everything okay?" I had to ask.

"Yeah, yeah, sure." Davinder didn't look at me. "This is me here." We stood in front of a three-story apartment building. It was lovely. The doors were painted blue and everything looked new, seldom the case in this neighborhood. This wasn't an apartment building, but a condominium. I instantly understood the financial burden this could entail for someone starting a new business with two small children. "Thanks for the great conversation," Davinder said. "It was really interesting."

Would I see him again? When? What did he really think of me? "It was my pleasure. I had a great time."

I watched him climb the first two steps to his porch, but he stopped and came back down to me. "Allan," he said, his voice catching in his throat.

"What is it?" I held his eyes to mine. He wanted to tell me something. It was right there in his stare. All of it. "What is it?" I asked him again.

"Um…I didn't show you my drawings."

"Okay, but you'll show me tomorrow," I said softly. "I can come by again if you want me to." I could barely keep from reaching out to touch him.

He nodded, and for a moment I thought he'd kiss me. The energy between us was beyond anything I'd ever experienced. My senses were on overload. "I'll come again?" I breathed.

He moved closer to me and gently pressed his forehead to mine until I felt his breath on my face. "Yeah," he said. "Please."

And with that, he walked away.

I had a strange feeling I'd watch him walk away from me many more times in my life.

CHAPTER EIGHT

School was officially out for Fay.

This morning, I'd called in sick again—a telltale sign that I was quitting this job before Christmas. Forget the bonus. I knew my usual routine: first sick days, then showing up but writing chapters of books that never went anywhere.

Fay and I had spent the afternoon together at the pool. She'd taken swimming lessons all winter. She'd finally graduated from the kiddie pool, and this meant I didn't have to sit around in three inches of water all afternoon, surrounded by mothers who shouldn't have been wearing bikinis.

Yes, I'd actually gotten to swim and tan today—a first in many years of going to the pool with my niece.

"Are you having supper with us?"

We sat on the balcony enjoying the late-afternoon sun and a Mr. Freeze. "No, Dayton's taking you out to dinner again, remember?"

Fay's lips were swollen and stained orange. "Is he your brother now?"

I didn't know where she was going with this. "Kind of, I guess. We're family now."

"Was my real daddy your family?" She wasn't looking at me.

Oh boy, this was not a conversation I wanted to have without Elsie around. I wasn't certain what I could or couldn't say. Gabe, Fay's biological father, had left my sister when she was five months pregnant, and after many sleepless nights of us talking, she'd decided to keep the baby. She wouldn't do it alone. I'd be there. Gabe wasn't a horrible guy, but a confused, tormented, and altogether unreliable man. They'd met on a trip my sister had taken to Cuba after graduation, and Elsie had fallen for him. They'd moved in together and I'd tried to like him. I'd really made an effort, but the guy wasn't right in the head. One morning, he'd left the apartment for a pack of smokes, never to return. Weeks later, we'd gotten a call from his mother. She was ashamed of her son's behavior and wanted to know if there was anything she could do for Elsie.

There was nothing she could do, my sister had replied, but stay away and never make contact with her again. Gabe had gone back to Edmonton, his hometown. We sometimes got a letter from him. He was married now. No kids.

That year of her pregnancy had been terrible for Elsie, and for me. She was lonely, pregnant, without a dime or hope. She wanted to open a florist shop and struggling with the paperwork and financing. I'd been with Anthony back then, and we'd been her sole support system. As my sister's pregnancy advanced and her dreams seemed more and more out of reach, I'd wondered if I could ever truly love Gabe's child.

And then Fay had been born, and I'd witnessed the whole bloody, terrifying, amazing thing. I was at my sister's side through the twenty-seven hours of labor and two hours of pushing. By the time Fay joined us, I was drenched with sweat and barely able to stand. I remembered Anthony's face when he saw me step out into the hall. He'd said, "You don't look the same." And I'd caught the fear in his eyes. No, I wasn't the same. I'd grown up in those thirty-one hours. With Fay's birth, the boy in me had died. And from then on, Anthony and I had slipped away from each other. Our carefree days were over and he couldn't deal.

Of course I'd loved my niece from the moment she'd curled her little fingers around mine. My fears of seeing Gabe in her eyes dissipated. I'd have killed a great white shark with my bare hands to protect her.

"Your real dad wasn't a friend of mine," I said at last.

"You didn't like him?"

"No," I replied. Elsie and I had one rule: Never lie to Fay. "I didn't like him, but I don't hate him either."

"Like I don't like shrimp." She turned her face to mine. She was a beautiful girl with strong features, like her mother. "But you like Dayton, don't you?"

"Absolutely."

"When they get married, he's gonna be my dad then."

"I think you should talk about this with your mom, huh?"

Fay sucked on her Mr. Freeze and nodded.

"Let's go inside and wash the chlorine out of your hair."

"Uncle Allan?" She followed me inside. "Can gay boys have babies?"

We'd always been open with her about my sexual orientation. She knew what the word *gay* meant, and when Anthony and I had been together, she'd seen us hug, hold hands, and even kiss.

"You mean, with our own bodies?"

"Yes."

I couldn't help laughing. "No, we sure can't."

"So then you'll never have a kid like me?"

"I have you, don't I?" I pulled her into my arms. She was still little enough to allow it. Soon enough she'd be a teenager and I'd miss holding her like this. "I don't need anything else," I said. "Don't worry about me, okay?"

She didn't say anything.

CHAPTER NINE

I sat around the house in my pajamas again. Elsie had invited me to join them for a movie, but I'd declined—I couldn't tag along all the time. They needed their space.

And maybe so did I. I wondered what to do with my evening. I'd tried to write tonight. But *trying* was never enough. I had an idea I wanted to put to paper, but no words for it. It would come.

But not tonight.

Truth was, I wanted only one thing—to call Davinder. I'd found out things about him—about his past mostly—that afternoon, after I'd dropped Fay at my sister's. And these revelations changed everything. I couldn't stop thinking about what Elsie had said. This week, she'd asked Dayton about his older brother, curious to find out what Davinder was really like.

Those very *things* were the reason I felt so instantly attracted to Davinder. The hidden secrets moving behind his eyes. I found myself walking closer and closer to the edge, wanting to see what was at the bottom.

Eileen had not been his first choice, Dayton had explained. Davinder met her in high school, they'd dated briefly and gone their separate ways. She'd even married another man. Davinder had studied for a few years, and in his mid-twenties, he'd shocked his family by moving to Paris with…a young *man*. Two years had gone by. Davinder didn't correspond much with his family. He'd told them he was living off crumbs he earned selling his drawings. How could a Canadian with no savings or contacts survive a two-year stretch in Paris? No one knew the young man's name.

One day, Davinder had shocked everyone yet again, returning to Montreal and getting in touch with Eileen, who was going through a nasty divorce. Six months after his return, he'd asked her to marry him. At their wedding, she was three months pregnant with Jude. His two-year "dabbling" in homosexuality was never mentioned again. Davinder had kicked his pot habit and became a stand-up family man.

So what happened in Paris? This was my current obsession. Homosexuality was not something one could refer to as a phase.

So what I'd seen in his eyes was real. What I'd felt around him was exactly what I'd thought it was. Was I going to do anything about it? He was my sister's soon-to-be brother-in-law. *Family*, really. The man had children, and Elsie had found out his family life was less than easy. Eileen was not adjusting well to going back to work after three years of being home. This year, she'd had to resume her career as a grocer because Davinder had quit his job as a graphic artist to start his own business. They had a very expensive mortgage, and their son Noah had mild learning disabilities.

So calling, pursing, or even tempting him would have been selfish on my part.

I looked at the phone in my hands and dialed his cell phone number. But I came to my senses and hung up before the first ring. Damn it, I just wanted to hear his voice. I hit the redial button and closed my eyes, leaning back into the couch.

"Hello?"

"Hey, it's Allan." I sat up, pressing the phone to my ear until it hurt. "Am I calling at a bad time?"

"No, I was just looking over some numbers."

I couldn't hear any background noise. "Are you home?"

"Yeah. What are you doing?"

Thinking about you. "Nothing much," I said. "I was trying to get some work done actually, but my mind's not on it."

"You shouldn't take your work home on the weekend."

"Well, it's not work per se." I couldn't believe I was going to tell him about my writing. I usually didn't tell people until they knew me very well. "I'm a writer," I said. "I'm working on a book."

"Fiction?"

"Yes, because if it was a memoir, I'd have two very boring chapters, at best."

"What's it about? If you want to tell me...or are you one of those superstitious writers?"

And here we were again, talking with ease.

I told him about my current efforts, and though my thoughts were still muddled, I managed to give him a pretty decent synopsis. It was basically the story of a blind man and his relationship with his estranged father, who was dying and wanted to donate his eyes to his wayward son. As I explained everything in spurts, Davinder listened without interrupting.

"It's just in the gestation stage," I said, a little embarrassed by my own enthusiasm. "I might change it."

"You've got a good idea there."

"Yeah, you really think so?"

"Yes, Allan," he whispered, his words coming sweet and slow. "I really think so."

I suspected we were talking about much more than this book. "It's not fair," I said, making sure I sounded as cute as I possibly could. "I told you about my book, and I haven't even seen your drawings."

Silence, and then, "I can't tonight."

I wanted to crawl under the couch. Had I flirted with him too openly? Had I come on too strong? "Of course, I didn't mean tonight."

"Eileen and I had a big fight and I can't take off—"

"Davinder, you don't have to explain." I'd composed myself. "I completely understand." I paused. "I understand about your situation, okay?"

"Okay, thank you."

"Sure."

"I'll call you."

"Sounds—"

But he'd hung up.

Chapter Ten

Another month passed.
  I kept the stupid job, but every day told myself it would be my last, and that's how I got through July—working, writing in the evenings, spending time with Elsie and Fay, calling up some old friends, trying to rekindle faded friendships. Everyone had settled down; even David and Kaliq were quiet. We weren't seeing much of each other since I'd stopped clubbing on Saturday nights. Dayton and Elsie had begun planning their wedding.

I had a feeling they'd be tying the knot the next year.

We hadn't talked about what would happen after that. Would Dayton move Fay and Elsie in with him, or would they move upstairs? I doubted they'd go with the second option. No, they'd start fresh, somewhere new, and I'd get a tenant.

My life was changing and there was nothing I could do about it.

I turned my computer on and checked my e-mail again. Anthony had been writing me in the last two weeks—usually late in the evening, when Lucas was asleep.

Anthony and I had been together for five years. We'd been the kind of couple who wore the same shoe size and shared a closet full of shirts and pants we bought together. We got our hair cut on the same day and stopped trying to figure out whose underwear was whose. We had fused into one man, and people often mistook us for brothers.

We tried to make it work, but our love died of boredom. The problems started before Fay's birth. Her coming into my world was a catalyst that freed Anthony and me of our unspoken contract.

I'd wanted to leave Anthony but he'd beat me to the punch, and I never forgave him. When I'd found Lucas's love letters, I'd broken down, but to this day my sister insisted I was more relieved than anything else. Maybe she was right. Lucas was everything I was not, and that was the part that hurt. He was outspoken, flaky in an endearing way, and could bend Anthony in two with laughter.

Well, not anymore, it appeared. And what was I expected to do about it? Comfort Anthony? Invite him over and be the shoulder he could lean on?

❖

"Allan?" Elsie called out from behind my front door.

I looked over at the DVD player. It was a little past midnight. I rolled off the couch and opened the door. "Is everything okay?" I was still waking up.

"Yeah, Dayton just left and I thought maybe you needed company." She showed me the baby monitor we still used to listen for Fay. "I want to talk to you." She came in and settled herself on the couch. "Is that okay?"

I plugged the monitor in and adjusted the volume. I heard Fay's slow and even breathing. "What's up?"

"Nothing really. I just wanted to hang out." She looked at me. "I don't know, it feels as if we don't talk as often anymore."

"You've got a boyfriend now. It's normal."

"I know, but you're still my brother. My best friend. Am I doing the right thing, Allan?"

"You're absolutely doing the right thing." I nudged her. "If you don't marry Dayton, I will."

She didn't laugh. "That's the thing, I feel like I'm abandoning you."

I didn't like the pity in her tone. "Elsie, I'm happy for you and don't need you to take care of me like some stray pet."

"That's not why I meant and you know it."

"Yeah, so maybe I'm struggling a little with all these changes, but they're necessary. We couldn't have spent our whole lives in symbiosis. Fay needs a father. You need a man, and I need—" But I stopped.

"And you need? What do you need, Allan?"

"I don't know." I took her hand in mine. "But I'll figure it out, and meanwhile, I'm enjoying the ride there, okay?"

She slapped my thigh. "Oh! I forgot to tell you…It's Dayton's birthday next Sunday and we're all going to throw him a little party. You'll come, won't you?"

Chapter Eleven

I'd taken the metro to Dayton's because I needed the short walk to calm my nerves.

It was an exceptionally hot day and I was glad to be in a light polo shirt.

When I saw Dayton's house, I stopped short, trying to see into the living room. Everyone would be there, including Dali and his new man. The kid had met someone, Elsie had told me this morning, and according to her and Dayton, this guy was *the guy.* Well, good for him.

Was there something fundamentally wrong with me? Had Anthony been right during all our fights? Was I too nice? Too accommodating?

"There you are," Elsie said once I was inside, grabbing the bottle of wine I'd brought. "Your face is all red. Did you walk from the metro station?" She seemed tense, jittery. "Listen, let's go outside and have a glass of something."

The living room was empty, save for Fay, who was watching a movie. Where was everybody?

"Hi there." I dropped a kiss on Fay's forehead. She barely looked up at me. She was watching *Space Jam*, and this was her favorite part. I turned to my sister. "Is everything all right?"

"Davinder and Eileen showed up without the kids and…I don't know, there was an argument." Elsie took my arm, pulling me to the patio door leading out to the balcony. "Eileen is in the bedroom resting, I think. And Davinder is in the kitchen with Ingrid. Everyone's pretty shook up."

"What's going on?" I wanted to go make sure he was all right. But it wasn't my place.

We stepped out onto the balcony.

Dali and Dayton were arguing pretty fiercely.

"Do you fucking know what kind of pressure he's under?" Dayton said, his face a mask of anger. I'd never seen him like this. "She's got him by the throat."

"Oh please," Dali snapped back, rolling his eyes. "Eileen went back to work so he could chase this stupid dream. Another one." He looked over at his boyfriend. The boyfriend was silent, clearly uneasy. "It's the same old story with Dav. It's always about him. She's got every right to be upset. She was there for him when he was trying to get clean."

"And he did, right?" Dayton threw his hands up. "Right? He got his shit together and has been working ninety hours a week for her, for those kids. Nothing he does for her is ever enough—"

"Anyway, you always take his side." Dali looked down at his empty beer glass. "Ever since Dad died. It's always been you and Dav all the way."

"Don't say that. That's not true. Dali, now come on."

Dali looked over at the patio door. "Things wouldn't be so fucked up if Dad were here."

Elsie and I exchanged a look.

Dayton pulled up a chair and sat by Dali. "Let's not fight, okay? Mom's gonna be upset." He looked over at Dali's boyfriend, who had yet to move or smile. "So what's your name again?"

"Theo."

Dali glared at his brother with suspicious eyes. "Don't embarrass him," he said in warning.

"I'm not gonna *embarrass* him. Just wanna get the guy to relax a little."

"Oh, leave him alone," Elsie said, laughing.

From then on, the conversation took another turn.

I made an effort to participate, but my heart wasn't in it. I kept looking sideways to the patio window, hoping to catch sight of Davinder. Was he all right? I could almost hear him calling me.

Did anyone here really *know* him?

Ingrid slid the patio door open and stepped out. "Pour me a glass, will you?" She sighed. "You guys okay?"

"Where's Dav?" Dayton handed his mother her glass. "What's going on, Ma?"

"He's in the kitchen." She sipped her wine. Her hand was shaking. "If you want to know what your brother is going through, then you ask him. All I can tell you is they're getting some counseling. They want to make it work, okay? Davinder loves those two boys."

"We know." Dayton took her arm. "Hey, don't worry."

I couldn't stand there anymore. "Excuse me," I said, moving for the door.

Elsie looked at me. I stepped inside and checked up on Fay. "Still watching the movie?"

She was drinking a soft drink, which she was allowed on special occasions. She was glassy-eyed but content. "It's almost finished," she said, her eyes returning to the screen.

"There's a park near here, and later, if you like, I'll take you, okay?" My voice sounded foreign to me. I didn't even wait for her reply—I walked to the kitchen, but then, at the door, stopped.

What was I going to say to him anyway?

I wiped my hands on my pants and walked in. "Hi."

Davinder had his back to me, but at the sound of my voice, he turned around. "Everything okay?"

He was asking *me* if things were okay? I made sure to keep a safe distance from him. I couldn't trust myself anymore. "Is there anything I can do?"

"Is Eileen outside?" He wouldn't look at me. He leaned up against the sink, closing himself off again. His white shirt was open at the collar. I could see the beginning of his chest.

"She's still in the bedroom," I heard myself say. "It'll be okay." I took a step to him. And then another. "Everything will be all right," I whispered again.

Davinder moaned, hiding his face in his hands. "What am I doing here?"

I couldn't have stopped myself if I'd tried. I pulled his hands off his face and made him look at me. "It's okay. It's all right."

For a moment, he just looked at me, and I came in a little closer still. "Allan," he said, "don't. Please, don't."

I moved back, my face hardening a little. "All right," I said.

"It'll fuck us up, Allan. It'll make us crazy."

"Fine," I said, my voice icier than I'd wanted it to be. I was hurt. Bruised. "I'm gonna go back outside."

"Allan, come on, don't be like that. I'm sorry."

At the door, I turned around. "Yeah, so am I." I was being hard on him. I could see it in his face. "It's too bad."

"You should know better, Allan. You really should."

Yes, I should have. "You're right. Let's forget this conversation ever happened."

"Yeah? Okay then. Let's do that."

"Fine." But I didn't move.

"Good," he whispered, taking a step to me. "Perfect."

We now stood eye to eye, every breath burning our faces.

I pulled on his shirt, drawing him close to me, digging my fingers in his hair. His kiss was hot and urgent, and I gripped his neck, banging the back of my head against the door, crushing our bodies together. I ran my hands along his thighs and ass, our kiss becoming more and more violent. We were losing control. We were going to do something stupid. "Davinder," I said, "slow down." I pushed on him gently, my hands shaking with passion.

He pressed his palms against the door behind me, leaning over me, as if trying to keep from passing out. "Gimme a minute," he said. He caught his breath and slowly moved back. "I'm sorry. I don't know what got into me."

"You're an amazing kisser." I ran my tongue over my lips, reaching for him again.

But he shook his head. "Allan, oh please, stop. I can't. I really can't." He stared at me with pleading eyes. "You're beautiful... You're...Look, this can't happen again. Please, okay?"

Didn't he know? At that instant, I'd have agreed to anything. *Anything.*

❖

The atmosphere was a little off, but Dayton's jokes were keeping things light. I noticed that he'd been given that role—he was the clown, the jester. Every time the conversation wanted to take a turn for the serious, he'd skillfully change the subject with humor. I'd found out Eileen suffered from terrible migraines since Noah's birth and she was still locked up in the bedroom. Once in a while, Davinder would go into the bedroom, stay in there for long minutes, and we'd all pretend we weren't waiting for him to return.

When Davinder was in the room with us, he was silent, fidgeting with his phone. He and I made eye contact a few times throughout the evening, but every time, he'd looked away before I could smile. No matter how much he tried to keep his true nature sealed up, I couldn't be deceived any longer. His kiss still burned on my lips, and as I watched his hands move over things, I could almost feel them on my face.

I understood why he didn't look at up at me.

We all sat in the living room, finishing our coffee. It was late and everyone had to be at work tomorrow morning. Despite the circumstances, we'd all had a good time. This was part of this family's charm—ugliness didn't seem to stick to them. It was obvious Dali had major issues with his older brother, but was here anyway. And even as Davinder and Eileen were on the brink of a domestic war, they'd come for Dayton's birthday.

"So, Allan, are you seeing anyone?" Ingrid asked. "You must have a boyfriend."

Why was she asking me this now? I cringed in my seat. I didn't look in Davinder's direction, but felt his stare. "No, not at the moment."

"But he was with a guy for five years," Elsie interjected.

Why did she feel like she had to come to my rescue?

"Oh, and what happened?"

"We just kind of grew apart." I looked over at my sister. "That was a *long* time ago."

"Getting older and being gay is hard to live with." Dali smirked at me.

"Depends what kind of man you are," I said.

"Yeah, but you have to admit gay men don't deal well with losing the ability to seduce." Dali kept looking sideways to his boyfriend. So, he was trying to impress him by taking on the mature gay man in the room.

Fine, I'll let him score some points. "That's true," I said.

Dali smiled, satisfied. "Anyway, you're not *that* old."

"Well, thank you." I dared a glance in Davinder's direction—he sat cross-legged, typing into his phone. He wasn't paying attention to the conversation.

"Ignore Dali," Dayton said, laughing. "He likes to antagonize people. Especially people he likes."

"It's all right. I don't mind."

"Yeah, a good debate keeps an old brain on its toes, right?"

"Don't push it." Ingrid gave her son a biting look.

I looked over at Dayton and Elsie. "Fay's got camp tomorrow."

"Yeah, we should get going." Elsie moved to get up.

"I'm sorry," Dali said, "I was just being—"

"A fucking arrogant youth?" We all turned to look at Davinder. He'd spoken those words with his eyes on his phone, still typing incessantly.

Dali's face got red. "Looks like Lazarus has joined the living," he muttered.

Slowly and deliberately, Davinder stuffed his phone back into his pocket and let out a long breath through the nose, staring at his little brother. At the look in his eyes, Dali shifted in his seat and reached for his glass, nearly knocking it over.

Without a word, Davinder went to the bedroom again. Dayton seemed to want to say something, but even he couldn't turn this around. It was time to go. We all gathered our things as Dayton picked up Fay, who'd fallen asleep in the guest room.

By the door, Ingrid squeezed my arm. "Dali gets confrontational when he wants to please. He misses his dad, you understand? You can't hold it against him."

"He's a good kid," I said, holding her hand in mine. "He'll grow out of this phase."

"You're so kind."

"My brother's a saint," Elsie said. "Didn't you know? A flesh-and-blood angel, right?"

Davinder stormed out of the bedroom, bumping my shoulder, dashing out the front door before I could move out of his way.

"What's going on now?" Ingrid left for the bedroom. We could all hear Eileen crying.

"I open my eyes," she was yelling, "and he's on his phone!"

"Shit," Dayton said under his breath.

Elsie touched his arm. "Come on, baby. Your mom's gonna handle this."

"What a surprise," Dali said, staying in the corner. "Another party ruined by their fucking childish shit."

Outside, we found Davinder smoking a cigarette. The street lamp shone on his face, and in that moment I found him so beautiful and so fragile that I had to stuff my hands into my pockets to keep from grabbing hold of him.

"What the hell is going on?" Dayton came close to his brother. "This is getting out of hand. You two can't keep this up much longer."

"What? The marriage?" Davinder threw his cigarette in the street drain. "Huh, Dayton? Is that what you mean? We should just throw in the towel and our lives along with it? Easy for you to say, you don't have kids." Dayton took Davinder by the shoulder and pulled him away. As they walked off, I heard Dayton whispering to his brother, trying to calm him down.

And somehow, I knew I could do it. Yes, I could soothe Davinder if only I could have a minute with him alone. I'd know what to do. What to say.

But I just stood there helpless.

"You know, he used to be a swimmer," Elsie said. "Dayton says Davinder could have made the Olympics."

"What?" My eyes were on Dayton and Davinder's dark silhouettes. They were at the end of the street. Dayton was doing all of the talking.

"Just before the provincials, he was at a pool party...and he fell off the board. Broke his neck. Davinder might have been drunk that night. Can you believe that? He spent half a year in some kind of neck apparatus."

"Jesus," I whispered. "That's a nightmare."

"And then there was Paris and—"

"What exactly happened in Paris anyway?"

"Big mystery. No one knows. He didn't tell you that night you guys went out?"

"No, I told you, we barely talked," I lied again.

Dayton came back to us. His expression was grim. "He's just exhausted," he said, not very convincingly. "He hasn't been sleeping. He needs a good night's sleep, that's all."

"And Eileen?"

"Mom?" In the backseat, Fay was fidgeting. "Can we go now?"

Dayton looked over in his brother's direction, opening the back door for me. "Eileen is overwhelmed with the kids and work. She's not doing too hot. It's a mess."

In the car, I took Fay's hand. "I'm sorry I didn't take you to the park like I said. But I'll take you swimming tomorrow."

Of course, when I mentioned swimming, the image of Davinder lying limp next to a diving board sent shivers down my spine. How horrific that must have been for him. The pieces of him were coming together, but somehow, the more I knew about him, the more I needed to know.

We passed him as we drove up, and Elsie rolled down her window. "Well, good night," she said.

Davinder bent to the window and smiled. His smile was full of sadness. "Don't worry, all right?" He looked at his brother. "It'll be okay. I'll call you."

I wanted some kind of sign he remembered the intensity of our kiss, but he walked off. I couldn't help turning around to watch him leave.

Then he stopped in his tracks and turned around as we drove away. With bated breath, I stared at him.

And for me—and only me—he waved discreetly.

Chapter Twelve

I couldn't believe I'd gotten myself into this.

"You look different," Anthony said. "You look...*mature*."

We sat face-to-face at the corner table of our favorite steak-and-fries place. Between us, a white candle flickered. Voices rose and fell. Forks clanked on plates. The dining room was crowded, as it usually was on Friday evenings, and all around me good-looking men sat with even more good-looking men, enjoying some of the best steaks in town before hitting the clubs.

"So how you been?" Anthony smiled, pouring more wine into my already filled glass. "What have you been up to? You never tell me anything in your e-mails."

He'd caught me off guard, that's what it was. He'd called me up as I'd turned the shower off, and I'd heard his voice trailing through my apartment as he left a message on my machine—he never called my cell—and I'd wondered how long it had been since we'd been in the same room together.

"Elsie's getting married, I'm sure I told you, and Fay is in summer camp. It's a circus school and—"

"Yes, I know, that's wonderful, but I'm not asking you about your sister or Fay." He touched the side of my hand. "I'm asking about *you*, Allan."

I moved my hand away. "There's nothing to say, really."

Anthony rolled his eyes and laughed. He was more relaxed than I'd expected. I thought he would have been frazzled and whining about Lucas's indiscretions, but he was in great shape, and it was *I* who felt uneasy and quite pathetic. "Your birthday is coming up," he said. "What are your plans?"

My *plans*? I'd do what I'd done the last two years he and I had been apart. I'd drop a hundred dollars at Chapters and read all day. My sister would pretend she needed help with something in the house. I'd go upstairs, and when she and Fay would jump out from behind the door, we'd all pretend I was shocked. We'd call in Chinese food, eat two marbled McCain cakes, and she'd manage to get a few of my friends to drop by for drinks. Later, I'd get a little drunk, tell some of my funniest stories, and we'd all promise to call each other soon. But this year, the whole thing felt old. As a matter of fact, my clothes, face, thoughts…they all felt old.

"The usual," I said, pushing my plate away. "I'm stuffed." I looked out the window. I didn't want to be here anymore. "Do you want to go for a walk or something?"

"Is everything okay?" Anthony asked for the check. When he'd paid and our waiter left, Anthony frowned at me. "I should have kept in touch more often."

"You left me, remember? People who leave their lovers don't usually call them up to hang out."

"And I'm sorry about that. The way it happened. The way I left. I'm sorry. I was a different man back then. I was young. I was—"

"Young? It was two years ago." I got out of my chair. I had a headache. "Look, you made a decision and it was the right one."

"Allan, wait." He chased me outside. "I wanted to see you…I wanted to tell you that—"

"Tell me what? You and Lucas are having problems and you think maybe you made a mistake? Well, it wasn't a mistake, Anthony. It really wasn't." I stared him in the eye. "I was hurt because you made the decision first. You beat me to the punch." I knew I'd hurt him.

"Is that really how you feel?" He moved closer to me. "Allan?"

I wasn't completely sure of anything. We'd had amazing times together. Five good years. I'd grown up a little with him. I'd faced many of my demons with him at my side. We'd discovered our sexuality together.

"Maybe we should go to your place and talk." Anthony spoke quietly, beckoning me as he walked to his car. "Come on."

If we went to my place, something would happen between us. Did I want it to happen? Yes, part of me did. "Okay, but listen—" But I stopped mid-sentence. My phone was buzzing in my pocket. I pulled it out and had a new text message.

"But what?" Anthony was at my side again, smiling. "You're gonna give me a condition, right?"

The message was from Davinder.

"What? What is it?" Anthony peeked at my phone before I had a chance to turn the screen off. "Who's that?" His voice jumped a little.

I stuffed the phone back into my pocket. "A friend."

"I see. A friend who's got you flustered with three words?" Those three words were *Where are you?*

"Anthony, I can't…We just can't go back to my place." I hugged him clumsily and kissed his face. "I'm sorry."

"Allan!"

But I was already hailing a cab.

❖

"Oh, man, what do I do?"

"Excuse me?" The cab driver looked up at me in the rearview mirror.

"No, sorry, I was talking to myself." I slid my finger across Davinder's message. He'd reached out to me tonight. I couldn't let him down. I hit the reply button and typed. *On my way home. Where are you?*

A few seconds passed.

Where's home?

He wanted my address?

Two words appeared on my screen and I knew there was no stopping this tonight.

See you?

With my heart in my mouth, I typed in the next word.

Yes.

❖

When I stepped out of the cab, Davinder was smoking in the shadows a few doors down from mine.

"Hi." I tried not to trip myself up on my own feet. "You were working late?"

"Yeah." He stomped his cigarette and nervously unwrapped a stick of gum. "I knew you lived around here, so I figured—" He stopped and ran a shaky hand through his hair. "Hi, how are you?" He smiled a little. "You look good."

I didn't know what to do. We couldn't stand here on the sidewalk. Elsie or Dayton could catch us here.

And I wanted to be alone with him.

"Do you want to come upstairs for a drink or something?"

"Yeah, well, it's the 'something' part that scares the hell out of me."

"You don't have to be scared. I promise."

"I don't mean it like that." He bit his lips, clearly at a loss for words. "Look, Allan, can I be straight with you?"

"Interesting choice of words." I smiled.

And he laughed at my stupid joke.

❖

Our beers sat on the coffee table, barely touched. We'd been talking about a variety of subjects—from religion to capitalism. I was finding out that Davinder was much more of an anarchist than I pretended to be. He didn't believe in government or any form of state control. He wanted to burn the whole thing to the ground and start from scratch. Though I'd heard all of that before, it was different with him. Davinder had a fire in his eyes that captivated me. He also had solutions to go along with the rhetoric. He'd actually thought some of this through. He hinted at eventually getting off the grid. Leaving society altogether.

We were talking about Monsanto and their disastrous genetically modified soya, and once again, Davinder was getting riled up. "When the time comes, the rulers of the world won't need a gun to get us down to our knees." He looked at his beer but didn't pick it up. He hadn't stepped out for a cigarette all evening either. "They'll own all the crops.

They'll have a fucking copyright on our food. And when they say, 'This is what you get, son,' then that's what we'll get and nothing more."

That sounded very grim. "So what do you suggest? I think we're a little past boycotts now."

"That's just it. Don't you see? There's no room for the usual pressure tactics anymore. No, we take back everything. We don't say please. We have to learn to live independently. To become self-sufficient."

"You really do make some good points," I said, getting up. I went to my computer and clicked on my favorite playlist. I came back and sat next to him again, but this time I made sure I was almost touching him.

"I love this song." Davinder leaned back in the seat, finally talked out. "Radiohead, right?"

"Yeah, 'Karma Police.'"

"Great title." He sighed, turning his face to mine. "Do you believe in that? You know, karma? Predefined lives?"

"Yeah, I think I do." In that moment, I did. I felt like I knew him. Like we'd traveled together before.

"You believe that our souls or quantum energy—whatever you want to call it—come back through another body, bringing with them all of their past shit?"

"Actually, I think that's the exact definition in the *Golden Bough*."

He chuckled softly, staring at the ceiling. "Yeah," he whispered, "I bet." Then he was lost in his thoughts again.

We sat side by side, my thigh half an inch from his. He wasn't giving any clear signals. I moved my leg over and when it touched his, he sat up and reached for his beer. "I should get going," he said, taking a long sip. "I told Eileen I was staying at the office, but I never stay this late."

I was staring at his shoulders. He still had a swimmer's body under that shirt. "You're parked near the office? I'll walk with—"

"No." He turned around. We were so very close again. "I don't have a car. Eileen does. I don't like cars. I don't like what it costs the world to fuel them." He wasn't moving.

"But how does your family get around?"

"Eileen drives. I don't even own a driver's license."

Davinder was pretty categorical in his opinions, and I had to admit he probably was a very difficult man to live with. "She must love that, huh?"

"I've made a lot of compromises, too, Allan."

What did I know about their marriage and the things Davinder had to give up in order to make it work with Eileen?

"I'm sorry," he said quickly. "I'm being a little too heavy, huh?" He forced a smile and got up, looking down at me. "I just don't get the chance to hear my own thoughts. Outside of my head, I mean."

"I love talking with you," I said in a breath.

"And I love talking with you."

I rose, meeting his eyes. "And the kiss? Was that—"

"I don't know. I don't know what to do about all that."

"So you don't feel—"

"Yes, I *feel*, Allan. I feel a million different things at once, and every one of those things pulls me in different directions."

"Okay," I said softly. "I'm not pulling, am I?"

"No, no, you're not."

I couldn't believe how vulnerable I felt around him. "You can be yourself with me."

"And if I chose to never to kiss you again, would you still feel the same?"

"Of course," I said without missing a beat. "We could be friends."

"You believe that?"

"Yes," I managed to say, holding his beautiful eyes to mine. "I think I do."

He held out his hand to mine. "Friends, then."

I shook his hand. "Of course," I blurted out, sticking my hand under my arm. "I'd like that."

"Man, Allan, you and I both know that's a bunch of bullshit." He touched my face and said sadly, "But we can try, can't we? We can try."

CHAPTER THIRTEEN

Summer days were as languid as the heat.

I took a few weeks off and took Fay to La Ronde, the water slide park, and hiking in Saint-Bruno. We spent a day in Tremblant and rode the cable car up the mountain. In between all of the trekking and driving—Dayton had graciously loaned me his car for the week—we played board games in my air-conditioned apartment or slept. Sometimes we hung around Elsie's shop and made her crazy.

We were both brown-skinned and our strawberry-blond hair had turned a nice shade of wheat. We were officially beach bums. "You bored?" I asked Fay, walking into the living room. She was drawing. "Who's this?" I looked at the four people she'd colored.

"Me, Mom, you, and Dayton."

"Why's my hair so big?"

"You have a big head." She laughed and lifted the picture up to me. "It's for you."

"Well, Mr. Big Head thanks you kindly." I sat down by her. "Do you want to go to the beach today?"

Her eyes widened and she clapped. That was definitely a yes.

"I'll check with your mom and we'll make some sandwiches." I called up Elsie, watching Fay run up and down my apartment.

"Everything okay?" Elsie answered.

"Yeah, her boyfriend just picked her up. They said something about Vegas."

"Very funny."

I told Elsie about my plans and she was thrilled. The shop was quiet, and so we talked awhile as I put lunch together.

"Hi, gorgeous," she said and I guessed Dayton had walked in. I heard her talking with him. She finally came back on the line. "Dayton says—"

"Does he want his car back?" I'd abused his goodwill. "We can take the metro to—"

"Forget the car, okay? No, Dayton was just telling me that Davinder took a few days off to be with the kids, and he's finding it... well, a *challenge*. He's got no car and is stuck in the city with two very bored kids."

Davinder and I had been talking every night for the last three weeks. He'd send me a text message around ten and I'd slip out on my balcony. I'd call him back five minutes later as we'd agreed. He'd also be outside for our ritual call, with his first and last cigarette. We talked for an hour every evening. About his day and mine. His kids. Eileen. I'd listened to the rhythm of his voice in the quiet evening.

Some nights, we talked about the books we'd read or his art. I'd been at his office late in the day twice and brought him dinner. We'd eaten at his desk, listened to music over a glass of beer. In those times, it didn't hurt so much. Yes, in those times, when he was in the same room as me, I almost felt as if I could stand this.

Whatever this was.

"Sure, I'll call him up," I said calmly enough, stuffing some baby carrots into a Tupperware container. "I'll call him right now."

"You have his number?"

My hand froze over the lid. "Um, yeah, I think so."

"Really. Since when?"

"I know what you're thinking, but we're friends and that's all."

"Well, that sounds wonderful, then." She didn't buy it, but didn't want to discuss it right now. I knew that tone. We discussed some minor details for the day. I agreed to everything and got off the phone.

"Hey, Fay," I called out, "you want to invite Jude and Noah along?"

From the living room, she cried, "Oh yes!"

I called Davinder to let him know our plans, and through the chaos of his home, I heard him say, "Oh God, thank you. We'll be packed and outside in seven minutes." I was going to spend the day at the beach with Davinder and his sons.

❖

The short drive to Notre-Dame Island had been difficult. Noah was in a terrible mood. He'd screamed most of the way, kicking his father's seat, and every time Davinder tried to talk him down, Noah covered his ears. He'd shut his eyes and shake his head—*no, no, no*. But Davinder had surprised me. He'd been calm and patient. He'd talked to him evenly all through the episodes. Davinder's original way of thinking obviously came through in his parenting as well. He spoke to his sons as if they were his equals—he was never condescending with them. During the drive, he said things like, "If you keep screaming, you'll keep embarrassing yourself and then you'll be screaming to cover up your shame."

When he fed him that line, I shot Noah a glance in the rearview mirror, not quite sure if a seven-year-old boy could grasp that concept, but the kid had turned quiet for a few precious minutes.

Now we were here at last.

"At least those two get along," Davinder said, tossing his chin up in Fay and Jude's direction. He swung his backpack over his shoulder and took hold of Noah's hand. We were in the parking lot. "You have everything?"

"Yeah." I shut the trunk and looked down at Noah. I wanted to make some kind of connection with him. This should have come easy to me. "I brought some buckets and shovels—" But Noah was hiding his face in Davinder's T-shirt. He didn't want to talk to me just yet.

"I'm sorry, he gets real tense when the usual routine changes."

"He's shy," I said as we all made our way to the entrance. "I was a shy kid, too. I used to hold my breath and get purple in the face every time my mom's friends tried talking to me."

"Yeah, well, this is different. This isn't a personality trait."

"Yeah, I know," I muttered, looking over at Noah. "I know."

Jude and Fay called out to us. They were already standing in line.

"But, Allan," he said, "thank you anyway."

And I understood what he meant.

❖

We were finally all set up.

All the kids had peed, drank something, removed their clothes, been thoroughly sprayed with sunblock, and been informed of the rules. At our signal, they scattered like mice and hit the artificial lake, save for Noah, who found a shallow hole in the sand and sat in it, shovel and bucket in hand. Davinder had told me Noah wouldn't touch the water and not to expect him to give in. Noah hated the feel of anything wet on his skin, and giving him showers or baths was an exhausting endeavor.

I watched Fay and Jude braving the cold lake. I hadn't even sipped a drop of water or removed my shoes yet. I was sweating under my shirt. "I've haven't been here in ages," I said, pulling my shirt over my head. "Since I was a teenager, I think." I stuffed my shirt inside the tote bag and squeezed some lotion into my hands. As I rubbed the cream on, trying to be as quick and non-erotic as I could about the whole thing, Davinder sat on a beach towel, resting back on his elbows, his eyes safely hidden behind his dark glasses.

I handed him the bottle, but he waved it off. "Don't need it."

Of course he didn't. He probably didn't believe in sunblock or any other form of commercial cream. After weeks of talking with him, I was beginning to get him. Some of his reactions bugged me, but they also stirred up my mind and forced me to think. Some of his opinions had already begun to rub off on me. I'd canceled two of my three credit cards—well, the ones I didn't use anyway—and had even registered to donate twenty dollars a month to Greenpeace.

He took out a thermos out of his backpack and drank from it. He offered it to me, and I sat by him, drinking out of it. This particular water, he believed, was the least tampered with. Something about the way we sat quietly, sharing water out of this thermos, our eyes on the same horizon, filled me with peace.

His phone rang and I saw the fine lines around his mouth tense. It was Eileen. It had to be Eileen. Davinder said she was in the habit of calling in excess of ten times a day. She needed to remind him about things. Or hear his voice. Or rehash last night's argument.

"Hi," he answered her, his voice deep and low.

While he was on the phone, I pretended to be interested in my book. It was *Naked Lunch* by Burroughs. Not a very wise choice for a light read on a beach full of children. I read the same line over and over, listening to the subtle anger seep in and out of Davinder's voice. Nothing much was said—at least, not on his end—but it was obvious from the way he briskly stuck the phone back in his bag that he was upset. "I don't get her," he said. He'd never been very keen on letting me know what the problems really were between them. "She's been complaining I don't spend enough time with the boys, and now she's pissed because I took them to the beach."

I chose to keep quiet.

"I guess she feels left out," he explained.

"But she's working today, no?"

"She hates it. She hates working." He sat up, folding his toned arms around his knees, and didn't say anything else.

Another thing I'd come to understand about him—if he went silent, it was best to let it be.

He'd eventually resume the conversation, and often pick up exactly where we'd left off. I went back to my book. I'd chosen to read Burroughs again because I loved the way he murdered language and resurrected it in the next sentence. I was a timid writer, still struggling to find my voice, and his was mighty and all-consuming—just the inspiration I needed. I'd been writing every day for two weeks now. Up to three thousand words a day. *New* words. This streak would end soon, but I wanted to get as much down as I could.

"But you know," Davinder said, "I understand why she hates it." He was back and willing to talk. "She works to pay off daycare and grocery bills. She works while another woman works to take care of our kids after school, but while that woman works, another person has to leave their kids with another, right?" He shook his head. "State-funded daycares and allocation checks, another invention of those bleeding-heart socialists."

"So, women should stay home and raise their kids?" I doubted that's what he meant. Davinder was a feminist.

"No, but instead of throwing money and social programs at people, the government should do like a black hole and implode on itself, and then we could choose what we want to do with our families, our time, our fucking minds." He took his sunglasses off and squinted. "Man, it's hot."

"Yeah, and I think the heat is getting to your head." I winked, knowing I could defuse the bomb ticking under his skin with a smile. "Why don't you go for a swim and cool off there, Mr. Anarchy?"

He gave me a sardonic grin. "Nothing can cool this soul off." He grabbed the book out of my hands and turned it over. "Ah, so this is how you get your porn."

"It's not porn, it's an obscene satire of—"

"Yeah, I've read it." He looked at the water again and at his son. His expression grew very intense, and I guessed he was thinking about Noah. He stood up and walked away. I tried to read a bit but was too distracted, constantly looking up at him and Noah. The two were digging up some kind of elaborate sewer system for their fortress and seemed to be bonding in their own particular way. I didn't see them talking much, but once in a while one of them smiled, and I found myself smiling, too. Jude and Fay were in the shallow water, playing crocodile and princess in distress. I put the book down and joined Davinder and Noah. "Wow, look at this," I said, staring down at the intricate connections of tunnels and ditches.

Davinder wiped the sand off his lip. "Pretty cool, huh?" He rubbed his son's hair. At the touch, Noah recoiled a little. "It's not finished," he muttered.

"Can I help?" I stooped down and looked at Davinder. "If you want to go for a swim, I can watch the kids." I dared a glance in Noah's direction. He was his mother's spitting image—fair-skinned and blue-eyed. "Can I do this with you?" I asked.

"Okay."

"All right then," I said. Finally, a breakthrough. "I'll start over here."

Davinder got to his feet and slipped his shirt off, dropping it by Noah. My hands fumbled for the shovel. He was better built than I'd imagined, and that was saying a lot—I had quite a dirty mind and imagination to spare.

"This lake is a sham," he said, rolling his sunglasses into his shirt. "But I'll take what I can get."

He walked into the lake. He kissed Jude on the head, saying something into his ear, and when the water had reached his muscular thighs, he dove under. I waited for him to emerge, but when at last he did, I was shocked at how far he'd gone without a single breath. He was more than halfway to the other bank. Granted, the lake was quite narrow, but his speed was impressive. So Elsie was wrong: he'd been swimming since his accident. By the time I'd dug another extension to the maze, he'd reached the other side and was on his way back to us. His strokes were long and powerful.

"Boy, your dad sure can swim, huh?"

Noah nodded. "He's like the girl on the Internet."

I had no clue what the kid meant, but he was talking to me. "And what about you? Do you want to try?"

"No, thank you." He threw some sand into a hole. "I don't like to try."

I laughed. "That's okay, I guess."

"But I tried oysters last Christmas."

"Now, that's impressive." Noah told me about his teacher and the mole on her nose. He told me about the girl who'd vomited in gym class. The cat who'd died under their balcony, and with every detail, I tried piecing him together, but there wasn't enough there to get a clear image of what the boy's world was really like.

Davinder came out of the water, his hair slicked back.

"So, are you ready to strike a peace treaty with the forces that be?" I stood up and walked to him.

"I'd have to swim across the Arctic Sea in my birthday suit." He shook the water out of his ears and smiled.

His smile stopped my heart. "Your brother told me you were on your way to the Olympics."

"Yeah well, my brother likes to exaggerate. I never even made it to the provincials."

"I know, I heard the story." I wanted to crawl under one of the buckets.

"Good, so I don't have to tell it again." He went to the towels and called out for Noah. "Come drink some water."

I convinced Noah to leave his creation and ushered him to the towels. We sat, passing the thermos around again.

"Notice how this lake doesn't move," Davinder said. He wasn't really speaking to anyone in particular. "Anything that's manmade doesn't have real life to it."

I searched my mind for an example that would contradict his statement, but found none. "You're a very somber mood," I couldn't help saying, a little under my breath.

He looked over at me with a touch of surprise on his handsome face. "I'm sorry. You're right." He sighed and said nothing more.

We spent the rest of the day with the kids, and nothing of real importance was said. We played ball in the water and tried manipulating Noah into joining us by any means available, but he would not concede. He seemed happy enough sitting by the lake, drawing in the sand with a stick he'd found or pretending he was a lion and crawling around on all fours, roaring.

Davinder was obviously making an effort to be as upbeat as his nature allowed him, but he had yet to relax. Sometimes I wondered if he even noticed how tense he could get. I was certain Jude felt it.

The day was coming to an end and the kids were played out. They were shivering from being in the sun too long, and grumpy from hunger. "We should get going," I said, turning to find Davinder already on his phone. I picked up our things and shook the sand out of everything. Well, it was over. And it had been nice, right?

"Eileen wants them back. She fixed dinner." He called his sons over and fussed over their clothes and shoes.

We began our trek back to the car. Fay and Jude had struck up a friendship this afternoon, and they walked ahead of us, talking incessantly. Noah dragged his heels and pouted.

"We had a good time, huh?" Davinder took him by the hand. "Mom's got a real feast waiting for you guys."

"What about you? Aren't you gonna eat with us?"

"I got lots of work, babe. But I'll be home later, okay? I'll come say good night."

Oh God, he was coming home with *me*.

"She made those chicken burgers you like with mashed potatoes." Davinder was struggling with the cover-up, and I felt for him.

But not enough to do the right thing.

Chapter Fourteen

S tay in the car." Davinder didn't look at me. He jumped out onto the driveway and hurried around to get his sons out.

What we were we doing? This was bad, very bad.

"Bye!" Jude shouted, his eyes on Fay. "Send me an e-mail if your mom says yes."

"What's he talking about?" I turned to look at Fay, but watched Davinder and Eileen at their front door. I felt the dirt on me already. I'd never been in this position before. To covet another person's lover, and with such easiness.

It was despicable.

"He's on Club Penguin," Fay said, looking out the window. "We'll meet there sometime."

"Sounds great," I said. "Wow."

Moments later, Davinder climbed back into the passenger seat. His whole body was taut. He smelled so good to me—the sand and sweat mixing with his cologne—and I was filled with desire.

"Okay, let's go," he said, anxiously.

"What did you say?" I drove out of the driveway and into the street.

"You're driving me to work."

Was I? Had I read this wrong? "Right," I said, my eyes on the street.

He looked out the window, chewing on his thumbnail. "Is Dayton with your sister?"

"Yeah, they're home waiting for Fay."

He was jerking his leg up and down. "Nina's at the office with one of our customers."

I didn't quite know what he meant. Nothing was clear.

Finally, he turned and looked at me. "You got a back door or something?"

I bit my lip to keep from smiling. "Yeah."

"Drop me off at the office and I'll call you."

❖

I dropped Fay off, but stayed in my sister's entrance. Of course, Elsie pestered me about my strange expression. She wondered why I wouldn't stay for dinner. They'd made pizza. Why wouldn't I at least come in for a bite? I faked a headache—*too much sun, you know*—and managed to escape.

An hour passed. I'd gone from excitement to concern to depression. Where was he? I'd called his stupid phone three times already, but there was no sign from him.

I hadn't eaten anything because I couldn't stomach it and was still in my shorts and dirty T-shirt because I didn't want to risk a shower. What if he called or rang the bell while I was in there?

"Oh, goddamnit," I whined, looking down at my brown feet. So, he'd obviously freaked out and changed his mind. I roused myself off the couch. I'd take a shower.

I stood under the jet for ten minutes, dried off, and slipped on my old cotton shorts along with my favorite sleeveless white T-shirt. I fell onto my bed and flicked my reading light on. He wasn't ready. He didn't feel the way I felt. What we had was good anyway. Sex would ruin everything. He'd made the right choice.

As I opened my book, my phone buzzed on the nightstand. The blood rushed into my head. "Where are you?"

"Downstairs," he whispered. "At the back."

"Coming." I ran to the door and slowed down. Didn't want my sister to suspect anything. I opened the back door quietly and let Davinder in. He went straight for the couch. He rubbed his face for a moment. "I'm sorry it took so long."

"Yeah, I called you like ten times." I stood there in my old shorts, peeved.

"I know, I know." He held out his hand to me. "Come here?"

I let him pull me in. "What happened?"

He held my hand in his, looking down at our fingers. "I went for a walk by the canal...I needed to think...And...well, here I am, Allan."

"Are you okay?" I tried to make eye contact, but he wouldn't have it. I could feel him coming apart. "Talk to me. What are you thinking about right now? What are you feeling?"

He hung his head. "I don't know what I feel. I don't know why I'm here."

"Okay." I pulled my hand out of his.

"Oh, come on, Allan, you know what I mean." He tried for my hand again. "The animal in me knows why I'm here. But I'm not talking about that. I'm talking about why I'm here tonight, with you, holding your hand, instead of being home with the mother of my children. Why have I come to this point? Why didn't I feel it coming, this turn in the road? This meeting of minds we have?"

"Davinder, I understand, I do." I touched his inner thigh and felt the tension in his muscles. "But all I really want right now," I said, moving my hand up to his crotch, "is you."

"And then what?" He slid his hand up my thigh. "What happens after tonight?"

"Nothing," I said, feeling the burn of his hand on my skin. "We go back to being friends."

He pressed his body against mine, his hand sliding into my shorts, reaching my erection. "I've broken every beautiful thing I've ever touched."

I bit into his shoulder and slapped his ass. "Would you just shut up?"

He looked down at me, surprised. And slowly, his mouth stretched into a smile. He squeezed my nipple through my shirt and laughed. "Yeah, why don't you make me?" His tone was playful. I pushed him and straddled his thighs. His hands moved frantically over my ass, pulling my shorts off. He stared at my cock, and his eyes met mine again. Teasing me, he kissed the tip of my dick, his eyes glimmering with delight, and slowly took me into his hot mouth. I'd fantasized about this moment—every detail of it, but in all of the scenarios I'd conjured up, I'd never imagined Davinder would blow me. He'd done this before—I could feel it. Breathless, I tore at his clothes and we rolled around, crazed with the scent of our sweat, our skin. Davinder knelt before me, looking down at my body, and I knew then—I'd give him everything tonight. I pushed my knees up for him and he pinned my hands down, leaning his weight on his elbows, staring at me— watching me go from pleasure, to pain, then back to pleasure again. His slow thrusting was sending me into a dreamlike state with reality fading in and out of focus. I could feel his every move, hear his every breath. He thrust faster now, his eyes glazing over with pleasure, his hold on my hands becoming stronger, and I moved my hand from under his, stroking my dick, letting him rock me as he needed, the orgasm building and mounting in me.

He groaned, his face looking boyish for a moment, and came in a long shiver. When he said my name in my ear, falling over me, I gripped his hair, holding back a cry, my own climax shuddering through me.

Davinder lay over me and I could hardly breathe, but at that moment, breathing seemed something I could delay. He leaned back. "Look at me," he said.

"I'm looking, handsome. And I like what I see."

❖

An hour passed and Davinder was still with me.

"Thank you," he said, setting his fork on the plate. His hair was still wet from the shower, darker and pulled away from his eyes. "You cook a lot?"

"Yeah. I enjoy it."

He nodded. In the last minutes, he'd grown more and more sullen. We both knew our time was up. We'd taken a shower together, staying in there until the hot water had run out. Over and over, he'd whispered my name into my ear, fondling me, holding me, and I'd felt him burning for me in a way no other man ever had.

But now I'd be going back to my bed, while he would have to go home to lie next to Eileen.

After what we'd done to each other.

"We need to talk, right?"

I sat up straight. Something in his manner made my stomach tight. "I think so, yes," I said. If he told me we couldn't see each other again, even as friends, could I take it?

"Eileen and me—we haven't had sex in a year. You understand? I've always walked the line for her. Never cheated. Not once. But in the last months...Look, Allan, I've been on overload over here, you know what I mean?" He glanced up at me.

I couldn't tell what he felt at that moment. "So, you're saying you've been horny and thanks for being of service?"

"You're a guy, you should get this."

"Okay, you can skip this part and tell me what you really want to happen now."

He was surprised, but his expression went back to blank. "I want to call this temporary insanity," he said. "I needed this. I wanted this. But it's bad for me. For you and—"

"Don't worry about what's good for me."

"You're getting pissed off."

"I don't understand," I said, my voice sinking along with my hopes. "What happened in there wasn't just fucking and you know it. I won't let you tell me that—"

"It doesn't matter what it was." He leaned back, getting ready to leave. "Or wasn't."

"Wasn't?"

"Stop." He got up and moved for the kitchen doorway. "I'm married, Allan! I have sons. I'm sorry, but you have no idea what that really means. The kind of responsibility that comes—"

"Oh, I don't?" I jumped out of my seat. "What do you know about my responsibilities, or anything about me, for that matter?"

"I don't mean—"

"You know what, I don't want to hear it." I was enraged, but I knew the anger would fade and I'd be in pain. "Go, Davinder. And you don't have to try to justify anything. Just go home. Yeah, maybe I don't know what it's like to be a father and a husband, but I've lived enough years on this earth to be able to imagine it."

"I'm sorry."

"So that's it? *I'm sorry?*" I stopped him from leaving. I stood in front of the door. "Look at me."

"I'm not gay, Allan, okay? I mean, even if I wasn't married, I wouldn't *be* with a man. I like the sex, I really do, but sporadically, when I get that itch—"

"I don't believe you."

He met my stare. "It's true."

"Oh yeah? And what about Paris?"

"Who told you about that?" His face blanched.

"Did he hurt you that bad?"

"Maybe it was the other way around," he said.

"I don't think so," I whispered. "You were the wounded party."

"It doesn't matter."

"It does matter, Dav. Everything you say and do *matters*."

"That's why I need to go home and try to redeem myself. I need to make my marriage work."

"And I understand that." I was drained by this conversation. "I just want you to respect me."

"But I do."

"Not when you fuck with my head because you think I can't handle the truth."

He looked at me—really looked at me. "Yes, and what is the *truth*?"

"You want me to hate you so that you can sweep me under your consciousness and go back to your sleepwalking."

He didn't say anything for a long time. At last, he let out a long breath. "Well, do you?"

"Do I what?"

"*Hate* me."

"No," I said, "I don't hate you. Disappointed?"

He held out his hand to me. "Friends, then?"

"I don't think so," I answered without thinking.

"But Elsie and Dayton, they'll wonder…We have to—"

"They won't know." I stepped away from the door. "Davinder, when we do see each other again, we'll be brothers-in-law, and that's all."

"So that's it, then?"

"It'll be okay. You'll work things out with her and you guys will be happy again."

"But what about you?"

I opened the door for him. If he didn't leave now, I'd break down and cry. "I'll be fine, Davinder. I'm happy we had tonight. It was wonderful."

"Please don't say it like that. It sounds so tragic."

"Yeah, I know."

"What if we're making a mistake?" He looked out into the hall, but didn't say anything else.

I slowly closed the door behind him.

Was doing the right thing our mistake?

Only time would tell.

PART TWO

Chapter One

H ey, babe," Vassilios said, walking through my front door. He was in the habit of showing up without calling first since I'd given him a key. We'd been seeing each other for ten months come next week. "You turned the phone off again, huh?"

I looked up from my computer screen. "What?" My mind was still miles away, conjuring up a landscape I'd never even walked through. I'd been writing since that morning, struggling to get in the zone. I'd finally escaped reality a few minutes ago, and here was Vassilios. I looked at the screen again. Dinnertime already. "I'm sorry, yeah."

He came up behind me and kissed my neck. He smelled like tar. "I bet you haven't eaten all day." He tossed a brown bag on the desk and strutted off in a way only he could. He had a sort of obscene walk. It was quite a thing to witness.

It was a miracle we'd met.

Last Thanksgiving, I'd been hijacked by Kaliq and David, driven to their house for a "soirée." Vassilios had been there. He'd stuck out like a bear at a tea party in his cheap button-up shirt a size too small, and within the hour a pang of life penetrated my limbs. His rough edges had brought me back from the dead. He was new in town, fresh off the prairies, and sometimes I could almost smell the hay on him.

He turned my computer screen off. "Max says hello," he said, watching for my reaction.

I didn't mind. I was done for the day. I peeked into the bag. "Thank him for me." I carefully slipped out the wrapped pita souvlaki—my new favorite—and began to unfold the wax paper. "He must be tired of feeding me, no?" I took a bite and tried not to make a mess.

Max, Vassilios's boss, was recently divorced. His wife and three kids had moved out, but he still fixed meals for five people and insisted we take the leftovers. He was the only one in Vassilios's team who knew Vassilios was gay. Vassilios had spent his life in the closet, and after many talks with him, I didn't believe he'd ever come out.

And where did that leave me?

Nowhere, I supposed, but nowhere was quite fine by me.

"Do you mind if I hit the shower?"

"Please do," I said with my mouth full.

"Oh, so I stink that bad, huh?" He smiled and looked down at himself. He was sweaty and covered with dust, his hair caked with dirt. His work pants could have stood up by themselves. "Yeah, well, it was hot out there today." He pulled his T-shirt over his head. He was all tension and brawn. I still couldn't believe I'd managed to snag this beast and make him my lover. "Not that you would know, right?" Vassilios rolled his shirt into a ball, staring at me with a whimsical smile. "I see you're looking at my tan marks there." He came in closer, until he stood right over me. "You haven't seen these," he said, tugging the waist of his pants down to reveal the contrast of skin tones.

I wasn't looking at that. I was looking at the beginning of his pubic hair and the way he'd trimmed it so close to his skin. I'd been sleeping with Vassilios for almost a year, but every time he came close to me, I still wanted to rip his clothes off. Vassilios came and went as he pleased, but we didn't live together.

"Maybe I'll join you," I said, rousing to meet his eyes. They were very pale blue, and one of the reasons I'd let him so close…so fast. Those eyes would never remind me of that long-ago night. They would never remind me of how much I'd hurt.

How much I still missed *him*.

Vassilios grabbed my hand and pulled me into the washroom. "Mr. Writer wants a rub-me-down. I can tell." Vassilios wasn't the most cultivated or worldly man I'd ever been with, but he was always frank with me, and kind. He was a roofer and spent his days working hard with men who used the word *fag* to describe almost everything under the sun. But Vassilios rarely complained. He'd been raised by very religious parents and his teenage years had been one big brawl. He'd never had it easy. The pain was there in his eyes. In his lovemaking, too. Sometimes I felt like he was on the run and I was just a stop on his getaway. He didn't talk much, but, I didn't ask many questions.

He wasn't bookish, but he did think I was brilliant and soon to become a famous novelist. He supported me and hung on my every word. And his praise fed my bruised ego. Of course, he was dead wrong about my success and intelligence, and with every rejection slip I got, the dream of seeing my first novel published faded more and more.

But he didn't need to know that.

No, Vassilios only needed to put his hands on me, and I would pretend for a few hours that I was happy.

❖

Fay chewed on her pencil, swinging her leg under the kitchen table. We'd been at this cursed problem for thirty minutes now and she was beginning to lose interest. I couldn't figure it out, and by God, I'd graduated from college. This was third-grade math.

"Maybe we put the A here and the C over there, in the corner."

"The M has to be touching the A and—"

"Right, right." I leaned back into my chair. I was sick of this. "They probably made a mistake or something."

"You said that last time, and Mom figured it out." She doodled a cat on the paper. "Sheila says I'm too old to be a flower girl. She says only five-year-old people get to be a flower girl."

"Sheila? Is that the one who told you Tintin was a woman? Anybody can be a flower girl, okay? The bride decides who gets to walk down the aisle and throw flowers. *I* could be the flower girl if your mom asked me."

She laughed and shook her head.

"Anyway, Sheila won't be at the wedding."

"Will Finnegan be there?" Fay kept drawing.

Finnegan was the name Elsie and Dayton had chosen for the son they were having. The baby was due in December. The wedding was going to be on September fifth, over the Labor Day weekend. In three weeks. "No, your brother won't be there, but he'll have a front-row seat in your mom's belly, right?"

Fay was happy about having a little brother. She didn't seem jealous or apprehensive about it at all. *So far.* Of course, Elsie and Dayton were being very careful to include her in everything—from choosing the color of the nursery to naming the baby. Fay had decided on Finnegan after she'd heard the name on one of her television shows. I was trying to get used to it. I was still a little in shock. They were thrilled and I was glad for it, but I couldn't imagine having a nephew who would be a Lamontagne—blood relative to me and Davinder.

We would be linked through this child, in some way. Would he look like him? Or what if he looked like me?

Or both of us?

In the last year, I'd worked so hard at forgetting Davinder. But how could I really? I heard his name every other day, mentioned by Elsie or Dayton, or even Fay. In the last weeks, Ingrid and I had been speaking occasionally—she was thinking of renting upstairs once Elsie and Dayton's house was ready to move into—and she often bragged about her eldest son. I knew he and Eileen were doing better, still seeing a counselor, and Davinder was breaking ground with his business. Ingrid never gave me enough details to truly satisfy me, but every drop of information tortured me.

Did he think of me sometimes? Did he miss me?

Now the wedding was coming up fast. In the last year, I'd been sneaky enough to get out of family get-togethers, and I hadn't been in the same room with him.

This was different.

There was no getting out of *this*.

On top of it all, Vassilios was coming with me. Elsie had insisted. She and Dayton adored him. My sister wanted me to dive in headfirst as she'd done with Dayton. If she only knew. But I couldn't tell her now. So I found ways to make my life make sense, day after day.

"It'll be a lot of fun," I said to Fay, getting up. "We'll have a blast. Now come on, let's take a break from this and go for a walk."

She didn't need much convincing. We threw on our jackets and headed out.

The book could wait. The world could wait. The pain and longing as well. All of it would be waiting for me tonight when I laid my head down on the pillow and saw Davinder's face.

❖

"Where are you going?"

I pulled away from Vassilios's possessive arms and got out of bed. "I just need to write this one scene down. I think I have it now." I found my pants on the floor and slipped them on in the dark.

"It's three in the morning."

"I know."

He sighed and rolled over. "Okay."

Was he upset? I'd been more and more immersed with my new project—a full-length novel—in the last weeks. The thing was still a jumbled mess, but there was something about the main character that kept me returning to it. "I'll be right back," I said.

"No, it's all right." Vassilios's voice was rich and smooth as his golden skin. "It's important you finish this book," he said quietly. "When you do, maybe we can—"

"It'll be a while."

"How long, do you think?"

I knew where he was going with this. He was trying to bring the future into our lives. Motion. Some kind of evolution. "I don't know." I wanted to sit by him and touch him, but if I did, then I'd get nothing done tonight. "I think maybe a year?"

He sat up. "That long?"

There was electricity in the air. He wanted to go deeper while I struggled to keep afloat in the shallowest of waters. "Well, that's how long a sabbatical year usually lasts." I regretted using sarcasm. Vassilios didn't deserve it. He'd come into my life at a time when I was at my worst, and somehow, I hoped that one day, he'd get the best of me.

"Allan," he said, holding out his hand to me. He seldom used my name, and to hear it now chipped away at the ice in my soul. "Can you come here?"

I did. I went to him and sat at his side. "What is it?" I asked, my defenses weakened by the warmth of his hand, the way he stroked mine.

"I wanted to tell you that…I just thought that maybe you'd want to know… I met someone."

I wasn't sure I'd heard right. "What?"

"You said you wanted us to be up front with each other, right? The thing is, I like him, but you know how I feel about you and what I really want—"

"You guys fuck, then."

"This is not like Anthony's bullshit."

"No? Sure feels like a déjà-vu to me." I snapped my hand out of his and rose. "So what is it, then?"

"This is me saying I wanna be in love with somebody and if ain't you, then it's him."

The brutality of his honesty was unexpected.

Of course he wanted to be in love.

God, didn't we all?

"Then go. Get out." The anger came like a stabbing, quick and deadly. "Get out!" I ripped the blanket off him. "You liar."

"Liar?" He jumped to his feet. He was a good five inches taller than me. I saw his body in a whole new light. What had turned me on now scared me a little. "I'm no liar, Allan. You're the one who ain't honest here. And you know what I'm talking about. *Who*, I mean."

"That's not true. I'm over him. I told you—"

"Well, I don't feel it."

"You said you were fine with this—"

"That was then and this is now." His voice sank low. "Allan, I been fighting all my life, man. I just wanna make something good here. Just wanna settle down."

What more havoc could I allow Davinder to cause in my life? He was gone. *Gone.* And for the first time since he'd walked out of my apartment that night, now I felt it.

The finality of it.

"I'm sorry, Vassilios, you're right."

"I don't care about the other guy. You know I'm just reaching for something here, trying to get a reaction out of you."

"Vassily," I said, using the name his friends and family did, believing I could earn the right to use it, too, if he let me. If he gave me that chance. "I don't want to lose you." And I meant those words. "Please."

"You can read me your books. I ain't stupid. You can show me the things you like. You can tell me what you're thinking."

"Yes, okay. Yes."

Our kiss was just like the first—but then, in some ways, it actually was our first real one.

CHAPTER TWO

I looked around my desk for my cup of coffee. The coffee was cold and bitter, but I drank it anyway.

I'd been locked inside my apartment for two days writing. I hadn't even seen Fay. In the last forty-eight hours, there had been many small breakthroughs in the book, and I'd finally connected with my main character. He'd been eluding me since the start. The man was secretive and unwilling to let me inside his head. It wasn't until I'd had an epiphany in the shower yesterday morning that I'd really understood why: I'd built him all out of resistance—made him into a man who would never compromise for anyone or anything, but these traits were false, fabricated. I wanted him to be everything I wasn't, and this afternoon, I'd finally let him go where he wanted to go. The scene had flowed and the story seemed to take flight.

But somehow, that change left me feeling hollow. This novel was my best writing yet, but I found no satisfaction in that. It didn't matter who would read it, because Davinder *wouldn't*, and he was who I was writing it for.

Every word on the page had been typed thinking of his reaction to it. As if he sat right by me through the whole process.

I put my shoes on and left my apartment.

Vassilios was probably home, and I'd surprise him. He'd like that. Maybe I'd like it, too. I turned down Notre-Dame Street and walked by the antique shops, never looking into their windows lest I catch sight of my lonely reflection in them. Lamontagne Inc. was just around this corner here. A mere hundred strides away. I slowed my pace and stopped, pretending to be interested in a book propped up in a storefront, seeing right through it, right through my own face looking back at me with a haunted expression. What was I doing with my life? Thirty years old and still completely lost. This sabbatical I'd gotten from the firm, this escape I'd managed from reality, would soon come to an abrupt end, and what then? The novella was being politely but steadily rejected and I was running out of small presses to send it to. I lacked the knowledge or will to self-publish, and I was sinking deeper into a relationship that felt wrong. Vassilios deserved a whole person, not some hologram of a man. The memory of Davinder's face tainted everything. I'd fallen hard for him. I hadn't realized how hard until he'd exited my life. Something about him had sunk its claws into my flesh, and since he'd touched me no other could compare. It was a meeting of the minds, Davinder had said, and he'd been right. I missed his scent and skin, but what I missed the most was our conversations, our long, heated talks. I missed the way he snorted his laughs, the sharpness of his words. I wanted to hear him tear through a subject until he'd destroyed my conventional point of view.

Had he found someone else to debate with?

I walked away from the bookstore and turned the corner. His office was within sight and now I leaned back, staying out of view, watching the building, the door. What harm would I cause if I were to cross this street and enter that building? Knock on his door. Ask him how he's been.

I retraced my steps and caught the bus.

❖

"Wow, okay, what a surprise." Vassilios looked over my shoulder at his street. "Come in." He made sure no one had seen me on his porch and ushered me inside his house. "You didn't call?"

I hadn't been inside his home but three or four times, and only at night. I glanced around a little. The living room was a mess, and from what I could see of his bathroom, it was worse in there. So much for gay men being neat freaks. "I wanted to surprise you. Not good?" I raised a brow.

"No, it's great," he said, not convincingly, throwing stuff off the couch. Shirts. Papers. "My neighbors—"

"No one saw me." I grabbed a beer bottle off the coffee table. One of many. I shook the bottle. "Any more of these?"

I'd gone from a married man to a paranoid closet case. Was I condemned to live in the shadows?

"Yeah, sure." Vassilios disappeared into the kitchen and I moved more stuff off the couch—a ruler, some kind of tape, and an empty pack of cigarettes. When I'd cleared a space for us, I sat down.

What would we do with our evening?

Vassilios didn't like to go out much. Since we'd met, we'd seen a few movies at the cinema, and once I'd convinced him to go to a bar, but our main activity consisted of drinking two or three beers in a row and having sex. I didn't really mind. Why would I? The sex was fantastic. In the last months, I'd woken up with bite marks and scratches, and the day before last I thought I'd strained a thigh muscle. Vassilios could get a little crazy in bed, but I was finding that I could handle a lot.

I looked at the pack of cigarettes and sat up straight.

Vassilios didn't smoke.

"Whose are these?" I asked as he walked back in with our beers.

"Max's." He sat by me and clinked his bottle to mine. "You were thinking they were that guy's, huh?"

"Can we stop calling him *that guy*? He has a name, right?" His name was Fredric. And *Fredric* was Vassilios's real estate agent. As a matter of fact, he'd sold him this house. Their fling was over now, or so Vassilios swore. Was I jealous? We'd never agreed on monogamy, but some part of me had naturally assumed I was the only one. Another blow to my ego. But who was keeping count anyway?

"Allan, I've had one of those days, so please don't start with that."

I decided to let it go. He did look like he'd been put through the wringer. It was Friday night and he needed a night off. "Okay," I said, nudging his leg with mine, "fair enough."

"I'm glad you're here. You've never done that…showing up without an invitation. It's kind of nice."

There were many things I hadn't done for him. But I'd change all that. I'd be a better man from now on. "You wanna get out of here?"

He leaned back into the seat and rubbed his face. "Man, I'm just beat, you know?"

He didn't spend his days sitting on his ass in front of a computer screen. Yet his lack of energy irritated me. I'd been cooped up all week. I needed to see a little action. "Maybe just a drink somewhere?" I played with his collar. "Come on, please. We won't stay long."

"No, Allan, I'm really not up to it." He stared at me. "Look at you, you're jumping out of your skin. Come here."

"No, come on, stop it," I said, pulling back.

"What?" He laughed, but his eyes darkened. "Come here." He tugged at my belt. "You didn't come here to nag me about a drink, now, did you?"

"Nag?" I let him unbuckle my belt. "I came here to see you."

"Well, I'm right here, babe." He slid his hand inside my pants and my dick betrayed me, but my mind wasn't on this. "I know what you need," he said, moving over me.

Maybe he did. Maybe he had the cure.

But really, how could he give me so much pleasure when I was in such pain?

CHAPTER THREE

D ark rain lashed the glass, and the wind rattled the windows.
"There's a storm rolling in," Ingrid said, lighting a candle.

We sat around Elsie's kitchen table, looking over the final details of the wedding. Everything was coming together. It would be a church wedding, followed by a small reception—sixty-seven guests were expected—and Dayton and Elsie would spend a weekend at Le Chateau Montebello.

This was it. Come Sunday, my sister would be a married woman.

"Oh, there she is," Elsie said, jumping out of her chair at the doorbell.

Yes, here she was.

Eileen.

My sister had thought it was a good idea to invite her for our "girls' night," she'd teased me. "You two never really got to know each other," she'd said that morning. "Eileen's actually really nice."

Eileen was seeing a therapist and being treated for minor depression. She was doing very well, Ingrid had promised. She was a whole other person.

"I can't believe how much that poor thing suffered," Ingrid said now, reading my mind again. She did that. She seemed to have this link to my mind I couldn't sever. "The kids are different people now. You remember Noah, right? The problems...well, he seems to be opening up these days."

I knew most of this was a concerned grandmother's wishful

thinking. Noah's issues were real and proper to the child itself. I recalled his eyes now, our day at the beach. I missed the boys sometimes. Maybe I missed a life that was never mine to live. "That's great," I said. "They're a beautiful family."

"Davinder just landed a big publicity campaign." She slapped my hand gently. "Did I tell you already?"

My stomach was now tight as a fist. "No, you didn't."

"It's for this organization, not sure what they're called, oh anyway, he told me, but I forgot. They have all kinds of halfway houses for people who are reentering society, and he's going to help them with ads and such."

"So he's going to help bring attention to marginalized people with his talent," I said in a hollow voice. He'd done it after all. Davinder had managed to make money and stand his ground. He'd make a living out of his convictions.

"It's so like him, isn't it?" Ingrid went to the kitchen door and called out. "Girls?" She turned to me again. "He was asking about you, Allan. You should give him a call. He thinks highly of you. You know, sometimes I think my son's a bit lonely for another man's company."

God, what did she mean by *lonely for another man's company*? "You think so?" I asked.

"Hi, Mom," Eileen said, walking in. She kissed Ingrid and looked over at me. "How are you? It's been so long." Her eyes were just as piercing and clear as Noah's. She'd gained weight and her face was less pinched and gaunt. She looked fantastic. She wore a white cardigan over simple black jeans, and a loosely wrapped silk scarf around her slender neck. Her blond hair shone like a Pantene commercial.

"You look great," she said, hugging me.

Was that Davinder's aftershave I smelled on her neck? "So do you," I said. "As a matter of fact, you look like an actress just off a photo shoot or something."

She released me and laughed. "Why, thank you, sir."

Ingrid offered her a glass of wine. "So, how are my boys tonight?"

"They were running around, playing Pirates of the Caribbean in Dav's shirts and ties, but I don't care." She laughed again. "I'm out of that asylum tonight! Dav is on his own. And anyway, he enjoys it. I think it's good for them all." She touched Elsie's belly. "And how's my nephew?"

As they cooed over my sister, I flipped through a wedding magazine. What was I doing here? Here with the wife of the man I still fantasized about every night. And his mother!

"I'm so glad you're here, Allan." Eileen squeezed my hand. "I just wanted to tell you…I know I wasn't very warm to you when we first met, but I was going through—"

"No, please, it's okay. You were very nice and—"

"That's sweet of you, but I wasn't. And I've been meaning to call you or—"

"Really, it's okay." I was mortified.

"Allan, she's trying to apologize and—"

"She doesn't have to," I said to Elsie. This was more than I could stand. I'd slept with the woman's husband. And she was apologizing to me? "Anyway, that was a long time ago." I raised my glass and hoped no one saw my hand shaking. "Let's have a toast."

"Good idea." Ingrid said. "Shall I? As the matriarch of the family." She winked and I saw Davinder in her clever expression. "To Dayton and Elsie. To love."

"Hear, hear." Eileen clinked my glass and smiled. "And what about you? Elsie tells me you've been seeing some kind of Greek Adonis? Will he be at the wedding?"

"Um, yeah, he will."

"Oh, good," Ingrid cried. "That's wonderful. It'll be so nice to see you paired up."

Eileen chimed in, "Tell us about him."

"Yeah, Allan," Elsie said, obviously loving this. "Tell us all about Vassilios the Great."

❖

Fay was running up and down the hallway, making me nuts. My hands were sweating and this bow tie was impossible. "Fay," I shouted, still struggling with the knot. "Stop that!"

"Jesus," Vassilios said, coming up behind me. "Relax, will ya?"

I watched our reflection in the floor mirror. Him so blond and

tanned, and me so frazzled and pale. "Can you help me with this thing?"
I turned around.

"You're asking this hick here?" He grabbed the bow tie, pulling
me closer.

"You're not a hick," I said, taking in the vision Vassilios was today.
He'd parted his hair to the side and was clean-shaven. He smelled great
and the tux fit him like a glove. "You look stunning."

He helped me with the tie and had it knotted perfectly within
seconds. "And this family is okay with us?"

"Dayton's kid brother is gay, remember?"

"True." He gave me a suspicious look. "And the other one plays
for both teams, right?"

I chose not to reply and stepped away from the mirror, looking for
my speech.

"Uncle Allan," Fay said, running in, "Mom wants you upstairs."

I slipped the speech into my pocket. "Coming."

"So how is it gonna be, seeing him today?" Vassilios stood there
looking at me with his arms crossed over his chest. He was nervous
about the wedding, and I knew his way of dealing with any unpleasant
feelings was to argue or fight.

"I don't care." I walked up to him and took hold of his hands.
"Okay? I really don't. I'll say hello—"

"*We'll* say hello."

"Yes, *we'll* say hello, and that's that."

"I don't know," he said, looking away. "I remember the way you
were when I met you, the mess your head was in. It's kinda hard to
believe that you're just gonna say hello and be okay with that."

I was finding out that Vassilios was much brighter then I'd given
him credit for. In the last days, we'd talked a little more often, and I was
beginning to see that what he lacked in finesse, he made up in intuition.
His sentences were short and often unrefined, but were always spot-on.
It was a little annoying. "Look," I said, trying to keep the impatience
out of my voice, "he's my sister's family. We are tied up in this for life.
Might as well try and be sensible about it."

"What do you mean, sensible?"

"I mean reasonable."

"All right," he said, simply.

I wasn't prepared for such a quick retreat on his part. "Good, then." I kissed him. "It'll be fun, okay?"

His response to my faked enthusiasm was a long sigh.

❖

I expected to find chaos upstairs, but when I walked into my sister's apartment, I was greeted by silence. Fay was in the bathroom with Eileen, getting her hair done, and Ingrid and Elsie were standing in front of my sister's vanity mirror, putting the final touches to their makeup.

I stopped in the threshold. Elsie had chosen a simple off-white dress, which draped her curves perfectly. Her belly was hard and round as a melon. The dress flowed down to the floor in gentle ripples of satin. She was wearing a crown of flowers instead of a veil. When our eyes met in the mirror, I got a little choked up.

"Hey," I whispered. "You look so amazing."

Elsie smiled. She didn't seem nervous at all. "Yeah? The lipstick isn't too much?"

"No, it's perfect, really." I kissed Ingrid's cheek. "Hello. You look beautiful as well."

"And you shine like a new penny."

I didn't feel like it. "Thanks," I said. "Everything's going well, I see."

"Yes," they replied together and laughed. In the last year, I'd been so obsessed with my own pain, I'd barely noticed anything else. Elsie had Ingrid had woven a strong relationship, and if our mother couldn't be here today, I was grateful Ingrid was.

"Can I take a picture of you two?" I took my phone out and they posed for me. "That's wonderful." I smiled and began to relax. "So, how's Dayton doing?"

Ingrid rolled her eyes. "The boy is so wound up, his brothers had to pour him a double shot of scotch for breakfast."

"They won't get him drunk, now will they?" Elsie fussed with her crown.

"Don't worry, honey." Ingrid took my sister by the shoulders, standing behind her, looking at their reflection. "Everything will be fine."

As we all stepped out, I took hold of Fay's hand. "You ready for this gig, Ms. Flower Girl?"

She looked serious, clutching the bouquet to her breast. "I know exactly what to do."

"I bet you do," I said, helping her down the stairs.

Everything was exactly as it should have been. It was time for me to move on and accept that. Today my sister would get married, and I would see Davinder, shake his hand, and bury his memory.

CHAPTER FOUR

We'd gathered in the very church where Elsie and I had been baptized moe than thirty years ago.

I sat in the front row with my aunt Viv and her new husband. Vassilios sat by me, fumbling with the prayer booklet. "Do you have a mint or something?" he said, stuffing the booklet back in its proper place.

I gave him a Tic-Tac and looked around the church. It was a beautiful little Gothic church in the Polish district. I never understood why we'd been baptized here, but that was another one of my mother's mysteries. "It should start any time now." I kept looking around, but didn't allow my eyes to focus on any detail or face in particular.

I wasn't ready to see him. Not just yet.

"Wow, the groom looks like he might pass out."

I looked up and saw Dayton standing stiff as a statue. Dali was teasing him. "He'll be okay," I said, waving at them both. "Dayton's pretty solid."

"Okay, so which one is he?"

"Dayton's the groom—"

"No, I meant Davinder." I sat up straight and glanced over at the left side of the church. The rows were filled. The Lamontagnes made up two-thirds of the guests. My eyes went from pew to pew until I caught sight of him. Davinder was standing with his mother, his back to me so I could see his profile. "There, that's him with Ingrid."

Vassilios snapped his head around. "The tall guy with the black hair?"

"Don't stare," I mumbled, staring myself. I wanted Davinder to turn around, yet I prayed he wouldn't. Not right now. Needed to control my heart first. "Anyway, that's him."

"Well, let's go say hi."

"No, the wedding's starting in—"

"Allan, come on." Vassilios rose. "Get it over with."

Could I do this? "Don't say anything to embarrass me."

"Have a little faith, will ya?" Vassilios fixed his tie. "Come on, stop stalling." Ingrid saw us as we approached. "Oh, hi," she said, looking straight at Vassilios. "We finally meet."

I stood away behind Davinder, and when he turned around, I looked down at the floor.

"Congratulations." I saw Vassilios's hand raise to pump Davinder's. "You're the groom's brother, right?"

"And you are?" Davinder said.

I had to look up at the sound of his voice. Yes, and there they were, those dark eyes I'd longed to look into for so long. "This is Vassilios," I muttered.

While Ingrid made small talk with Vassilios, I stood there, my ears buzzing.

"How are you, Allan?"

I kept fussing with my jacket. "Fine. Just fine. You?"

He didn't answer me. Just smiled a little.

How I'd missed his scent. His voice. His way. "I've heard that you're all doing really well. And that you landed a marketing—"

"Your sister looks beautiful." Davinder's eyes broke away from mine as he looked over at Elsie and Dayton. "They're happy."

There was still a vague melancholy about him, and it made him more beautiful to me. There were so many layers to Davinder. "I've been meaning to—"

"Oh, it's starting!" Ingrid pulled away from our group. "Go take your seats."

"We better go," Vassilios said. "Nice to meet you." He tossed his chin up at Davinder.

I walked over to my row and sat. When the music started, we all turned our heads to watch the church doors open. Fay and Jude entered, making a fabulous little couple, followed by three pairs of ushers and bridesmaids. Elsie had asked me if I wanted to walk her down the aisle, but we'd decided she'd walk alone in memory of our deceased parents. When she appeared, I heard a few sighs and whispers around the church.

As she passed me her eyes met mine, and we winked at the same time. I'd expected her to shed a tear or two, but she smiled and kept herself together.

I followed her until she'd reached the altar, and couldn't help looking over.

Was he stealing a look at me, too?

No, Davinder stared straight ahead, his arm safely wrapped around Eileen's shoulders.

❖

"Whew," Dayton sighed, loosening his tie. "Your sister sure can dance." He called the barman over and grabbed my shoulder, shaking me. "Hey, having fun?"

"Yes, absolutely."

"You still haven't seen us Lamontagnes line dance." He took the drinks from the barman and handed me a glass. "Cheers. So where's the boyfriend?"

"Over there, talking with your mom." Vassilios and Ingrid had hit it off. Ingrid appreciated beauty, but was also interested in people. Vassilios was indeed an intriguing man—refreshingly honest and always up for a laugh. He made people feel better. I was proud to introduce him as my boyfriend.

Yet my stare kept returning to Davinder's face time and time again.

"You think my mom's really gonna move upstairs from you? Do you think that's a good idea?"

"I think it could be all right."

"Are you okay?"

"Yeah, sure, why?"

"Nothing." Dayton nudged my shoulder. "How's the book going?"

Davinder was walking up to us. To me. "It's coming along," I mumbled before draining half of my scotch and soda.

"Beautiful wedding," Davinder said. "You did good, kid."

"I'm gonna go see my sexy wife," Dayton said, pushing his glass up. "See you guys later. And remember, I'm paying for this open bar."

Davinder snorted softly, watching his brother walk away. "There goes a happy man," he said. He leaned his elbow on the bar top and looked over at me. "And *he's* something," he said, gesturing his head in Vassilios's direction.

"Something?"

"Where did you meet him, anyway? It wasn't at a conference on Spinoza."

Oh, so he *was* jealous. "No, actually," I said. "We met at a bathhouse. He's the lube boy there."

Davinder snorted again, looking away. "Right." He was trying not to smile.

We stood side by side, oddly at ease. "So what's this contract your mom was telling me—"

"Let's go for a walk?" He shook a pack of DuMaurier cigarettes at me. "Still hooked."

"Don't think so, no."

"Please, come take a walk with me. I really want to talk to you."

His face was so full of genuine affection and his eyes, so insisting…I couldn't say no. "Five minutes," I said.

"Five minutes." Davinder touched his chest. "Swear to God."

CHAPTER FIVE

We walked across the lawn, passing clusters of people, and stopped by the artificial pond. From where we stood, we could see the stone house, its large windows brightly lit with silhouettes dancing behind them.

Davinder frowned at me. "Why are you smiling like that?" He took a drag of his cigarette and blew the smoke out through his nose.

I'd never really liked the smell of cigarettes, but it was different with him. "So, what did you want to tell me?"

His jaw clenched. He took another drag. "Shit, where do I put this?"

"Throw it in the pond. I'm sure the plastic fish won't mind."

He ignored me and crushed the stub against his heel. He stuffed it into his jacket pocket.

"That's gross." I looked at him. "I have to go back inside soon."

He ran a hand through his hair and nibbled on his lower lip.

I was trying to keep calm as best I could, but being so close to him was putting my self-control to the test. Vassilios was going to notice I'd slipped out, and he'd come find me any minute now. He'd be pissed. "Look, Davinder—"

"Allan, I—"

"I don't think I want to hear this." I backed up.

"I won't say anything reckless. Listen to me, please."

"I can't, Davinder." Contradicting emotions rolled over me. "I really can't."

"You're right."

"Okay, tell me. I don't care. I think I need to know."

"You love this guy?" His voice was barely above a whisper. "I mean, you're *with* him?"

"Yes, I'm with him, whatever that means."

"But do you *love* him?"

If I answered yes, I'd put an end to this. "No, I don't." I'd been with Vassilios for ten months and had lied all that time? "I'm not proud of myself, I'll tell you that."

"We do what we can to survive."

"At the expense of others? Vassilios is a good man and—"

"But he isn't me."

"You're so full of yourself." I turned away.

But he stopped me by standing in front of me. "But he isn't me," he said. No, Vassilios wasn't Davinder. Wasn't the man I burned for. The man I loved.

"No, he isn't," I said, sighing out the words, my shoulders dropping. Why fight this? I loved Davinder, period. There wasn't much I could do about it.

"Do you know it doesn't matter what we say to each other right now? Do you understand?"

"Yeah," I said. "I understand." No one had ever looked at me the way he looked at me then. "Tell me what you need to say." I took his hand and held it tightly. "And we walk away."

"I love you, Allan. You stayed away from me and I love you."

"Are you sure?" I said.

He looked confused, but laughed. "Of all the things I imagined you'd say, that wasn't one of them. Yeah, I'm *sure*."

I couldn't speak.

"You don't…You don't feel the same?"

"What? No, I mean, yes, of course I feel the same." He loved me. *Loved* me. "Davinder, what the fuck?"

"What the fuck, what?"

"Oh my God! I spent a year in absolute fucking misery."

"Yeah, and mine was all sunshine and lollipops."

"There you are." Vassilios walked up to us. "I was looking for you."

Davinder cleared his throat, stepping back a little. "I should go back inside."

Vassilios stared him down until he'd turned away and left. "What are you doing?" he asked me. "What are you doing out here with him?"

"Just talking." I sounded like a schoolboy.

"Right, okay." He kicked the grass, spun around, and threw his hands up. "What the hell, Allan? You tell me one thing and then turn around and do the exact opposite. What is it with you and this cocktease anyway?"

"He's no cocktease."

"Whatever. He's *married*. Okay, I'm leaving."

"No, don't." I walked up to him and tried to make him look at me.

"What am I doing here, anyway? Huh? Why did you bring me here? To humiliate me?"

"Vassily—"

"Don't call me that."

"We were just talking."

"I'm going home." He walked away in great strides.

I stood there for long minutes, shaken. Let him go? Chase him?

Before I knew it, I was running to the parking lot. When I reached it, wheezing, he was already climbing in his beat-up sedan. "Vassilios," I shouted, grabbing for the handle of the driver's door. "Oh, come on, don't be like this," I whined, leaning to the window, which was rolled up. "It's my sister's wedding."

He inched down the window a bit. "Something about us ain't right," he said. "Just ain't right."

What could I say to that? "Come back inside with me. Please."

"Tell 'em I felt sick." He put his hand on the stick shift. "I'm sorry, Allan. I'm not even mad. Just messed up." He put his hands on the wheel and the car began to move back.

"Damn it!"

How could I have been so careless?

"Who are you waiting for?"

I turned around to find Noah standing a few feet from me. What was he doing here in the parking lot? "Where's your mom?" I said, looking around.

"Inside."

"Well, then, let's go find her." I put my arm around his shoulder. "How you been? I missed you, you know."

"Who were you waiting for?"

"No one. I was watching someone leave."

"The frog?"

I remembered how confused this kid left me sometimes. "Frog? What frog?"

"The one I was chasing."

"Yeah, I think it drove right out of here."

Noah looked up at me, serious. "I think it's that kind of frog, yes."

We found Eileen and Jude by the fountain.

"Where were you?" Eileen frowned at us. "Your father's looking for you out in the back. He caught a firefly."

"Want to go check it out, Noah?"

Noah ran ahead of me the whole way. We passed Dayton and Elsie, and grabbed Fay on the run. "Dad caught a bug and her butt's on fire!" Noah said to her.

Outside, Davinder was having a conversation with Dali and his latest boyfriend. When Noah and Fay rushed up demanding to see the bug, Davinder produced it from inside his pocket. It was actually still alive and glowing in his hand. "I have to let it go now," he said to the kids, holding his hand open. But the firefly lingered on his palm.

"It wants to stay with you," Fay said. She looked up at me. "See, it's not moving from his hand."

"Yeah well, it's probably a little woozy, that's all. God knows what's in your dad's pockets."

Dali laughed. "Allan's got a point." He asked Noah to blow on the bug and soon, the firefly flew off Davinder's hand. "His mom's gonna be happy to see him, I bet," Dali said.

"Yeah, and his grandmother, too." Noah watched the sky, lost in his imaginary world once more.

Fay trotted back to the house and called out to him. Noah soon followed her. She had a way with these boys.

"Allan, you look great," Dali said. "Elsie says you wrote a book?"

"You're a writer?" the boyfriend said. "Like, you write novels and stuff?"

Davinder muffled a laugh by pretending to be coughing into his hand.

"Brendan loves fan fiction," Dali said.

Brendan explained how he'd been reading some Sherlock Holmes fan fiction, and became quite enthused. He was passionate and quite entertaining. I watched Dali's eyes as Brendan spoke. He was lovestruck. Oh yes, this could be the one.

"Anyway, you have to check it out yourselves," Brendan finally said, a little winded.

"I will." Davinder was obviously humoring him. "Let's get a drink?"

We all went back inside.

"You gonna tell me about this book?" Davinder waved Dayton over.

"Yeah, some day."

We piled up at the bar and ordered two rounds of B52s shooters for all.

As the evening progressed, ties were pulled off and left to hang on chairs, jackets were thrown on tables, and high heels were scattered around the room.

On the dance floor, there were moments when Davinder's body brushed mine, and I was conscious of Eileen, always nearby. He was never anything but discreet. I would have given anything, truly *anything* to take him home tonight. Strip him bare. Lay him down over my sheets. I'd take it so slow. Wouldn't rush into it like I had the only time we'd been together. I'd show him what I was made of. He'd want no other lover.

I danced with these thoughts running through my hazed mind.

Did he feel me watching him?

When the night finally ended and it was time to go, I hugged Elsie and wished her the best and climbed into the car, eager to be in my bed. As I rolled by Davinder's minivan, I stopped to wave at Eileen, but didn't dare look over at Davinder. Those three words he'd confessed by the pond consumed me more and more. He *loved* me. I still couldn't understand what that meant for him. Or me. He'd said it didn't matter.

We'd do nothing about it. It would be there between us, this secret life never to be lived, and I'd have to accept that.

"I'll call you this week," Eileen called out to me before yawning. "I'd love to go have a coffee with you or something. Lunch maybe?"

What? Had I heard that right?

"What do you say?" She smiled at me, waiting.

I glanced over at Davinder and saw the shock on his face. "Okay, sure," I said. "Of course, I'd like that."

"Great!" She rolled up her window and drove away.

I sat there for a few seconds, my foot on the brake, staring at the steering wheel.

Was this how Judas had felt?

CHAPTER SIX

I rolled over, stuffing my face into the mattress. "Hon, get your stupid uncle a glass of water, please?"

"You're not stupid," Fay said, running off. "I fixed you breakfast!"

"Breakfast?" I squinted, trying to read the time on the digital clock on the nightstand. "That's so sweet, Fay. I'll be right there." I sat up, groaning at every movement. I was still in my tuxedo pants. I wasn't hungover, just very tired.

"Here." She gave me the glass and drew open the curtains. "Come to the kitchen," she said, running out again.

Davinder is in love with me.

I slipped on a T-shirt, my mind clearing up by the second. Yes, and Vassilios had left. I found my phone and checked for messages. There were none. I texted Vassilios the words *call me* and went to find Fay.

She'd prepared a huge bowl of Cheerios, drowned them in milk and decorated them with sliced strawberries.

"You cut these? You have to be careful with a knife when—"

"Yeah, I know, Uncle Allan." She rolled her eyes. "Do you like it?"

I pulled up a stool to the kitchen island. "It's great, thanks." The strawberries were overripe and soft with the milk. The Cheerios could have been oatmeal. But she'd made this for me, and I'd eat it.

"Uncle Davinder was here this morning."

I sat there with the spoon to my mouth. "What do you mean? When?"

"When you were sleeping. I was watching TV. He knocked and I looked in the peephole like you showed me and I knew he was him because he wasn't anybody else, so I opened the door."

I set my spoon down. "What did he say? What did he want?"

"Nothing."

"He didn't say anything at all?"

"What's wrong? You look funny."

I jumped out of my seat. "No, I'm fine," I said before dashing out of the kitchen to find my phone. Vassilios had texted me. I read his message and fell back into the couch with a pitiful sigh. *I'm sorry* was all he wrote.

I needed to take care of this before I even thought of calling Davinder.

❖

Ingrid slipped Fay's bag off my shoulder and tossed it in the front seat of her BMW. I wondered what Davinder thought of his mother driving around in a luxury car. "We'll have a great time together," she said before dropping a kiss on my lips. "Bye, gorgeous. And don't worry."

"I'll call you to say good night," I said to Fay, who sat buckled up in the backseat. Elsie had arranged for Fay to spend part of the weekend with Ingrid.

I waved them off and watched the car turn the corner.

It was still very warm for September, and the air was sweet with the scent of newly mowed grass. All though the yards here were small, my neighbors always tended theirs religiously. I liked this neighborhood. I hadn't at first, but Anthony had promised it would grow on me. The mix of old and new dwellings, the clash of architecture, the traffic of the Atwater market, the proximity of the bridge—all of this had seemed to me too much. Years later, I saw the charm of this area. Where else could I ride my bike in peace along the beautiful canal, and yet be five minutes away from downtown?

I looked around, taking a few good breaths, content to stand on the sidewalk, under the setting sun, taking in the light, the sights and smells of my street. I had a home here. If only I could share it with someone.

As I climbed the three steps up to my porch, my phone rang. It was Vassilios. I sat on the last step. "Are you still mad at me?"

"No," he sighed. "How'd the rest of the night go?"

"It was a lot of fun."

"Good, then." There was a trace of anger in his voice.

"Vassilios, we need to talk." I wasn't going to end our relationship over the phone. "Can you come over?"

"No, tell me now."

I waved to a neighbor, a retired police officer whose name I always forgot, and played with my shoelace. "I think it would better—"

"Better for who?"

"You said it yourself, something isn't right with us, and—"

"And you said you wanted to give us a try. Remember that?"

"There's something missing between us and I don't think—"

"So you've made up your mind."

I rose and stepped into my apartment. It was dark in here…and cold. I walked around with the phone pressed between my ear and shoulder, opening windows. "Maybe we should just spend some time apart for a while," I said, turning the air conditioner off. "We could—"

"You'll regret this, Allan. You'll think back on this day and regret it. What do you think he's gonna do for you, huh? Nothing, man. He's a taker, I could see it in those eyes of his. He's the guy kind of guy who'll tell you all about the rules while he breaks—"

"You don't know him." I was shaken by his words. "You don't know what he said to me."

"Oh yeah? Lemme guess. He's in love with you. Can't stop thinking about you. He's dying for you. Am I close?"

I stood by the living room window, looking out. "Yes," I said.

I heard his sharp intake of air. "Don't come crying to me when he's through with you. I won't wait around for that."

Why was Vassilios being so nasty? Why couldn't he have been mature about the whole thing? "Don't worry," I said. "I won't."

He hung up on me.

Yes, he might have been right about Davinder. Most likely, I'd be used and lied to, and my mind would be tampered with.

But sadly, I didn't care.

Chapter Seven

Bright dots danced at the corner of my eyes. It was time to pull away from the computer and eat something. Earlier, I'd taken a short power nap, but my very critical inner voice had ordered me to not waste this evening. So I'd brewed some coffee and settled down for a writing marathon.

Time and again, I'd found myself staring at the screen, my fingers quiet on the keyboard, lost in my thoughts. I hadn't written anything worthy. I was stuck. My main character had decided to give me the silent treatment. Served me right. I deserved this sudden blank—I'd treated Vassilios badly.

I walked around my apartment, going from the bedroom to the kitchen, looking into the fridge for something to eat. It wasn't too late to call David and Kaliq and be their third wheel tonight. It was still relatively early...

Or I could go out *alone*. There were a few places I'd visited in my early twenties, places where the shadows moved around you and the air was pungent with the scent of cologne and sex. I'd been in those corridors before. Not often, but it had been a rite of passage for me.

I had bound myself up in rules and limitations because I spent most of my time with Elsie and Fay. I'd found comfort in being a good, decent, responsible man. But tonight, my sister away with her new husband, Fay taken care of, my apartment clean and organized, my life perfectly frozen and not going anywhere, I felt it—my body had its own story to tell.

Now my body wanted Davinder, and no stranger could satisfy it. I had waited long enough. Tonight, I would not be denied.

Flushed, I found my phone and called his mobile.

He answered on the first ring. "Where are you?" He was home and he'd been thinking of me.

"I want you to come over," I said.

"What do I tell Eileen?" He wasn't really asking me, but thinking out loud.

"Davinder, come over."

"Gimme an hour," he said and hung up.

❖

Our clothes lay scattered around the bedroom, and my sheets were wet with our sweat.

I lay in bed, naked. Nothing moved around me. My heart beat quietly. My mind had been unhinged and freed to wander, leaving me in peace with my flesh. It was as it should be. I'd turned the tables on Davinder tonight, been the one to possess him this time. I'd made him scream and come in a way his body hadn't let him before. I'd made him see what it really meant to give. He'd resisted it, kissed me, cajoled me, clinging to all of his safe notions on masculinity, until what I wanted had become what he needed, and what he gave me became what he could take.

This was the point from which we could not return.

He was still in the bathroom. He'd been in there for a while. I wouldn't allow him to feel shame. I slipped my underwear on, not bothering with cleaning up, and went to him.

I listened at the bathroom door. "Davinder?"

"Just a second."

I walked back to the bedroom and waited. Five minutes passed. I knocked on the door. "You okay?"

He didn't answer me.

I knocked again and jiggled the handle. "What are you doing in there?" A slight chill ran through me. "Okay, open the door." I saw the handle turn and he opened the door a wedge. "Let me in," I said, pushing myself in. "What's up?"

"I'm fine."

"Do you need to go home?"

"You know I've never let a man do me like that," he said, not looking up at me. "I never even wanted to."

"I know." I leaned in and kissed his chest. "I know," I repeated softly.

"What do you think of that? I mean, what do you think of a man like me?" Something had come undone inside him, and he needed time to find all of the loose ends.

"I want you to go home and get some rest. Okay?"

"I don't feel right."

"I know, Davinder." I guided him out of the bathroom, into my bedroom, and collected his clothes. "But you might feel better tomorrow."

"You're calm."

"I'm just not scared anymore." I helped him with his shirt, buttoning it up for him. "I can't explain it to you, I'm sorry."

"I love you."

"I love you, too."

He smiled, but he still looked shocked. "I'll call you this week?"

"Call me when you can."

When he'd left, I wrapped myself in the sheets we'd soiled and fell asleep.

CHAPTER EIGHT

S unday evening, and I sat around the living room with Elsie, Dayton, and Fay. They'd had a wonderful weekend.

"So, how was your night?" Elsie said, playing with Fay's hair. She'd missed her. "You look like you had a good one."

"I wrote a lot."

"Ah, I see."

"Any news from the press in Vancouver?" Dayton asked. "The one you said could be a possible yes?"

"Still waiting," I said. "But I'm confident." This was my automatic response to any questions pertaining to my submission process.

"Thanks so much for babysitting Fay." Elsie stifled a yawn. "Let's have dinner tomorrow night. I'll make the curry I made the other time."

"That sounds great," I said with as much enthusiasm as I could fake. "I'll bring dessert."

At the entrance, I hugged Fay. "You look all grown up with your new haircut." Ingrid had taken her to the salon and shopping. They'd had their first ladies' day out. First of many to come, I suspected. Fay needed a grandmother.

"Hey." Dayton was flipping a shiny object between his thick fingers. "This is my brother's Zippo lighter."

"Yeah?" I looked at the lighter. "Hmm," I said, ordering myself to calm down. *Stay cool.* They didn't know. "I must have taken it by mistake at the wedding. Take it back to him, I'm sure he's looking for it."

Dayton put it in his pocket and Elsie opened the door. "Thanks again."

"Maybe he dropped it when he came over yesterday." Fay swung on Dayton's arm. "Do I have to got to bed right now?"

Elsie's cheeks colored slightly. "No, you can stay up a little," she said to Fay, her eyes on mine.

❖

I shut the door behind me and wiped my face with the back of my sleeve.

I was drenched from head to toe.

"Look at you," Davinder said, glancing up from the mess of papers on his desk. "I'll get you a towel."

It was a little past nine and his office was closed. Lamontagne Inc. now had three full-time employees on the payroll, and two part-timers. But Davinder seemed to be overloaded. He still worked every day of the week and stayed late in the evening.

"Here." He gave me a large bath towel and went to the window, peeking through the closed blinds. "Shit, it's really coming down hard out there."

I hung my jacket on the door and toweled dry. "How come you have a bath towel here?"

He waved dismissively, walking back to his desk. He looked so beautiful tonight. I loved him in this gray shirt. "A customer gave it to me, I think."

"Busy day?" I still stood in the entrance. I'd been seeing Davinder for three weeks now, almost every day, but every time we met I spent the first few minutes in this state—embarrassed, a little awkward, unsure of myself. He was never warm when he greeted me. Never hugged or kissed me. Never showed any sign that he'd missed me.

"I finished the suicide hotline thing." He clicked around on his computer. "I think I like it." He'd been working on this particular campaign for a while.

"It's very good," I said, looking at the image of the baobab tree more closely. "I love the green here."

"Green is the color of hope." He stared at his work. I could tell he was proud. He'd nailed it again. "Every branch snapped off, big or small, slowly kills the tree, you know?"

"Yeah, I get it," I said softly, standing behind him.

"I know you do." He cleared his throat. "So, should I send it like this?"

"Yes."

He did, turned his computer off, and looked at me.

"What?" I smiled.

"Nothing," he said, still looking at me.

I knew what he wanted to say. I saw it all in his stare. *I love you. Thank you. I'm scared.* I didn't need him to speak the words out loud. "You want to go have a drink to celebrate?" I went to him. "Come on."

"Not more than an hour." He sat facing me, his face turned upward. "I told Eileen that—"

"An hour's fine."

Finally, he leaned his head against my stomach. "I'm sorry, Allan."

I made him look at me. "Stop it. Come on, let's go." I pulled him up.

We grabbed an umbrella and our coats and stepped out into the deluge. The rain still came down, pounding the sidewalk, filling the street drains quickly. We tried to keep the umbrella over us and wrestled with the wind, but eventually had to give it up.

"Fuck it," Davinder said, his voice almost lost in the rain. He closed the umbrella and we dashed for the nearest pub.

❖

The place was empty except for the staff. It was Wednesday, and raining. No Montrealer would be seen out of their home tonight. I was glad we had the place to ourselves, but I also knew it didn't change anything. There could have been ten thousand people or none— Davinder wouldn't relax. He'd sit across from me, never letting his eyes linger too long on my face, and wouldn't touch me.

I didn't mind his paranoia. I was finding out, I didn't mind anything Davinder ever did.

"So what did you tell Eileen today?" He moved the ice around in his drink. "She's starting to think you don't like her, and man, I don't know what to tell her."

"And you think I do? I'm not going to have lunch with your wife. *Ever.*"

"I'm not asking you to, but I don't know what to tell her when she asks me why you don't like her."

"I'm doing so much lying that I don't even—"

"I know." He sipped his drink and looked away.

We never talked about it. Never acknowledged the immensity of our betrayal. "My sister could be on to me... on to *us*, but I'm not sure."

"But you told me she bought the explanation about the lighter and me coming over."

"She hears me coming and going."

"So, you could be going anywhere." He pushed his drink up and rose. "I need a smoke."

"It's still pouring."

"I'll stand under the awning." He didn't look at me and left. He didn't want to talk about it. He and Eileen were doing fairly well, he'd told me. Eileen was much more lenient since she'd cut back on her hours and made new friends. She went swimming in the evenings and had started a yoga class. Ingrid watched the boys a lot, so Eileen didn't need him so much anymore. Wasn't so dependent on him. And that was fantastic. But for whom, I wasn't certain. The better the two of them got along, the less chance I had at a future with him.

I finished my beer and slipped my coat on. He was still out there, under the awning. He'd lit a second cigarette. "Do you want to call it quits?" he said, his voice trailing off with the wind. He turned and looked at me. "I'd understand if you did."

"You mean us?" I took the cigarette from him and tossed it in the flooded gutter. "Not right now. Not today." Discreetly, I touched his hand.

He sighed. "I'm tired. Just tired of feeling like this."

"This situation is poison for you, do you understand?" I hadn't planned on talking to him like this. "You married Eileen because you loved her and you did right by her for years, but now you're not doing right by her anymore, and that's the truth."

"She'd take the boys from me." He turned his collar up, shivering.

He'd actually thought about this?

Davinder shot me a sidelong glance. "She wouldn't give me a divorce. Especially after all of the progress we made this year."

"Let's go inside or to my place. I'm freezing."

"I have to go home." He took a step into the rain and looked at the end of the empty street. "No chance for a cab, I think."

"It's early," I said. "Come to my place for a few minutes and we'll call a cab from there." I knew logic was a sure bet with him.

He agreed and we walked to my home in silence.

"I'll toss your jacket in the dryer." Inside the apartment, I turned the corner lamp on and took his coat. "And your socks?"

"What if I stayed here for the night?" He sat down on the couch with a blank look in his eyes. He stared out into space. "I could call her right now and tell her I'm here and spending the night with you."

I sat on the coffee table, facing him, and took his hands in mine. "Your hands are frozen. And you're exhausted. You need to stop thinking."

"Am I allowed to feel things even if they disgust or hurt others? I can't put my heart through the sausage machine, right? Can't make it obey like a good little tinker solider, now can I? I tried, you know? I did the things they told me, and walked the road they pointed to, and look at where I am today."

"Where are you today?"

"In fucking hell, Allan."

"It's that bad?"

"Worse."

"Okay, you want to try telling each other the truth?" I sat by him now, not letting go of his hand. "I'll start, okay? I don't think I'll ever get a book published in my life. Not enough talent or balls for it. I think Dayton and my sister made a mistake getting married so fast and having a baby, but I wonder if it's because I'm jealous. I don't remember what my mom's face looked like or the sound of her voice and I don't really feel any remorse about it."

"That's normal."

"I'm not finished."

"Okay, go on."

"I didn't love Anthony. I loved how he made me feel. I think Vassilios is crazy and he's been leaving messages on my phone for days now, writing me very nasty e-mails, and——"

"What? Since when? You didn't tell me."

"Still not finished. I can't sleep at night because I lie there thinking of you. I don't really care about things anymore. That scares me a little. I used to have my head on right, and now, well…I could sit in the dark all day waiting for you to call and that would be my life, and I might be all right with it."

"People get obsessed with things they can't have."

"Is that what you are, then? Something I can't have?"

He didn't answer me, of course. He slipped his hand out of my grasp and looked around, still with that blank look on his face.

Was he an *obsession*? "Maybe you're right," I said.

"No, you see very clearly." He sighed and leaned back on the seat, closing his eyes. "Tell me about your book. What's it about?"

He'd already read my novella last week and given me some positive feedback. Granted, his sharp insights into the weaker aspects of my writing had torn gashes into my ego, but I was glad he'd cared enough to read it so attentively.

I wanted to tell him about this book. "Okay, well, it's about a struggling actor who gets caught up in an underground agency whose secret agenda is to build careers by bringing their clients to the summit and then destroying them through media, only to give them the ultimate comeback and cash in. And they've got all kinds of people on the payroll, from the paparazzi to senators to famous news anchors, you know?"

Davinder was staring at me with vivid interest. "You have some chapters I can look at?"

"It's a rough draft. It needs——"

"Allan, this idea is so contemporary. You have to hurry up with this one. It's all about timing." He was getting excited. "Read," he said, sitting up. "I want to get a feel for it."

"Yeah? You sure?" It was late. He'd get in trouble.

"I have fifteen minutes."

I rose and turned on my computer. I sat with my back to him and read the first two very short chapters, trying to keep a good pace and my voice clear. As I read my own words out loud, I began to feel excited, too. This was good. This could turn into something if I kept at it.

When I was finished, I didn't turn around, afraid to see his expression. He'd listened without interrupting, but I couldn't tell if he was quiet because he'd liked it, or was just sleeping. "That's all I have for now," I said.

"It's very good."

I slowly spun my chair around and faced him. "I'm going to write this book and I'm going to self-publish it." Yes, that's exactly what I'd do. "And you're going to design the cover for it."

He laughed. "That would be fucking awesome."

"You'll do it, then? If I write a book worthy of your artistic talent?"

"Yes." His face grew serious. "We'll be bound by ink and paper forever."

I wrapped my arms around him and felt the stirrings of his desire for me. "I read for eleven minutes," I said, half in jest. "Now, in certain circles, I'm known as the Fabulous Four-Minute Man."

He laughed. "You're crazy." He kissed me again and I knew he had to go. I watched him saunter down my back steps, but in the yard, he turned around and stood there for a moment, looking up at me. "I love you," he said quietly. "Give me a month."

He left me there with my mouth hanging open.

CHAPTER NINE

B ut three months passed.
　　Davinder and I saw each other every few days—never on weekends—and our meetings became the core of my life. Sometimes we met at his office late in the evening and I helped him with some data entry, sales confirmations, translations (my French was better than his even though he'd lived in Paris for two years). Other times, we'd sneak into my apartment and spend an hour in bed. Some evenings, we just lay together and talked. Davinder began to open up to me. He never would discuss what happened to him in Paris or if he'd ever been with other men aside from that boy and me. He did tell me about his accident and what it meant for him. The lessons he'd learned from it. He would never again be careless. Would never take his health for granted. We talked about Noah and Jude more and more. He was very fond of his sons. We seldom discussed his childhood. I knew he'd been his father's favorite. He was a restless soul and his mind was constantly working on a problem he shared with no one.

Was I part of this secret problem or part of the solution?

My answer changed from day to day.

"Dav," I said, caressing his arm. He'd fallen asleep in my bed, but our time was up. "You have to wake up." It was close to nine p.m. Eileen's patience with his long hours had run out last month. In the last fourteen days, we hadn't seen each other but twice a week, and had cut our time together by half. Davinder was like a windmill in a tornado. All I could do was try to get him to relax when we were together. I was wrapping up my novel, *The Agency*, and finding I loved editing more than I did the actual writing. I spent a lot of time with Fay, as Elsie and Dayton were getting their new home ready and preparing for Finn's birth. Ingrid would not be moving upstairs after all—what a relief that was—and in the last weeks, I'd been interviewing potential tenants. On weekends, I tried to keep busy by going out with friends, and I'd recently gotten a yearly subscription to the Centaur Theatre. I'd seen a few plays and was discovering this dormant passion in me.

Yet all of these distractions were merely that—things I did to fill in the gaps.

"Do you want me to make some coffee?" I stroked Davinder's hair. "Come on, you really have to get up."

"I know." He rolled over and wrapped his arm around me. "Oh man, I'm so comfortable right now." He closed his eyes.

I was usually the voice of reason, but tonight, I didn't feel like being sensible. Didn't feel like worrying about what Eileen would think. She had him every day and barely touched him. She'd stopped her medication as soon as she'd felt better, and the depression was creeping back into their lives. Noah wasn't doing well in school, despite the tutors and specialists, and Jude had begun acting out at home, clearly feeling the tension between his parents. Their family was off balance—there was no real harmony in their house. Eileen must have sensed Davinder was not faithful to her. Every argument was a disguised attempt at rousing the truth out of him, and their kids were unwilling participants in this charade.

"I'm up," he said, sitting.

"Are you taking the metro or a cab?" I got out of bed and collected his clothes. This routine was second nature to me now. "Here," I said, handing him his pants.

He dressed in silence while I stripped the bed. He went to the window and stared out. I saw the neighbors' Christmas lights reflected in his eyes. Everything was covered in snow. Maybe I'd wrap some gifts tonight and that would keep me sane.

"I found the science kit Noah was asking for," I said, meeting him at the window. "I had to go to a few places, but I found it."

Davinder nodded. "He'll like that." The street was a blanket of white and silent as a still picture.

I leaned my chin on his shoulder. "So how's that going to be?

Christmas Eve, I mean." We were all invited to Dayton's. "You're sure you don't want me to fake a stomach flu that day?"

"No, there's no way you're spending Christmas Eve alone." His tone left no room for debate. "It's really quiet out there," he said. "Like when I was a kid and everybody in the house slept. Except me. I'd sit up in bed and look out the window like this."

"And what did you think about?"

"I wondered if we were real or some little people in a giant's model."

"I used to look up at the sky and make myself crazy thinking about what was at the end of it."

He turned around. "It's getting harder to leave you. I'll call and tell her I feel feverish and would rather stay at the office and lie down in the back room."

"That's a horrible excuse. You can't tell her that."

He shook his head. "Fuck, there's only so much I can put up with before I crack."

"I'm here, okay? I'll be here tomorrow. Don't get yourself worked up like this." I wanted him to flip out and call his wife to confess everything. God, how I wanted him to break free from all these lies! I was worried about him. This situation was taking a toll on his mental health. But part of me—the better part—knew that he wasn't strong enough to withstand the consequences of telling Eileen the truth. Not right now, at least. Not today. "Give it some time," I said.

"What are you reading?" He picked up the paperback novel on my nightstand and flipped it over. "*Swann's Way*," he whispered. He found the page I'd bookmarked. "Page thirty-seven."

"Yeah, it's a tough read. It's a long stream of consciousness and—"

"How long do you think it'll take you to finish it?" He glided his hand over the cover and set it down again. "Days, weeks?"

"I don't know…Maybe two weeks. Why, you want it?"

"No, I've read it." He inhaled sharply. "Listen to me, I know I made a lot of stupid promises to you in the last couple of months, but this is different." He touched the book once more. "By the time you finish this book, I'll have asked Eileen for a divorce."

"What if I read it all tonight?"

"You think this is funny?"

"I'm sorry, Dav."

He whipped past me on his way to the entrance. I watched him throw his coat on. His jaw was set as he tied his boots, and I knew he was angry. He opened the door and a gust of wind blew in.

"Read the fucking thing in one night, I don't care," he said, standing in the doorway.

I looked at him, but held my tongue.

"You think you know everything, don't you?" His stare could have killed me. "It's easy for you to be kind and patient because you're fishing with a full stomach. You've never really known what it's like to lose or go without."

"Is that so?" I said.

"See, like right now…you won't argue with me. Won't even put up a decent fight. Because you know I'll be back and I'll be sorry. And you'll say the right things, and do the right things—"

"I don't know where you're going with this."

"You know how hard it is always being wrong?"

"Is this what this is about?" I pulled him in and shut the door. "Right and wrong? What about happiness, huh? Where does that fit in?"

"And what makes you think we'd be happy together anyway?" I turned away, but he caught my arm. "Allan, I—"

"Just leave me alone," I said, breaking free.

"I didn't mean that, and you know it."

"Do you think you're the only one who suffers?"

"No."

We stood face-to-face, both on the verge of tears. "You better go," I finally said. "There's no use talking about this tonight."

"What if we didn't see each other for the next few days? What if we took some time to think?"

"If you stop seeing me, you'll kill me, you need to know that."

"I wouldn't," he whispered, coming closer. "I'd never leave you." Why did he have to be so intense all the time? "Allan, I just meant that I need a few days to think."

"When will we see each other again?"

"Christmas?"

"At Dayton's house? That should be interesting."

"Allan, come on."

"I'm going to go crazy," I cried. "Is that what you want? You're telling me I won't see you for almost a week and then when I do see you, you'll be with your wife and kids!"

"I need time to think!" His voice rose and we both looked up. Every time he was here, I wondered how long our luck would hold out. One time, Dayton was coming down the front steps as Davinder went down the back. That had been the closest call. My sister never asked me anything about my comings and goings in the evenings, and whenever anyone mentioned Davinder, she'd avoid looking at me.

"I can't think clearly when we're always together," he said, more softly. "I need to gain some perspective on this."

"And what if you discover that you don't love me as much as you thought?" I'd spoken my worst fears. "What if you realize this is a mistake? That *I'm* a mistake?"

He snorted a laugh. "Please, I've made a lot of mistakes in my life, but trust me, you're not one of them."

I bit my lip, looking down at my feet. "That's good to hear."

"I could never do without you now. It's way too late for that."

"All right," I said. "I'll see you at Christmas, then."

CHAPTER TEN

I couldn't believe how much work Dayton had done on their house. I vividly remembered the atrocious pistachio-colored kitchen, the pink halls, the thin, aging carpets in every room, the curtains, the dusty stairs…I'd tried to forget the bathroom lest I have nightmares about it. But he'd stripped the carpets and varnished the floors, given the walls a fresh coat of paint, changed every fixture, curtain, cabinet. It was a sunny sort of little house in one of Montreal's oldest neighborhoods. They'd be happy here.

"And now," Elsie said, pulling on my arm, "the bathroom."

"Oh God. I don't think I can take it." I followed her down the hall. My sister was wobbling, I noticed. Her belly had dropped low. She insisted the baby wouldn't be here until New Year's Eve, but Dayton had packed her bag anyway and it sat in the trunk of his car.

"Ta da!" Fay said, jumping in front of the new bathtub and striking a pose. "I can swim in here!"

"You did this?" I asked Dayton, who'd joined us. "The plumbing, too?"

"Yeah. It's nice, huh?" Dayton looked around as if seeing everything with new eyes. He'd come here every evening for weeks and weeks, grading papers in the kitchen and rolling up his sleeves to renovate this house for my sister and their kids.

I took Fay by the shoulders. "You like it?"

"Yes!" She ran out and up the stairs to her room.

They were moving in on January fifth. Their timing, although they hadn't planned it, was perfect. My sabbatical was up, and that meant going back to work in two weeks, but with a new tenant upstairs, maybe I'd extend my time off for another few months—if my boss let me.

"Okay, we should go," Dayton said, shutting the light off. "Gotta check on the turkey."

"I'll get Fay." My hands had begun to sweat a little. I hadn't seen Davinder or heard from him in the last five days, but I'd been good about it. I'd resisted calling him or writing him. I'd used our time apart to work on the book.

I climbed the stairs up to Fay's bedroom and stopped on the last step. He'd be with his wife today. There would be no chance to be alone with him. But that didn't matter.

One look at his face and I'd know if he still wanted me.

❖

Elsie lit the last candle and looked around Dayton's living room with a satisfied expression. "I think that's everything." She smiled at me. "Are you feeling all right? You seem nervous today."

"I'm fine, but I wouldn't mind a drink." I picked up one of Dayton's bottles and a glass and poured a shot. "Sure you don't want one? It'll put some hair on Finn's chest." I winked and drank. I was drinking more than I should these days.

"Come here." She sat on the couch, sinking into it, rubbing her belly. "Hurry before Dayton comes in."

"What is it?" I sat by her.

"Dayton wants to ask Davinder and Eileen to be Finnegan's godparents."

"And you don't want that," I muttered, not sure where she was going with this.

"Do you think it's a good idea?" She was calm. "Considering."

Considering. Yes, considering everything. "I don't know," I said.

"You don't? Hmm, I think Dali and Brendan would be the better choice in this case."

"The church would allow that?" I was eager to steer the conversation away from Davinder. "I think only Dali can sign the registrar."

"I still think he's the better choice." There was anger covering her carefully chosen words. She didn't respect Davinder. She didn't think much of him.

"I think Dali's a good choice, yeah." I rose and looked down at her. "I suppose he's the better man, huh?" I left the room before she could say anything and walked into the kitchen. Ingrid was helping Dayton with dinner.

"Am I interrupting?" I said, watching Dayton stick his hand up to the elbow inside the turkey. "You and the bird are obviously busy."

"Gimme the sauce there." Dayton hadn't gotten my stupid joke. "Thanks."

"Can I help with anything?"

"Can I help with anything?" Elsie echoed my words, walking in.

Dayton laughed. "Why don't you two set the table?"

I looked over at her and saw the ice inside her eyes. "Sure," I said, shrugging. "Come on, sis." I gave her a big phony smile.

We piled up the dishes and carried them to the dining room. We set the table in complete silence, both of us staring down at the cutlery and plates. She knew, then. Yes, she knew and judged us.

"Eileen was asking about you," she said, folding a napkin. "Asking if you'd met someone. She has a friend at work who she thinks would be a perfect match for you."

"I'm not interested." I straightened the forks and knives.

"It's been a while since you and Vassilios broke up."

"I'm not interested."

This time, she looked up at me. "It's nice of her to think of you, isn't it?"

"I never asked her to."

"But she does it because she's a good person."

"Being good is highly overrated." I held her eyes. "I'll take hell with my lover over heaven any day."

"You've changed." She looked away, shaking her head.

"So have you."

She seemed shocked. "Yes, but in a good way."

"If you say so." I flipped a glass over and wiped it.

"Allan," she whispered, touching my arm. "What are you two doing with your lives?"

I took her hand in mine. "I'm not leaving him. I'd rather die."

"This is my family, Allan. Did you ever think about that? You're my brother. He's my husband's brother!" She clutched the chair, her face growing pale.

"Elsie." I held her arm, afraid for her. "It'll be okay, I swear to you."

"They'll hate you."

I hugged her. "I don't care."

"But I do," she said, crying against my shoulder. "I do."

❖

"She's okay?" Dayton pointed at my sister, who was seated by Ingrid, looking over pictures. We sat around in the living room. Davinder and his family had yet to show up.

After our secret talk, Elsie had a little meltdown, but blamed it on hormones, lack of sleep, and the insanity of the holidays. "She's fine." I looked at my watch again.

Around me, conversations flowed, but I couldn't focus enough to join in. Dali and Brendan had brought their new puppy and I played with it as he chewed on my shoes.

"Don't let him do that," Brendan said, scooping the dog up. It was a Jack Russell. "Dali, I think he needs to go out again."

"It's your turn." Dali smiled and raised his glass. "Bundle up, babe, it's cold."

Ingrid jumped out of her chair. "They're here."

When I heard the boys' voices, I rose and turned around. "Hey, guys," I said, walking to the entrance. Everyone had gathered around Eileen and Davinder. Hugs and kisses were being exchanged. I was lost in the swell of their excitement.

"Merry Christmas," Eileen said, hugging me. "So glad you're here."

I mumbled appropriate words, shaking her hand. I said a few insignificant things to Noah and Jude, and finally held out my hand to Davinder. "Hi, how are you?"

"Nice to see you," he said, shaking my hand, his voice and manner under perfect control. He looked away from me and greeted Dali.

I felt sick.

I hung around the living room for a few minutes, but my stomach lurched and I couldn't trust myself anymore. Discreetly, I went to the bathroom and shut myself in. He could be so cold. He could be so distant. I'd been torturing myself all day, and here he was, Mr. Ice Man, completely unaffected. I'd have taken anything. Anything to let me know he'd thought of me in the last days.

Outside the door, I heard his voice—he was laughing with his brothers, talking as if I wasn't in this stupid bathroom.

As if I didn't exist.

I looked at my face in the mirror and remembered the day I'd stood here, more than a year ago. "Don't be an idiot," I'd told myself that day. I wished I could go back and change the course of my life.

CHAPTER ELEVEN

Before dinner, we'd all toasted Finn's imminent birth with a glass of brandy eggnog, played with the kids, listened to their long lists of what they thought Santa would bring them in the morning, laughed at Dayton's new jokes, and through it all, I'd smiled and played nice. I wanted to grab Davinder by the collar and demand he tell me how he could be in the same room with me for three consecutive hours and not make eye contact.

However, Eileen wanted to talk to me *plenty*.

"I guess you've been busy with your book," she said. We sat side by side at the table. Dinner was over, but no one wanted to get up yet.

"Yeah, I have." I looked at her and across the table to where Davinder was immersed in conversation with Dali. "I'm sorry if I've been so unavailable," I said.

"Maybe when you finish it, we can go out for a drink and celebrate or something."

"Sure, that sounds like a plan." I shot Davinder another quick glance. He still wouldn't look at me. "I'd love to go out for a drink," I said, louder. "I know this great place I go with a friend of mine all the time. You'd love it." I looked at Davinder again. This time, I detected a vague tension in his jawline.

Eileen called out to him. "Hear that, Dav? Allan's going to take me out." Her laughter was full of bitterness. "He doesn't even care," she said under her breath, to me. "Look at him...nothing excites him. Sometimes I pity him."

"Excuse me," I said, standing.

"Are you okay?"

"Nature calls," I said, leaving the table.

I stumbled through the living room, tripped on a toy, and dashed for the washroom. But the door was locked. Fay was in there. She'd be a while, she told me. I looked around and decided on Dayton's home office. The kids were playing and everyone else was sitting at the table. No one would come looking for me for a while. I shut the door and fell into a chair. I needed to get out of this house.

Long minutes passed and to my great surprise, Davinder entered the office without a word, shutting the door behind him. He opened his mouth to speak.

"Hi," I said angrily. "How are you?"

"I know, I know."

"You do? No, I don't think you know what it's like for me tonight. As a matter of fact, I think you're pretty fucking clueless to what I'm—"

"You think this is easy for me," he said between clenched teeth. "You think—"

"You make it look like a walk in the park."

"What did you want me to do? Stick my tongue down your throat?"

I leaned back against the wall. "I wanted you to give me *one* look tonight," I said, softly. "That's all."

"I couldn't."

"Fine."

"You don't understand, do you?" He came closer. "I can't look at you without selling myself out. She'd see it in my eyes. She knows me. Probably more than she lets on. When I saw you tonight, I thought I'd do something crazy. It took every ounce of my self-control to shake your hand and let it go."

I met his eyes and saw he was telling the truth. "You still want me, then," I said.

"Want you?" He leaned his forehead against mine. "Allan, I need you." He moved back, looking at the door. "I've thought about all this during the last days, and no matter how much I try to convince myself that I could forget about you if only I chose to, I can't do it."

"I want to be with you," I said. "I want you to get a divorce and I want to be with you."

"But I wouldn't make you happy. Don't you get that? This is beautiful because it's forbidden and new. It'll get old and—"

"So that's it? I get to be your fuck of the week for the rest of my life?"

"That's all I can give you."

"You need time," I said. "With time you'll see we could be happy together."

"As a couple?"

"You don't believe in us?"

"I believe that in another place, another time—"

"But what about now? What about this life here?" I wiped my eyes with my sleeve. I didn't care if I was crying. He couldn't do this to me. Not so soon. "Davinder?"

"Please don't cry." He reached for my face, but I slapped his hand off.

"Don't touch me," I growled and rubbed the tears off my cheeks. "And don't tell me what to do."

"Weep, then. Make a fucking scene."

"Maybe I should."

"I think we've come to the end of the line," he said, at length. "This is where I get off."

"You'll never touch me again."

"You'll be okay."

"Don't tell me I'll be okay!"

"Keep your voice down."

"Fuck you!" I shoved him. I hadn't planned on it, but I shoved him. He stumbled back a few steps, shocked, his eyes darkening as he quietly adjusted his jacket.

"I hate you," I sneered. "I hate your—"

"What do you want from me!" he shouted, pushing me into the wall. "Huh? What? I can't move around in my own life!"

"What's going on in here?" Elsie walked in and grabbed Davinder's arm. "I could hear you in the bathroom," she said under her breath. "You're lucky your wife wasn't in there instead of me." She released him and looked at me. "I want you to go home right now or I swear to God—"

"Okay. Okay." I nodded, fixing my shirt.

"*Now*, Allan. I'll tell everyone you were sick." She threw a finger up in Davinder's face. "You couldn't keep away from my little brother, huh? Why did you have to go and do that?"

"Elsie, don't—"

"Oh," she moaned, grabbing her stomach. She looked down at her feet and her face reddened. "Oh, shit, get Dayton. My water just broke."

Chapter Twelve

I sat on the couch, coffee in hand. "Wow," I said in a flat voice. "A Fashionista Barbie." I couldn't even move. I was beyond tired.

"I love her!" Fay tossed the doll aside and grabbed another gift from under my makeshift Christmas tree—a plastic plant I'd decorated with a paper man string last night—and tore through the paper with frenzied hands.

Last night, after Elsie's water had broke, chaos had erupted, and through it all, it had been decided that I'd take Fay home with me. She didn't want to go to her own house. She wanted to sleep in my bed. Eileen had offered to drive us here, and I'd reluctantly agreed, leaving with Fay snuggled up against me. Leaving Davinder behind.

He'd never leave Eileen.

"When can we go see my brother?" Fay was not her usual perky self. "Can I call Mom now?"

I'd been up all night, sitting with my phone in my hand, waiting on news from Dayton. Finally, at six this morning, he'd called. Finn was here. He was a big boy, weighing nine pounds, four ounces. Elsie was doing fine, according to Dayton—exhausted and a little nauseous from the epidural, but fine.

I had a nephew. A little boy named Finnegan Lamontagne.

"Your mom might be sleeping," I said, dialing my sister's hospital room anyway. "Here."

Fay took the phone and spoke with Elsie, pacing the living room. I heard her voice, but couldn't follow the conversation. I stared at the mess of papers and toys.

I'd never felt this lost in my life.

"She wants to talk to you." Fay gave me the phone. She was probably thinking her uncle was losing his marbles.

"Hey," I said, choking up without warning. "Congratulations." I held it all in and smiled. "I'm dying to know, who does he look like most?"

"Allan, I'm sorry about last night." Her voice was thin. "I shouldn't have meddled."

"Meddled? Shit, Elsie, they're your family."

"It has to stop. The affair, you know that, right?"

"Yes," I lied. "It's over. I promise you. It's over."

"He looks like you a lot." She paused, and said, "Oh, Allan, Finn's perfect."

I'd get Fay ready and we'd be on our way to meet Finn soon, I promised her.

❖

We walked through the maternity ward and found Elsie's room. I'd told Fay to be as quiet as she could, but as soon as we'd crept into my sister's room, she screamed and ran to her mom.

"Is that him?" she asked, poking at the bundle of blankets inside Elsie's arms. "I can't see his face."

I unzipped my coat and slipped my hat off. I hadn't expected a room full of people. Everyone was here.

Dali hugged me. "You look like you've had a rough night. Have one of my mother's madeleines." He scooped a yellow pastry out of a box and offered it to me.

"Thanks," I said, feeling hot and dizzy. "Let me see this little boy." I moved to the bed. This whole scene was surreal. I looked down at my nephew. He was a chubby baby with a healthy face. His eyes were closed and he was frowning. Maybe he did look a little like me. He had a dent in his chin as I did. "Hello, Finnegan." I touched his pudgy little hand and shook it. "Welcome."

"You look worse than I do." Elsie brushed my hair back. "Why don't you go home and crash?"

"No, it's okay," I protested.

"Honestly, Allan, you should get some rest."

I turned to find everyone staring back at me. Did I look that bad?

"Go," Dayton said, squeezing my arm. He was sipping his coffee out of his plastic cup. "I'll call you later, don't worry." He hugged me. "Thanks for watching Fay."

"Okay," I said, my voice not quite right. "I'll call you, I mean, call me."

"Say bye, Finn." Elsie waved the baby's hand. "Bye, Uncle Allan."

I walked out of the room. I found the exit and stepped out into the cold air. I looked around, getting my bearings back. I'd walk home. It would do me good. I stuffed my hands into my pockets and set out for the street.

"Allan!"

I pretended not to hear him.

"Wait," Davinder said, catching up to me. "Wait."

The wind blew into my eyes, making them water. He stood there in his flimsy shirt, the snow getting caught in his black hair. "Can we talk?" His face was pale. "Please?"

"What?" I said, opening my hands.

Without a word, he reached out and pulled me into his arms. He was shaking and I held him.

"I can't do it," he said. "I can't."

"Can't what?" I made him look at me.

"Can't leave you." He moved back and lit up a cigarette. "Just like I can't quit these." He smiled and his face was serious once more. "I have this life, you see, this life I started once, and never finished."

"You mean Paris?"

Davinder didn't say anything.

"Why are you afraid to be loved? What scares you so? What is it that you're hiding from?"

He looked at the cigarette in his fingers and sighed. "I don't know."

"You end us because of Eileen, I'll take it. I'll die a little, but I'll take it. But if you end this because you're afraid of happiness...I'll never forgive you for it."

"It's gonna get ugly, Allan. You know that, right?" He shook all over and crossed his arms around his chest. "She's gonna tear me to pieces. This will be the nastiest divorce in the history of the fucking world."

"But I'll be there. I'll be right by you through it all."

And what would happen to Elsie in all this?

I couldn't think about that.

"What if we made a life together," he said. "I'd never leave my kids. I'd take care of them, you know that. I'd give her everything she wanted." He inhaled sharply, glancing around. "And you'd give me time? You'd be patient?"

"If you swear you won't take me for a ride."

"I swear, Allan." I believed in *us*.

CHAPTER THIRTEEN

I walked down my street, returning from the market, glad to have been out of the apartment for a few hours. There was a general excitement in the air this late afternoon. People were outside on their balconies, and kids were chasing each other up and down the sidewalk. Grass poked through patches of melting snow. It was five and the sun was still out. My God, spring was here. This year, winter had seemed longer than ever.

"How are you?" My neighbor, the retired police officer whose name I'd forgotten again, waved to me. "Look at this," he said, smiling. "And it's only gonna get better."

His genuine satisfaction with the weather made me laugh and I waved back at him, but didn't stop to talk. I ran up the three steps leading to my porch, hurried inside, and slammed the door.

Davinder would be here in an hour. I threw everything in the fridge and pantry and stripped as I walked to the washroom, leaving a trail of clothes behind me.

In the shower, I closed my eyes and just stood under the jet, relaxing.

Tonight was special. Tonight was our first actual dinner together, here at my place. Davinder was spending the night with me. Eileen was in Bromont, set up in a five-star hotel with six other lucky colleagues, as a thank-you from their bosses for their great year. Ingrid was watching the kids tonight, Lamontagne Inc. was officially closed tomorrow, and we were going to know what it was like to wake up together. Since Finnegan's birth three months ago we'd been seeing each other every weekday in small doses. He could no longer count on Eileen's patience, and if he was indeed going to get a divorce—

But I didn't want to think about that tonight. I wouldn't even bring it up. It seemed every time we met lately, that's all we talked about: his divorce, Eileen, his kids, my book. No, tonight, we'd put all that to rest for a while.

I splashed a little lotion on my neck and face and checked my reflection in the bathroom mirror. I looked better than I had all winter. I washed the stubble out of the sink, cleaned my hands again, fixed the towels on the rack. If he didn't show up soon, I'd either start drinking or cleaning. I walked through the living room and plugged my iPod into the speakers. I clicked on our song, "Karma Police," and stared out the window.

There he was, coming up the stairs.

"Hi," he said, smiling coolly. "Here, I brought this for us later." He handed me a bottle, but I didn't even look at it. I set it on the coffee table and stood there, taking in all of his dark, sexy energy. "Wow, you're horny as hell," he said, laughing, grabbing my collar gently, pulling me close.

I wasn't going to deny it. It had been a while since this kind of tension had been felt between us. And he felt it, too, because in an instant, his tongue was discovering mine again, and I kissed him hard, riding my hands up and down his lovely ass. "Allan," he whispered. I loved to hear him say my name. I kissed him again, my tongue lacing with his, and soon we were pulling our shirts off and I was shivering with every one of his slow, sweet moves. I was lost—didn't know where I was anymore.

We lay over the sheets, and I went down on him, knowing he was relaxed enough to let me open new doors for him. I refused to hear the word no and licked and teased him until he rolled his head back and the contraction of his thighs shook my shoulders. He was loose and docile then, and I moved up to push myself into him. There was no more resistance.

We made love for hours.

It was nearing midnight and I was weak as a kitten.

"Oh, man," Davinder said, "I need a cigarette badly."

I looked over at him. "Light up, I don't care."

"Too lazy to get them." He snorted a laugh and kissed me. "I'll make you dinner if you go get me a glass of water and a smoke."

"Better yet, I'll get you your poison and a take-out menu." I rolled out of bed and stumbled out of the room naked. I got his cigarettes and a glass of water, found a few take-out menus and came back with those. I slipped into bed again. "What do you feel like?"

"I don't care." He took a long drag and blew out a curl of smoke. "You decide." He looked over at me and winked. "You've been deciding everything else tonight."

"Okay then." I settled on pizza. After I'd ordered, I tossed my phone on the nightstand. "You'll get the door," I said, throwing my arm over his chest, pressing the length of my body against his.

He smoked his cigarette, stroking my shoulder absentmindedly. "Yes, I will. Close your eyes and sleep if you like."

I watched the smoke cling to the air, pale blue in the moonlight.

"I don't think I'll sleep tonight." Davinder sat up and crushed his cigarette in an empty cup. "I'm gonna get cleaned up." He got out of bed, taking all the warmth with him. "We'll stay up all night and make every minute count." He collected his clothes and turned around in the doorway to look at me. "We get along, don't we? I never knew it could be like this."

"Easy?"

"Yeah, easy." He smiled and shook his head, bewildered. "Maybe because you're a guy, I don't know."

"Maybe."

He held the bundle of his clothes against his naked crotch, looking more vulnerable than I'd ever seen him.

"Why did you marry Eileen after you came back from Paris?" I'd been yearning for this talk for so long. "You said you loved that man, but that you lost him…what did you mean by that? What happened, Davinder?"

"We were young and fired up about changing the world."

I held my hand out to him. "Don't stand in the doorway like that. Come."

He slipped his pants on and came to sit on the edge of the bed. "Why do you want to know this?"

"Tell me his name."

He looked down at his hands, hesitating to speak, but inhaled deeply and said, "His name was Renaud."

"Go on, tell me. I want to hear it, and I think you want to tell it."

"Maybe you're right…Okay, here it is…Renaud was a diplomat's son. His father was a millionaire and Renaud hated him for it. He hated the aristocracy. He was a bourgeois, don't get me wrong, but at heart, Renaud was really a punk kid who was way too smart for his own good and had too much free time on his hands. I met him here in Montreal, and two weeks later, I was on plane with him back to Paris."

"You lived together there?"

"No, we didn't. His father would have disowned him, and Renaud, although he liked to complain about the rich, sure *loved* his daddy's money. It kept him drinking his espressos in the best cafés in the city and kept him the center of attention in Paris's jaded underground scene. No, he set me up in a crappy apartment, like some kind of rent boy he saw when the kids he hung out with didn't impress him anymore."

"He wasn't good to you, then."

"He was better than good to me. Renaud treated me as I deserved. I was living off him, dabbling in my art, smoking way too much weed, and throwing shit fits like a true aspiring artist."

"But you two loved each other."

Davinder shut his eyes for a moment. "Yeah, in our own selfish way, we loved each other, but Renaud was always torn between being a diplomat's son and being an anarchist. He'd spend two days with me in which time he'd organize meetings for left-wing student groups, all in the name of leaving scars on Paris's beautiful face, but then he'd tire of it quickly and disappear on me for weeks. I couldn't be seen going up to his penthouse apartment, couldn't talk to him, couldn't reach him…I'd go mad then. I'd paint for days, forgetting to eat, forgetting to sleep."

"And your paintings? Your drawings?"

"He dragged me to some openings and art shows. Nothing ever came of it. No one was interested in my art. It was the nineties, and art was being replaced by video games."

"And you lost him?"

"One day, after I hadn't seen him in weeks, he showed up…I'd been miserable as a dog, so when I saw his face, I hated him for humiliating me. But it was me I hated, really. After all, I'd made the choice to follow him there. I'd lived off his money. His contacts. I was a taker, I realized that day, and it made me sick. I'm not proud of that, Allan."

"That was a long time ago," I said. "You've learned your lesson."

"Have I?"

"You're not taking anything from me."

"And Eileen?"

I slipped my hand out of his and sighed out impatience. "She's taken plenty from you, too. Tell me why you lost him."

"His father found out about Renaud's little meetings and shady friends, and when he finally understood what his pretty queer son did with his spare time, he beat him and threatened to cut Renaud out of his will. In short, he was going to leave Renaud to fend for himself unless he quit everything. And I remember that day, I remember it like it was yesterday, Renaud stood there in my hall, with a fat lip and a shiner, just stood there and looked at me, like a child who's lost his house key. That day, he asked me if I could love him if he was to forsake all of his money and future. If we could go back to Montreal and start anew."

"He was ready for that?"

"I think so, but I never got a chance to find out. Because I laughed at his naïveté and told him he could never survive without his father's money. That in the real world, he was just a little faggot boy amongst millions."

"You were cruel because he'd humiliated you."

"No, I was cruel because I loved him so much at that moment it scared me, and I enjoyed breaking his heart."

I didn't know what to say. My sympathy went to Renaud. I felt close to him in that moment. I wanted to say to him, "He didn't mean it, my friend, and you'll survive him."

And if *I* had to lose Davinder one day, would I survive it?

"Pretty ugly, huh?" Davinder couldn't look at me. "I bet you see me differently now," he said, his voice shaky.

"What happened after?"

"I never saw him again. I looked for him for days, but never found him. Here I was, my rent due in a week, and no Renaud in sight. Then, one afternoon, a mutual acquaintance of ours told me he'd left Paris for

Germany. Rumor was, Renaud had forsaken all of his father's money and fled to Berlin."

"Alone?"

"No one knew. My time in Paris was up and I had nothing to show for it but a broken heart and a smashed-up ego. Anyway, years later, after Jude was born, I looked Renaud up."

"And?"

"He's a journalist and an advocate for gay youth rights. When I saw his picture, I couldn't believe it. He's a man now. A great man at that."

"You never wrote him or tried to make contact?"

"Why would I? No, I broke what we had, and you can't put a shattered thing back together again. When I came back to Montreal, the first thing I wanted to do was call Eileen and forget what I'd done, who I'd become."

"She knows about all this?"

"Yes, not in detail, but she knows."

I was shocked. "She does? You mean she knows you're bisexual? She's known all this time?"

"Of course. She's my wife. I couldn't keep that from her."

"Do you think she suspects me?"

"I don't know. Sometimes I think she does, and then I think she's the sweetest woman who ever lived and could never imagine such a betrayal. She gets emotional, and granted, she can get a little crazy, but she lives with me, and that's enough to make anyone nuts. She's honest, Allan, and the best mother my boys could have."

"You talk about Renaud," I said, watching him slip into his shirt, "and you talk about Eileen, and the more you talk, the more I feel lost in the crowd. What am I in all this?"

"You're Allan."

"Don't patronize me, please."

"What's wrong?" He stood over the bed, looking at me seriously. "What did I say?"

"It's what you're *not* saying. Not once did you say, 'But what I felt for Renaud was nothing compared to what I feel for you,' or even, 'I don't love Eileen anymore, it's you I want to be with.'"

"Why do you always need me to reassure you? After what we did tonight. No one has ever gone that deep into me, physically, emotionally, *whatever*...Don't you know that by now?"

"So what do I get, a gold star?" I held his smoldering stare.

To my surprise, he laughed. "Are we gonna fight?"

I looked away, shrugging.

Maybe.

"Baby, I only told you my story because you asked me to. Believe me, if you never want to bring it up again as long as we both live, I won't."

The doorbell rang—pizza was here—and Davinder stepped out of the bedroom.

I could feel the doubt spread through me.

❖

I stared at Davinder's face as he slept.

I'd never seen him sleeping in the sunlight. My eyes traced the creases of his brow, the arc of his nose, the fine lines at the corner of his mouth. He had freckles below his eyes and I'd never noticed the scar across his temple—pale and straight, probably a childhood accident. He slept on his side, with his arms locked around him—even in his sleep, he seemed to be protecting his heart. He didn't snore, but he talked in his sleep and moved around a lot.

I leaned in closer and kissed his mouth, knowing he wouldn't wake up. His eyelids fluttered a bit and he mumbled something, pouting. I'd never seen that expression on his face before. For a short moment, he looked like a boy again.

I touched his face. "I love you," I whispered. "It doesn't matter what you did."

I tried to believe it.

Still sound asleep, Davinder sighed and slapped my hand off his face.

I crept out of bed, leaving him to his boyish dreams.

CHAPTER FOURTEEN

I stood in the bathroom doorway, watching Davinder brush his teeth. That was another new experience for me. I'd never seen him do any of these everyday things.

I'd found out he hated eggs, only drank his first coffee after he'd had a glass of orange juice, didn't butter his toast and liked it black as tar. He ate standing up at the counter and definitely wasn't a morning person. He read the obituaries and made funny but disturbing comments. Every little thing he said or did was a discovery. He thought it was cute that I ate oatmeal. He'd never known a grown man who liked it. His mood brightened after his second cup of coffee, and I was glad to see he didn't smoke in the morning.

"What time is it?" he said, his toothbrush hanging out of his mouth. He was nervous now.

"Nine."

He rinsed and cleaned the sink. "Okay."

"So what should we do?"

"I was thinking…you know, since you're so good with words… would you help me write a letter to Eileen? I wouldn't give it to her or anything, but—"

"No, I see…yeah, that's a great idea." There went my morning of lazy sex in the sun. "Sure, I'll do that for you. Come on, let's pick your brains first."

"Scary thought." He joined me in the living room and sat, fidgeting.

"Okay, here we go." I sat by him and spread some loose sheets of paper on the table and gave him the pen. "What would you start with?"

He rolled the pen between his fingers, staring at it. "Sometimes people meet and travel together for a while, down the road they've chosen together, until one of them decides that maybe that road isn't leading him anywhere."

"That's very good," I said. "But I wouldn't use the word *anywhere.*"

"Right, that makes me sound like a pretentious prick." He tapped the pen on his front teeth. "But the road they chose," he went on, "was never a mistake. It was part of their long path to self-realization."

"Now you're getting a little too heavy. Keep it simple. Speak from the heart." I touched his chest. "From here, Davinder. Tell her what you really want to tell her."

"Dear Eileen," he said, not writing. "I'm in love for the first time in my life."

I felt the sting of a blush on my face. "You mean that? Really?"

"Yes."

"You've never said it quite like that before."

"I don't think I knew it until just now."

"Let's keep going," I said, taking the pen from him. "Don't stop, just let it come out the way it wants to."

And he did.

I listened to him, jotting down his words. They came fast at times, but then he'd slow down once more. He was confessing his sins. He'd married Eileen for the wrong reasons, but he'd believed they were right. He'd loved her as best he could, and when they'd become parents, he'd taken on all of the responsibilities his role demanded. He'd never allowed himself to listen to that voice inside him telling him there were other ways to love and live.

I looked at the loose sheets we'd filled. The side of my hand was stained with ink and cramping up. I hadn't written anything longhand in years. "How do you feel?"

"Strange," he said, leaning back into the seat. "But good."

I gave him the papers. "This is yours."

"I know. It's all mine. All of it, and I'm going to have to do something about it, now aren't I?"

"Yes."

"I'm standing at the gates, Allan. I'm right there, just a step away."

❖

Elsie crept out of Finn's bedroom and put a finger to her mouth. "Let's go to the living room," she whispered. She'd finally gotten him down for the night.

"Tea or wine?" Elsie began to put away the dishes.

"Tea, thanks." I sat at their new table and looked around the kitchen. "So, how have you been?" I hadn't seen my sister in a while. I missed when she lived upstairs from me. I missed how simple my life had been back then. I'd thought it boring, when it had been beautiful and clean.

"It's been kind of hectic since Dayton had to go back to work." She sat across from me, waiting for the kettle to sing. "I'm just tired, I guess." I hadn't seen her smile since I'd arrived an hour a ago. "Listen, Allan, we really need to talk."

My jaw tightened. "Okay, what is it?"

Elsie took my hand in hers.

Did I know Davinder and Eileen were doing much better?

Did I know Eileen had been mending her relationship with Ingrid, and that she'd been opening up to her mother-in-law more? Yes, Eileen had been telling her *things*. She and Davinder were reconnecting lately, making love again. They'd been reserving Saturday nights for date night, going out for dinner together…

Did I know this?

How could I not?

What was he telling me?

And what did I expect out of this?

I sat there, listening, trying to keep my face from betraying the emotions raging through me.

"I know you've always been there for me," Elsie said. "I owe you so much. That's why this is tearing me apart, Allan. Because you sacrificed a lot to take care of me and Fay when we needed you the most."

"You don't owe me anything." I was so shaken I could barely speak.

So Davinder was sleeping with Eileen.

"Listen to me, please." The kettle sang and my sister turned the burner off, standing with her back to me. "He's not going to leave her," she said. "And even if he did, what do you think would happen next? Do you know what kind of disaster this would mean for you?" She turned around. "For me? Do you really believe you guys could be together after the explosion?"

"Is this about you, then?"

"Yes! My God, Allan, I'm married to his brother! And I love Dayton. I love his family! They're *my* family now. *Mine!* How long did I have to wait for this, huh?" She composed herself, but her hands shook as she poured the water into our cups. "I don't want you to blame me," she said, the tears finally spilling over her face. "But I can't let you destroy my family over a man who doesn't even deserve you."

"What makes you think he doesn't deserve me? You think I'm a fucking angel, right? That he's the big bad wolf that corrupted your perfect little brother? Well, I've got news for you. I'm not this—"

"I know you're not a saint. I know that." She sat and held her cup in both hands. "You're in love, and love makes us blind sometimes. Do you remember what you said to me when I told you I loved Gabe and nothing could ever stop me from it?"

"I never tried to stop you."

"Yes, you did. In subtle ways, you did. And you were right, weren't you?"

"He's not Gabe."

"No, he's not. He's worse."

I wanted to throw my cup at the wall and leave. But I couldn't. Because no matter how much this hurt, a part of me wanted to hear it. The better part of me?

"I can't live without him…I swear, I'll die."

"You won't. You won't die. Look at me. Allan, you're addicted to him, but you can get him out of your system, you can, and you will. You have to."

"He loves me." I wiped my eyes. "Do you understand? He loves me like he's never loved anyone, and he needs me."

"I believe that. I'm not questioning that. But that doesn't make it right. Does it? I mean, can you honestly sit there and tell me that what you two are doing is right? How can you guys look Jude and Noah in the eye? How can you?"

"They're not my sons."

"Not your problem, huh? Eileen, the kids, me, Dayton...Finn." She nodded, her eyes icing over. "Not your problem. As long as you get your daily hit, right? And Fay? What about Fay, Allan? What are you going to tell her when she asks why Dayton doesn't want to be in the same room as you? Why everyone in her family hates you or doesn't want anything to do with you? Is she going to have to choose? What do you think this mess will do to her? She's young, but she'll catch on, and she'll feel betrayed. Abandoned again."

Fay.

No, I couldn't think about that. I'd explain things to her. She'd understand.

"He's not going to leave Eileen, and you're going to waste away waiting for him, and even if he does have the decency and courage to do the right thing, you'll lose everyone and everything."

"I only need him."

"Is that so?"

I was in shock. Couldn't recognize my own thoughts and words.

"You're my baby brother. I always thought we'd stick together. Why are you doing this to me?"

"You got your man. Let me have mine."

She rubbed her face and stared me down. "He isn't yours to have."

"Are we done here?" I got up.

She had her little picket-fence dream. Her kids. Her business. Her loving husband.

And what did I have? I'd given her and Fay nine years of my life. I was done with giving. "I'm leaving." I turned for the door.

"I'll tell them all...I'll tell Dayton first. He's my husband and I can't lie to him anymore."

I stopped, my hands turning cold, but didn't face her. "You wouldn't."

"Yes, Allan, I would. And I will. If I'm going to lose everything,

I'd rather do it now then to spend every day wondering if this is the day it all goes down."

I spun around. "I won't let you."

"You going to kill me or something?" She was leaning back on the counter. The room moved around me and I had to lean my hand over the chair behind me to steady myself. When I'd backed away, she hid her face in her hands and sobbed. "Get out of my house!"

I had to sit down. But she slapped my shoulder. "Get out!"

Ashamed, I grabbed hold of her waist and pressed my face into her maternal soft belly. "I'm sorry," I said. "Elsie, please, I'm sorry." She didn't hold me. What had I done? I looked up at her. "What do you want me to do? Just tell me. I don't know anymore."

She pushed my hair back from my forehead. Her tenderness made me feel even more ashamed. "Leave him. End it." She didn't say the words as an order, but as a plea. "Sell the duplex. Go away. Start new somewhere else. You know this is the only way. You look so tired. You look so miserable."

"I thought he and I could make it."

"This is something that should have never started in the first place."

I didn't want to say it, but I did. "You're right."

It was guilt that tortured me, not love for Davinder.

Yes, *guilt*. Every time we'd made love. Every time we'd met secretly. Guilt. Always.

I didn't want to feel it anymore. "Give me some time. Please."

"No, Allan, time will only weaken you even more. No, this has to be done quickly. Do you understand? The minute you see him, you'll go right back to denial and everything we said tonight will seem stupid."

"I'm supposed to leave him just like that." I snapped my fingers.

"Yes. Just like that. You call him, you tell him, you come to me. I'll be here."

"No, give me time." I shook my head. "I need time."

She inhaled a deep breath and nodded. "Don't take too long, please."

Leave Davinder?

Was I really going to do this?

How could I?

"I need to think, Elsie." I pulled away and stared at the floor.

"Think about this, then…think about Davinder making love to his wife as we speak about how much you need him."

I shot her a cold glance.

"Huh? Think about that, Allan. Then think about Fay asleep in her bed and the peace she feels for the first time in her life. And when you're done thinking about that, think about what it would feel like to be able to look yourself in the eye again."

CHAPTER FIFTEEN

Davinder hung his coat on the rack and rubbed his hands together. "Whew, it's cold out there." He pulled his boots off. "Sorry I'm late."

It was Friday night, two days after my conversation with Elsie, and I stood there in my living room, my heart in a vise. I'd been sick for the last two days. I'd not been able to keep anything down and had slept on and off. I'd wake up on the couch and wonder how I got there, or look up at the kitchen clock and realize I'd been sitting in front of a sandwich for minutes, staring out into space.

"Hi," he said, kissing me. "I called you last night. Writing a lot?"

"Yeah," I heard myself say.

"You feeling okay?"

"I'm a little sick." I grabbed a cushion and hugged it for strength.

He sat by me, on the edge of the couch, nervous. "Yeah? What's wrong?"

"Davinder…" But I couldn't say anything else.

"What's up?"

"I've been thinking…making myself sick over what I'm about to say." I couldn't look at his face. "Davinder, I can't do this anymore."

Out of the corner of my eye, I saw him fold his hands together. "*This?* You mean us, right?"

"You're still sleeping with your wife."

"What?"

"You're still sleeping with your wife," I said again, looking straight at him.

"Is that what this is about?" He tried to look unaffected, but I'd seen him flinch. "Me sleeping with my wife? You think I can get away with not having sex with her for a year?"

"No, I don't think so. Because you're married to her."

"For now, yeah." He reached for my knee. "But I'm working on—"

"Don't, Dav…Don't say you're working on getting a divorce." I moved closer to him, tossing the pillow. "Look at me, let's—"

"I think you need to eat something or—"

I grabbed his hands. "No. *Look* at me."

He did, but his whole body was closed off to me again. "What? What are you saying?"

"Be honest with me," I said, softly. "Be good to me. Tell me the truth, please. I need it, Davinder. You don't know how much I need it right now."

"Don't do this," he said. "Don't give me an ultimatum. Not now, please. If you love me, don't—"

"I'm not giving you an ultimatum. I'm leaving. I'm putting the house up for sale, and I'm leaving Montreal."

"What? No, what?"

"I have to."

"You don't *have* to do anything. What are you talking about? No, you can't." He got up and looked down at me, pacing. "No way. This is crazy. This is bullshit. You can't just—"

"Davinder, sit down." I held my hand out to him. "Come, please."

He did. "Baby, what the fuck are you saying to me here?"

"I'm saying good-bye."

His face blanched and he shook his head.

For two days, I'd agonized over this moment, fearing I'd weaken at the sight of his pain, but I felt strong. "We can never be together and you know that," I said calmly. "Never. Even if you did get a divorce. It could never work. Do you know what it would do to my sister? To your brother? Your mom? Think about your kids."

"You said you'd give me time." His eyes were hard again. "You said you loved me. What was that, huh? Lies? Did you fucking lie to me all this time? Did you make me cheat on my wife and risk everything—everything, Allan!"

"I didn't make you do anything. You made those choices."

"Why have I been coming here, then? For sex? Is that it? You think that's all this is? You're gonna try and sell me that?"

"I need to get away from all this," I said.

"What am I gonna do? You're gonna leave me? What am I supposed to do? I'm supposed to just go back to my life and forget you?" He reached out and skimmed his thumb along my mouth. "How am I gonna do that, Allan?"

"Don't do that," I said, pushing his hand away gently. "Help me."

"Help you what? Help you leave me?"

"Yes! You owe me that much."

He stared at me for a long time and nodded. "I felt it, you know. In the last month, I could feel it. I knew you would eventually get sick of this."

"You know it's the right thing to do. I have nothing here anymore. My life is going nowhere. I want to move and give myself another chance. I don't know how I'll do it, Davinder. I don't know if I'll even be able to, but I want to try." I couldn't help taking his hand. "Will you let me try?"

His face contorted as he held back from crying. "Goddamnit," he said, pulling me into his arms. "It hurts."

I held him tighter, knowing this was the last time. "Yeah," I said, crying into his shirt. "But it'll be okay. It'll get better."

"Allan, please. Please, don't do this."

I looked up at him. "You have to let me go," I said, looking into his eyes. "I don't want you to feel guilt when you think of me," I said, breaking away. "Promise me that. No matter what happens, I want you to think back on what we had and see it for what it was."

He sniffled, wiping his eyes. "I don't know what I'm gonna do without you."

"You'll fix your life. You'll make amends. And so will I."

"I'll miss you," he said, the tears coming again. He leaned in, resting his forehead against mine. "Where will you go? And when?"

"I'm going to Toronto...Davinder, I got a book deal for *The Agency*." I'd gotten the e-mail today. The publishing company was offering me an advance and wanted me to commit to a three-book series. It wasn't a big advance, and it wasn't a big company, but it was a book deal, and a door opening where one was being closed.

"You're gonna be published?"

"Yes."

"You're amazing." He looked around as if waking from a dream. "Will we keep in touch? Will you let me know what's happening in your life?"

"No." I rose. "Not for a while at least. We'll know what's going on through Dayton and Elsie, and that's going to have to be enough." I pulled him up. "I'll call you a cab."

"Allan, please—"

"You have to go," I said turning away from his face.

"It doesn't have to be—"

"Davinder, it does." I faced him. "Give me a hug." I wrapped my arms around his chest and listened to his heart. "Get your life together," I said, unable to pull away. "It's not too late."

He wouldn't let me go. I looked at him, hoping I could remember his face the way it was now, when those cold, lonely nights would come haunting me later.

"So this is it?"

"Yes," I said, taking my phone out to call him a cab.

"No, I'll walk." His eyes were swollen and he looked so lost. He fumbled for his coat and slipped it on. When he was dressed and ready, he stood by the door, waiting.

"Go home, Davinder," I said, firmly but gently. "To your wife who loves you and your children who need you, and be a good man to them." I touched his face. "And try to be good to yourself."

He bit his lip. "I don't know what I'm gonna do. I thought you'd give me more time. Didn't you say you'd give me—"

"I'm sorry, I can't." I opened the door for him and looked out.

He seemed to be in a state of shock, backing up into the night. "Good-bye?"

"Good-bye." A sob gripped my throat. "I won't forget you, okay?"

"You promise?" Davinder looked at the street and, without another word, stepped out of my home and out of my life.

Chapter Sixteen

Here," David said, handing me a cup of coffee. He looked around the airport terminal and clapped his hands. "Man, I love airports, you know?" He sat by me in the empty row of plastic chairs. "That feeling…like everything is possible, like I could just take off."

"Yeah, I'm sure Kaliq would *love* that." I smiled and raised my plastic cup. "Thanks for driving me. I really appreciate it." My flight to Toronto was less than an hour away. That evening, I'd be in my new apartment on Yonge Street. The place was pretty small, but was all I needed for now. When the agent sold the Montreal duplex, I'd maybe buy something in Toronto. But I was going to be away from everyone I knew and loved. I was going to be a stranger in a city I had only visited a few times.

I'd write, that's what I'd do. I'd write, and maybe… I'd heal.

"So, how do you feel?" David brushed something off my cheek. "You had an eyelash there." He winked. "Come on, kid, it's gonna be okay. Hey, you're gonna be a big shot pretty soon, huh? And the boys are gonna be lining up at your door. You'll be like Truman Capote or something."

"I doubt Capote had boys lining up at his door." I sipped my coffee, trying to keep it together. I'd asked David to drive me to the airport because I needed his sense of humor to get me through this. "Anyway, this press is so small, it's not even on Google."

"Shut up." He laughed. "And you're lying. Listen to me, that's something you're gonna have to change if you want to make it in Toronto—this modesty thing. Look at you, you're one of the most fuckable guys I've ever met."

"Yeah, right." I sighed, fidgeting with my cup.

"Wow, that jerk really did a number on your head, didn't he?"

"Please don't call him a jerk."

I hadn't slept since the day before. I'd sat in the darkness of my bedroom, with the phone in my hands, watching the screen light up with Davinder's phone number every half hour. He'd called all night, but I hadn't answered. He knew I was leaving today. Every one of his messages had been heartbreaking.

"I'm sorry," David said. "I know he probably isn't the prick we've all built up in our minds. I mean, if you loved him—"

"I still do." I finished my coffee and crushed the cup inside my hand. My eyes were dry. I'd cried so much in the last three months—I couldn't recognize myself anymore. I hadn't seen Davinder in *three months*. He'd called and written incessantly. And last week, he'd even knocked on my door in the night. I'd stood there, holding my breath, listening to him say my name.

When he'd finally walked away from my door, I'd broken down in a way I never had before.

"For what it's worth, I'm proud of you, Allan. Really." David tapped my knee. "You make us look good. You're making a statement here. You're saying, 'The gay man will no longer be the married man's side dish,' and that's—"

"David, be quiet, please." I tried to smile. "Honestly." I rose and threw my cup in the trash. I couldn't sit anymore. I'd had way too much coffee since the morning. "You should get going. I can—"

"No, I'll stay until your plane flies into the blue."

My phone rang and I jumped. "Oh, God," I said.

"It's him, right?" David got up and snapped the phone out of my hand. "Don't let him do this to you."

"Give me that." I grabbed my phone. "What if it's important?"

"Don't, Allan."

I watched the screen light up with Davinder's phone number and clutched the phone tightly. From what Elsie had told me, Davinder had been sick with the flu for a month. Three weeks out of that month, he'd been bedridden. Everyone was concerned for him. But I knew it wasn't only the flu, no. He was coming off me, like I'd been coming off him.

The phone went silent and I stuffed it back in my pocket.

"Come here." David pulled me into his arms and squeezed me hard. "Good boy." He kissed my head.

"How am I going to do this?"

"You'll do it one day at a time, okay? One day." David took my arm and my carry-on and guided me to the security checkpoint. "Once you get there, I want you to try to open up to people more. This will be good for you, Allan. You've been taking care of your sister and niece for so long, you forgot you're still young." He grabbed my chest through my jacket. "You still have all this energy inside you."

"You think I'll be okay?"

David leaned in and planted a kiss on my lips. He didn't care what people thought. "Are you kidding me? You'll be stellar out there."

"Here I go, huh?"

"Here you go," he said softly, looking into my face. "Go get 'em, kid."

I turned away and walked toward the security line.

"Allan," he called out, "maybe, one day, I can say I knew you when."

I spun around and flashed a smile. "Yeah, maybe."

When I'd turned the corner and was safely out of his sight, I stopped and leaned my hand on the wall. My head spun and I thought I'd be sick.

"Sir? Are you all right?"

I nodded, leaning back from the wall. "Too much coffee," I said.

"Yeah, that happens." The woman smiled and walked on.

I stood in the middle of the short hall, halfway between here and there. I could turn back right now. I could run to him.

"Sir?" The woman—a young brunette dressed in an army jacket and black jeans—was stepping back to me. "Do you need help?"

"I feel a little out of it," I said.

"Well, give me your arm and I'll walk with you."

"Thanks." I took her arm. I didn't know who this girl was and why she was being so sweet to me, but I needed her, yes.

"I'm Julia," she said, walking along with me.

I straightened up. "I'm Allan...Thank you."

"Sure, Allan." She smiled. "So, what do you say we get you on your plane?"

"Yes," I said, my heart swelling with excitement and sadness. "I think that's the plan."

But I still wasn't sure if the plan was mine, or part of the Karma Police's design.

PART THREE

CHAPTER ONE

I gathered the copies of the books I hadn't sold and stepped out of the bookstore.

I'd done better than I'd expected today. More people had turned up than at my last signing two weeks ago. It was a damp November day, so perhaps the people who'd showed up this morning had nothing better to do with their time. Regardless, my agent would be happy. My sales had gone down a little with this third installment in *The Agency* series, but the market was in turmoil and yes, I hadn't been as aggressive with marketing this book compared to the other two. I'd been neglecting the promotion part. In the last five years, I'd been blessed enough to live off my writing. *The Agency* series had been translated into many languages—I couldn't keep track of them all. At the apogee of my success, three years ago, I'd quit my day job and now lived off my two tenants and royalty checks. By keeping an extremely tight budget, I managed to keep out of the rat race. The downside was I spent most of my days alone and, aside from my writing, made no significant contribution to the world. I toyed with the idea of working part-time or even volunteering somewhere, but never got around to it. In the last months, I'd been in quite a rut. Truth was, I was tired of *The Agency* and its plot. I'd put the main character through more drama than a daytime soap-opera hero, and short of killing him, there wasn't much else I could do with this guy.

And I was tired of playing it safe.

There was a story I wanted to write, and in the last days, it had been creeping into my soul. Two nights ago I'd finally sat down and begun plotting it on paper. I'd never written a romance novel. Resisted it with all of my intellectual might. What did I have to say about love anyway? Love was like a car accident to me. I was just glad I'd survived it. It was tragic and vicious. Yes, but maybe taking vengeance on two poor unsuspecting characters would quiet the rage I still felt inside sometimes. I'd write an anti-romance. I'd put them through hell, yes. There would be no happy ending for these two people—they'd live their whole lives apart and die without ever seeing each other's faces again. They'd breathe their dying breaths thinking of the nights of their youth, the times they'd made love in the dark and whispered promises they never kept.

I'd been in this melancholic mood for months now.

"Mr. Waterhouse," a young voice called out behind me.

I turned to find a good-looking kid with a copy of my book in his hands. He wore a fedora and a Cindy Lauper T-shirt. "Yes?"

"I'm a die-hard fan, and you know, like, I was late for the reading, 'cause I had to help my mom with the dryer, but could you sign this for me please?"

He was very cute. And very young. "Of course." I took the book out of his hand and opened it to the first page. "What's your name?"

"Alexander."

"That's a good name," I said, signing. "Thank you for showing up. Everything worked out with the dryer?"

"You look different from the picture." He took the book back.

Ah, the picture.

"It was taken a while ago."

Try ten years.

"Disappointed, huh?" I winked, trying to be cool and mature about it. In the picture, I had a full head of hair and a thin face. Since then, I'd gained some weight. I wasn't porky, but I *was* fighting off the pot belly with both hands. And when my blond curls had thinned out, I'd started keeping my hair really short.

"Alex!" A girl tapped the kid's shoulder and wrapped her arms around his neck, jumping on his back. "What are you doing here?" she cried happily.

"Gen?" He grabbed her ankles and swung her around.

I left them to their reunion.

"Mr. Waterhouse," the kid yelled as I was walking away. "Thanks for signing my book."

I waved to him. "Thanks for buying it."

❖

I got out of Wellesley Station and walked home.

I lugged the half-full box of unsold books up the stairs, but when I put the key in the lock, the door opened. "Oh, really?" Cameron said, taking the box out of my arms and looking dejectedly into it. "Man, how come a famous writer like you has to carry his own books back and forth?" He dropped the box in the entrance and went straight for the kitchen. "I'm getting us a drink," he called back.

"It smells nice in here," I said as he came back with two Boris beers.

"Yeah, I cleaned." He looked around, but something in his eyes was different. He wasn't smiling, and Cameron smiled through everything. Even his anger. "I aired everything out, and what you're smelling is this candle." He picked up a blue candle from the coffee table. "Berry Madness. You like it?"

I'd met him six years ago. I'd just broken up with Robert then— lover number three in a series of seven failed affairs that ended last month when I broke up with John—and had found myself wandering down Church Street, dangerously depressed. I'd entered a bar, sat there and guzzled down beer after beer. At the end of that very blurry and embarrassing night, Cameron, who was the head waiter there (and still was today), had peeled me off the bar and driven me home. We'd slept together for a few months, until we'd come to realize we'd do much better as friends.

And here we were, six years later, complete opposites, with nothing in common but our shared sense of humor, closer than ever. Cameron had a place of his own, but he didn't like being there much. As a matter of fact, he'd been staying with me for three days straight now. I didn't mind it.

"Yeah, it's nice." I took the beer from him and plopped down into the couch. "I saw this kid today…God, you should have seen him." I snorted bitterly and drank my breakfast. "Anyway, I felt like an old fag blimp of a writer."

"Ugh, you're in one of *those* moods." Cameron turned around, shoving his tight little ass in my face. "You like me in these jeans? Two pairs for two hundred."

"Dollars?"

He stood on his tiptoes and faked a grin. His heart wasn't into it. What was wrong here?

"What are we doing tonight?" he asked, faking another smile.

"Don't you work?"

"Yeah, but only until midnight." He sipped his beer, looking down at me. "Oh, *right*, you'll be in bed by then, huh?"

"Thank you for cleaning my apartment."

"You haven't been doing much lately," he said, sitting by me. He smelled like baby shampoo. "You write all night, sleep most of the day."

"Why do you smell like baby shampoo? And I'm writing a book, *hence* the writing. Gimme a break, Cam, all right? I don't feel like being perky."

"Is it because you're gonna be forty next week?"

How could I be turning forty already? Impossible. I was twenty-nine years old yesterday. *Forty?* I was well on my way to being fifty. And then sixty, seventy, and then I'd die.

Alone with only my mediocre books to show for it.

Cameron grabbed my chin and snapped my head around. "You have that look on your face. Are you thinking about death, growing old, failure, losing your teeth and hair, and that your cock's gonna fall off and then you'll sell it on Craigslist, and—"

"Yes, and I'm enjoying it, so leave me alone." I smiled a little. "What about you? You've been here for three days, and unless there's a guy tied up in my guest room, I'd say you've been celibate for seventy-two hours—"

"I don't know," he said, looking away. "Just needed some time off the meat train."

Really now. That was hard to believe. Since I'd known Cameron, he'd been either getting over, pursuing, being pursued by, sleeping with, or dating some man. Any red-blooded queer man who hung around the bar scene knew the cute little waiter Cameron. He had a smile that made you feel important and a walk that made you feel alive.

But looking at him more closely, I saw he didn't look good. "Hey, everything okay?" I asked him, standing. I needed to eat something. The beer was making me sick. "Is there any stew left?" I took his arm and ushered him into the kitchen. I pushed a plate of leftovers into the microwave and slammed the door shut.

He still hadn't said anything.

"Cam?"

"Will you come to the clinic with me this afternoon?" He went to the sink and rinsed out his bottle. His shoulders had tensed under his fitted T-shirt. "I have an appointment at two. It's just around the corner here." He dropped the bottle into the empty beer box and looked everywhere but at me.

The microwave beeped and I stood frozen, with nothing to say. Cameron was always so careful. He was twenty-seven years old and knew all the rules. "I'll come with you," I said at last, nearing him.

"Thank you."

I turned my back to him, getting my meal out, burning my fingers on the plate in the process.

I stared at my fingers, my head turning.

Chapter Two

Cameron was high as a kite, sitting by me with his hand in his pants. I couldn't blame him for celebrating his negative test results.

I'd had a few scotch and sodas myself. My mind was hazy, and as I stared at the screen, the images I saw didn't relay back to my brain. There were simply colored dots and shapes put together to form men fucking. Maybe I'd seen this part too many times before. To Cameron, porn was like chicken soup—comforting and safe.

"I'm gonna get another drink," I said, getting out of the couch with effort. Truth was, I was going to get myself a glass of water and creep into my bedroom. I had work to do, and sometimes I worked best when I was depressed and on the verge of intoxication. There were feelings I could only unlock in this pathetic state.

Cameron didn't say anything.

In my bedroom, I picked up my notebook and stood by the window, watching the last of the leaves in the elk tree fight off the wind. I probably felt like this because of lack of sun.

Or whatever.

I looked at the box left open by my bed.

I'd read the letters so many times. There was no use in reading them again.

I sat on the edge of the bed, staring down into the box. This was my chicken soup. This was the only comfort left. When I read these letters, I heard their voices. Voices of the people I'd loved and known. Voices from another life—one that still ran side by side with mine, a parallel existence steaming down the tracks, a blessed life that went on without me.

Before I knew it, I was reaching down to lift the papers out. I curled my legs under me and unfolded the first letter. It was an e-mail from Elsie, sent a few days after I'd left Montreal ten years ago.

Subject: Miss you already

Dear Allan,

I keep looking at Finn and seeing you. I still can't believe you're gone. Isn't that sad? I always thought you'd live downstairs from me, or a phone call away. I guess that's what people mean when they talk about taking others for granted.

I don't think I ever want to see him again.

Tell me how you are. Don't lie.

Fay asks about you all the time. You were like a father to her. She cries for you when Dayton tries to console her.

Don't shut me out.

Elsie

But I had shut her out.

Through the years, my sister had written and called, and though I'd written back to her and visited them a few times, I'd never allowed Elsie through the invisible bars I'd built around myself. She stepped around my cage, aware of my inaccessibility. I'd watched Finn and Fay grow up in pictures and videos, painfully aware of the permanent rift between us. Fay resented me. As she'd blossomed into a young woman, she'd made it clear that I was unworthy of her affections. Her refusal to communicate via e-mail or other means had hurt me beyond repair. She was now a beautiful, outspoken girl of nineteen, unwilling to pursue her education despite good grades, and was planning on moving out come summer. There had been a string of questionable boyfriends in the last year. She'd shaved her hair and pierced her tongue. Dayton and Fay were constantly fighting. I knew he loved her, but Dayton was a simple man with simple expectations.

And there was nothing simple about Fay.

I pulled out another letter, this one from the middle. It was a longhand letter from Ingrid. She wrote me from time to time, always in green ink on lavender. This letter was dated September 2007. Five years ago.

After Davinder's divorce.

After he'd gone and lit up a powder keg in his life.

Allan,

I know we haven't been in touch in the last two years. Thank you for the wedding gift and the card. You truly do have a way with words, don't you? Lionel and I missed you that day, but I understand why you couldn't make it.

Now more than ever.

It's important that you know I write this letter in secret. No one knows I've made contact with you. Allan, you are not my family's favorite person at the moment, and that's putting it gently.

But, no matter how much Dali and Dayton need to blame you, I can't cut everything down to black and white in this story. Because I know my son. No one can make him do anything he doesn't want to do. And if what he says is true, then I also know he loved you and you loved him. I try to hold on to that, because I don't want to be angry at you two. I will not lose anyone else in my life.

But what were you thinking? He was a married man. Your brother-in-law. And his children? Your nephew and niece?

Your sister?

He swears it only lasted a year. A year, Allan? I watched over his sons those evenings, thinking he was going to work. Had I known what you two had made me an accomplice of, I'd have denounced you both.

My heart breaks for Eileen. She thought she was competing with a mistress (yes, she was suspicious), a young intern of his, but how could she win with you as an opponent? A man. A man she admired and cared for.

My son is broken. I don't recognize my child anymore.

He believes this is fair punishment for his mistakes. Do you?

The only thing keeping him from destroying himself is the love he has for his boys. Eileen has the grace and wisdom to allow him to spend time with them. Jude is sixteen and giving his father a very hard time. No, they don't know about the true reasons behind their parents' divorce. Everyone has agreed to spare the boys the additional trauma. God knows Noah doesn't need it. At fourteen, he is struggling more than ever.

But they are loved and they will make it through. I'll make sure of it.

As for my son, my Davinder, he's been talking nonsense about Germany of all places, and a friend he has there. Saying perhaps that what Jude and Noah need is time away from their father and his mistakes.

Do you still talk to him? He says you two haven't communicated since you left here. I have trouble believing that...

If you do still talk, I'm asking you, as a mother, please reason with him. There is no need for him to sabotage what little he has left.

Germany? What possible good could come from it?

In closing, I need to tell you...I saw it sometimes...in your eyes, and in his. There were moments when perhaps, we all saw it. Eileen included. And of that, we are all guilty for letting it go on as long as it did.

Davinder is forty-seven years old. I worry about him.

You were fortunate enough to be far away when the bomb went off in our lives. But I'm here to remind you of the responsibility you have in this.

Ingrid

I had the same reaction every time I read this particular letter. Just as a child sleeps through thunder in order to find silence, I felt like rolling into a ball and hiding under my blankets until the sickness passed.

He'd told Eileen about us. He'd told his brothers and his mother. It had taken him five years, but he'd done exactly what I'd wanted him to do all those years ago. Except it was too late. Prior to his divorce, I'd gotten news of him through Elsie, and it was always the same: Davinder was barely holding on. He was aloof, quiet, his eyes vacant of joy. Our separation had caused him too much pain, and he lived his life by going through the motions, nothing more. So, no, he hadn't told the truth out of *bravery*, he'd done it because he needed to quicken himself one last time.

And then he'd run to Renaud.

Not me.

"Allan?" Cameron poked his head in the doorway. "Can I come in?"

Davinder had spent three months in Germany before returning to Montreal. My sister's letters began to reveal the changes at work under the surface. Davinder had returned with something she couldn't describe in his eyes. He'd gained weight. Didn't smoke as much. Was drawing again.

"What is it?" I folded the letter and dropped it into the box.

"Why do you do this to yourself?" Cameron's green eyes had cleared up. He sat by me. "It's not healthy."

"I don't want to hear it, Cam."

"Read one to me, then."

In the six years we'd known each other, he'd never asked me that.

"Come on, read one to me. One of his."

His letters weren't in this box. Davinder had only written two letters to me. One shortly after we'd parted, and another two months ago. I hadn't opened that one yet. "No, I really don't want to." I lay back on the pillows, staring up at the ceiling. "Lie down with me."

Cameron crawled up to me and nestled himself in my arms. "Why can't we just fall in love already?"

"I don't know," I said, stroking his hair. "But come here." I rolled on top of him and slid my hand down his smooth chest, surrendering to my urges, and undid his jeans. This would be another one of my selfish mistakes, of course it would, but I needed him right now. His body. His affection.

"Fuck me like you would him," Cameron said into my ear. "Show me."

I flicked the light off and fell on him, holding him as close to my body as my heart could allow.

❖

Safe under the cover of darkness and rolled into my sheets, I listened to the water running in the bathroom.

Cameron was reasonable—he'd understand why we'd trespassed this boundary tonight.

He'd been too affected by the emotions of the morning, and I'd been tipsy, stupid with self-pity, and horny. I was worrying for nothing. Cam was probably in the bathroom thinking of a way to let me down. He was rehearsing his "it's not you, it's me" speech right now. He was young, beautiful, and sweet.

So why was I lying here finding ways to turn him down?

Because Cameron used his body as a conductor only. He tried channeling love and dedication with it. I'd experienced it once more tonight and remembered why I'd ended our sexual contacts almost six years ago.

I heard him coming to the door. For a second, I wondered if pretending to sleep was the solution.

"Um," he said, standing in the doorway. "Do you want me to sleep in here or—"

"Do you mind if—"

"No, I don't mind." He turned away and I heard the guest room door close. What had happened to me in the last ten years? Could I really blame my attitude on a broken heart? Every day, people got their hearts smashed—some lost their kids, a wife, a husband…did they walk around with a grudge against the world?

I had to change. *Needed* to change.

I jumped out of bed and ran down the hall to the guest room. "Cam," I almost shouted, opening the door.

"What the hell?" He sat up, a trace of light shining over his shocked face. "What's wrong?"

I stood there, with nothing to say.

"Allan? What is it?" I crept to the single bed and crawled into it. Cameron looked at me for a moment.

"I'll sleep here," I said, turning to my side, facing the wall.

He rolled over and away from me. "Hey, it's your house."

❖

I'd been living in seclusion for three days. Cameron hadn't called or shown up since our night together.

I couldn't stand being in the state I was in. I was on overload. I couldn't write. Couldn't read. Couldn't even sit still long enough to watch daytime TV. I perused my e-mail, moving the cursor around subject titles, seeing unread messages from my agent—*when's that first draft coming?*—or David—*hey, big forty next week*—a few new friends—*Allan, drinks tomorrow?*—and even fan letters—*loved your last book*. I left them all unmarked and unread, resisting the urge to delete them all.

Allan Waterhouse, the writer of thrillers.

I went to my bedroom closet and grabbed the box, tossing it on my unmade bed. Everything real and important was in here. This was my life's work, except I was still that blurry secondary character—never quite on the page. I'd never responded to any of these missives. I'd told myself it was out of respect for them.

I flipped through the letters and pulled out the only three letters I'd ever gotten from Eileen. I knew them almost by heart, but this afternoon, I'd read them differently.

The first one was dated two months after Davinder had revealed our affair to her.

It was an e-mail with no subject.

> *So that's why you never wanted to be alone with me.*
> *You slept with my husband? You slept with the man I loved? You slept with the father of my kids? Did you?*
> *He says you're not to blame. He says he was the one...*
> *I don't care. I really fucking don't.*
> *I know you're the one who seduced him. Because you're the one who left in a hurry.*

If you ever make it as writer, I'll make sure everyone knows who you really are.

But she never had. Three years later, I'd received this e-mail:

Allan,
Is it true that you loved him?
Eileen

I'd just moved in with John back then, and in the midst of writing, the second in the *The Agency* series. I'd felt I'd been given a second chance at happiness. John and I had met at a coffee shop I went to in the morning when writing at home was taking its toll on my nerves. He was a "corporate slave," as he referred to himself, and after a long and tedious courtship—I hadn't been attracted to him physically initially—we'd begun sleeping together.

I'd made myself believe it was possible to love again and form a relationship with another man.

When I'd gotten this particular e-mail, the possibility of moving on had been destroyed with such violence it had left me sobbing behind closed doors for half of the night. I don't know why her question had cut me so deep.

After that, John's optimism about our future had dwindled more every day. He'd finally understood I had a marooned heart and preferred it that way. For the first time since John and I had split, I wanted to call him. He'd left it up to me to make contact.

I retrieved my phone from under the letters. But before I called John, I read Eileen's last e-mail again. I'd twist the blade in the wound.

She'd sent this one only three weeks ago.

Hello,
I hope this e-mail finds its way to you. I read your books, well, I'm finishing the last one right now, but I started a new job so I haven't had a lot of time. You're a good writer. I usually don't like those kinds of books, but yours are different, I guess. Anyway, congratulations on your success. It must be

tough being a writer. I don't know, seems like a tough job, but I guess if you like doing it, then it's not so bad.

I used to write a journal when Davinder and I were going through the divorce, but I stopped because what's the point in writing down things you already felt during the day. It's like suffering twice for no reason.

When I read your books, I was looking for hints or clues to what happened between you and Davinder, but your characters are very different from you, aren't they? Except maybe I think the detective is a little like you, and maybe that guy who killed the big actor in the second one is like Davinder? I don't know, I think I saw some of Davinder's way of talking about conspiracies in him.

I don't really know why I'm writing you and I'm sorry if I'm rambling.

We're friends now. Davinder and I. It took a long time, but he's a great father and our sons love him, even if sometimes, Jude and him don't get along. I'm proud of myself for not destroying their bond. You know, when Davinder sold his business and left for Germany, I was scared for him. I mean, I hated him still, but I was scared. I thought maybe he'd lost his mind. I think he did.

I blamed you and it was easier that way.

I don't know, Allan, the years have passed now, and they say time heals, and I guess they're right. I'm happy now. Happier than I was, is what I mean. My boys are growing up to be nice men and they're both really smart, like their father. They question things around them. They're very curious and resourceful. Noah plays the piano beautifully and he's also an amazing artist. Jude wants to join the Red Cross. He wants to travel to Haiti. I think he got the bug when Davinder took him on a road trip down to Louisiana last year. But I don't know if Jude could really leave. Because of Fay. Have you heard from her lately? Elsie tells me that you and your niece didn't keep in close contact in the last ten years. I guess that explains Fay's attitude. She's really into older guys and I think she's looking for a dad or something, no?

What a mess you and Davinder created. It was very stupid.

But you never answered my question five years ago. It doesn't matter, because I figured it out on my own. You did love him. Probably more than I ever did.

It took me a long time to accept this, but I know he loved you, too. More than he loved me. I'm okay with that now. It hurts, but I'm okay with that.

He's been good to me in the last years. He's changed so much. It's hard to believe how angry and suspicious of everything he was before. He's toned down and is always trying to see the silver lining in things. It's annoying. :-)

Him and Fay are really tight. I think she kind of clung to him after you left and I guess he took her under his wing because that was the only way he could be close to you and repay you for choosing to leave. He treats her like she was his own. They do have the same kind of personality. He's been trying to get through to her, but lately, she's been angrier than ever and even he can't slow her down.

Davinder's been talking about going off the grid. You know what that is?

Actually, I believe he can do it. In the last five years, everything he said he would do, he did. It's funny, I used to be in love with him, and then I hated him, and now I admire him. It's a strange evolution of feelings, don't you think?

Elsie says you've been alone for ten years. That you had boyfriends, but none of them stayed. Because of Davinder? Is it?

Allan, a lot of water has gone under the bridge. We've all moved on. Including myself. No one hates you here. It took a long time, but we came to understand what happened, and why it happened. And you know what? In some messed-up way, we all miss you. You left and I guess it was the right thing to do, but we're still a family, aren't we? Dali asks about you all the time. For years he didn't speak to Davinder. He blamed him for your sacrifice. That's what it was, wasn't it? I think so.

You're tuning forty soon, Elsie told me. That's big. I turned fifty last month. I still look pretty good!:-) But Davinder must be swimming in a secret fountain of youth he won't share with us...He's fifty-two years old and looks better than ever, that bastard!

I have to tell you something. Davinder said he was going to write you a letter. And it was just then, the way he said it, that I knew you two had never kept in touch. I hadn't believed that until then. And my heart broke for you two. I might be stupid or too nice. But it really did.

Ten years?

Allan, please, if he writes you, you have to write him back. You have to.

Because...I know it's not my place to say this, or maybe it is, because he loves you. Never stopped. You know he's never really been with anyone else. I think he had a girlfriend once and maybe a boyfriend, but it never lasted and he never spoke about it.

No, it was always you.

What are you going to do about it?

It's funny, I'm his ex-wife and I'm asking you to write him! Life is pretty unpredictable.

Please let me know what is going on in your head,

Eileen

PS: Jude wants to read your books too.

My hands were shaking. I placed the letter back in the box and sat there, staring into space. I looked at the nightstand—in its first drawer were Davinder's two letters.

I glanced down at my phone and it rang.

It was Cameron.

"Hey," I answered. "What's up? How are you? Why did you leave and—"

"You sound strange."

"Cam, I'm sorry, okay? I'm really sorry."

"I know."

"You're so amazing and—"

"Allan, stop it." He sighed. "I don't know," he said, flatly. "Do you want me to come over or something?"

"Yeah." I leaned back into the pillows. "I'd love that."

"Have you eaten today? I'll bring pad thai and a bottle of sake."

"That sounds so good." I closed my eyes and rubbed them.

"I want to read all your letters, Allan. All of them, and you can't say no."

I nodded, but didn't say anything.

"Good then."

"See you in a few," I said and hung up.

CHAPTER THREE

I sat on the edge of my seat, finishing my third beer, trying to watch *Hoarders*.

We'd eaten and drained the sake bottle a while ago. Cameron had been locked up in my bedroom for almost an hour. Once in a while, I heard him say something to himself, but I wasn't allowed in there until he'd gone through the dozens of letters and e-mails in the box. We'd never really discussed my past. I'd told him what I wanted him to know, but mostly, what I needed to believe about myself.

I've been had, I'd told him before. *Taken for a fool by a married man.*

There had been a few times, especially after I'd had enough to drink, that I'd tripped myself up on my lies and the truth had come leaking out of me. Cameron was clever, and he knew my victim act was a role I played to avoid admitting the depth of my feelings for the man I liked to paint all black.

I turned the TV off and drained the last of my beer. It was Saturday night. Come Monday, I'd be forty years old. This was no way to celebrate a milestone. At home, watching TV, while my only real friend spent the evening rummaging through my past?

But the past seemed to be breathing down my neck these days. Something was changing. My exile was coming to its end.

And the answer I sought was in that envelope I refused to open.

Cameron stepped out of my bedroom, but I couldn't read the look in his eyes. He plopped down next to me on the couch and said nothing.

"You're done?" I asked, keeping my voice as cool as possible.

"It's like I traced all these people's evolution without ever even meeting any of them." He looked over at me and his eyes were fiery with emotion. "Eileen, his ex-wife, she's the one who surprised me the most. No, *surprise* isn't the right word. She actually shocked me. You know, we usually assume what people can and will forgive."

"I guess so, yeah."

"There was a letter from one of the brothers in there. Dali, the youngest one, right?"

Yes, Dali had written me after he'd left for Oregon when Brendan was given a scholarship to study osteopathy. It was a beautiful letter written by a wonderful man. In it, he'd given me his absolution and wished me love and healing.

"You never wrote him back? Or Ingrid? Or—"

"I couldn't. I didn't have the right."

"Bullshit." Cameron sat up straight, looking down at me. "I'm sorry, but I think it's pretty bad you never wrote these people back. They obviously need you to."

"They just needed to let me know what they were going through. My responsibility was to listen and to let them express their—"

"You're not their priest or shrink."

"What did you want me to do? Huh? What am I supposed to write back to them? 'Hi, it's Allan, the man who wrecked your family, I'm very sorry but I don't care all that much because if you think you're suffering, well, you have no idea what suffering really is'?"

"Is that how you feel?" His tone was gentler.

"Yeah, that's how I feel. That's how I *always* felt. I know they all went through a lot of pain, but they had each other, and me to blame. What did I have? I left, Cameron. I left everybody and everything I knew. I left so my sister could have the life of her dreams. I left the man I loved more than life itself."

"And you did it alone." He touched my hand. "I'm sorry."

"Do you know how many times I spent the night holding myself down, fighting the need to reach out to him? To see his face? To hear his voice?"

"Why didn't you? It's been years, and from what I've read in the latest letters, you've been forgiven, and more than that, you're understood. He's written you. What did he say in the letter?"

I picked up my beer, but it was empty. I rose and left for the kitchen.

"You didn't read it?" Cameron had followed me. "Allan?"

I took a large sip of my new beer, drinking to numb my emotions, and shook my head. No.

"You're not dying of curiosity? Shit, how can you not be?" Cameron took the beer from my hand and drank from it. "You're more fucked up than I thought."

"Thank you." I gave him a sardonic grin and drank again. At this rate, I'd be drunk soon.

"Where's the letter?"

"No," I said. "Don't even think about it."

"And why not?" He didn't move. "I think I have a right to know what's in that letter."

"It's none of your business, Cam."

"No? Don't you think I should know what my chances are?"

I set the beer down. I'd been very good at not having this conversation with him, but there was no getting out of it tonight. "What do you mean?" I asked.

"Why do you think I've been hanging around you for six years?" He was nervous. "I mean, I love sitting around, drinking beer and listening to you type all night as much as the next guy, but don't you think there's a little more to it than that?"

I liked the way he slicked his hair sideways. There was always that one rebellious strand that refused to comply. I liked his small hands and the way they moved over objects—carefully, yet willfully. I liked that his two front teeth overlapped slightly and when he smiled, he often stuck the tip of his tongue out.

"You're not saying anything."

"I don't know why you still come here. That's my true answer. I don't know, Cam. I don't know why you're still wasting your time with a guy like me."

"Wasting my time," he said bitterly. "Is that what I'm doing?"

"That's not what I mean." I went around to him. "What I mean is, I'm much older than you, not to mention more jaded and cynical and—"

"I like cynical better than *vain*. I can't stand the guys my age. The ones at the club, the ones who—"

"I'm not talking about the club scene. I'm talking about, there's a world out there, beyond the clubs and me. And I think it's time you gave it a shot."

"Do you love me?" He threw his chin up defiantly. "Do you?"

"I do love you, I really do. But not the way I think you mean."

He bit his bottom lip, reddening it, looking away. "It's 'cause I don't read much. And I'm flaky, I know that."

I grabbed his hand, drawing him closer. "What are you talking about? This has nothing to do with you, and I know people say that all the time, but it's true in this case. You're fucking fantastic...You need to stop trying to please so much—"

"Am I good in bed?" He was serious. He hadn't been a great lover to me, but I probably hadn't been a good one for him, either. "You're amazing," I said, smiling.

"And you're a good liar." He sighed, pulling his hand out of mine. "I guess most writers are."

"Writing isn't lying." I stepped away, a little bruised. "Anyway, good writing isn't."

"I'm sorry. I'm just so tired of wondering what's wrong with me. Why am I still single?"

"What's wrong with being single? What is this obsession you guys have with pairing up? In my day—"

"In your day? You make it sound like you and Rock Hudson used to hang out."

"Look, there's nothing wrong with you. Just relax. Let it happen."

He was quiet for a moment. He let out sharp breath. "I have to be at work in twenty minutes. Do you want to come and hang around for a few hours?"

"The club? No way." I went back to my beer. "I can't do that anymore." It was the honest truth. I hated the music. The lights. The smell.

"You're gonna stay here all night?" He looked around, confused. "You'll be lonely."

"I'll write."

"Those people aren't real."

"Hmm, you're definitely not a writer." I winked and raised my bottle. "Have a good night, okay?"

"Can I come by after?"

I wanted him to, but the boundaries had to be set, and I had to be mature enough to do it. "I think you should take Brian home and make him French toast tomorrow morning."

"Brian? The shooter boy?"

"Yeah."

Cameron tilted his head, staring out into space for a moment.

"Isn't he into chicks, too?" he asked.

Bisexuality was on Cameron's long black list of undesirable components in his perfect model of the twenty-first-century gay man.

"He *is* hot, though. Most bi guys are for some messed-up reason."

I laughed. "You're telling me, buddy."

"Read the letter, Allan. You have nothing to lose anymore."

❖

It was four a.m.

Cameron had stopped texting me half an hour ago. So, he'd taken my advice. He was home, in bed, with Brian. Young, sculpted, and baby-faced Brian.

I blinked, my eyes bleary from watching TV, and sipped the last of my beer. I'd gone through six of those tonight. I was passing out, here on the couch. Good going.

My mind kept showing me images I didn't want to see: Cameron kissing Brian's mouth, pulling his shirt over his head, biting the smooth skin of his shoulder. Man, I really needed to go to bed and sleep off all this stupid misery. After all, I was the one who'd driven him right into Brian's arms tonight.

I was good at sacrifice. Allan, the disappearing act. The man who will cease to exist the minute happiness shows the tip of its nose. The man who will shut up and hope you forget him so you can have what he deems worthy of you.

Drunk and wretched, I got up and stumbled to my computer, knocking my chair out of the way. I scrolled through my files, reading titles of novels I intended to write in the coming years. I drained my beer, selecting all of the folders at once.

With a few clicks, I deleted them all. I dragged the cursor to the bin and emptied that as well. Everything was gone. Drafts and ideas. Plot lines and character charts. But I felt nothing. I stood with effort and stumbled back to my bedroom. I fell on the bed, flat on my back, and threw my arm over my eyes. It didn't matter. I was done with writing fiction anyway. I'd find something else to do. Besides, it was about time I got a day job. My royalties just weren't cutting it.

I turned to my side, hoping the room would stop circling my head.

I'd go back to being a clerk and start wearing ties again. I'd lose some weight and grow my hair out. I'd go back, always back, until I was myself again. Before all of this happened.

Through my heavy lids, I stared at the nightstand. Cameron didn't understand. They'd all moved on with their lives, Cameron had said it himself after he'd read the letters—they'd *evolved*.

And I hadn't.

Now, from what I'd been able to piece together, Davinder had changed the most of all of them. He'd come into his own and led some kind of charmed life.

I didn't know that man. I knew my Davinder. The man I'd loved had been dark and moody, and he'd believed in himself almost as much as he'd doubted. He'd been pretentious and volatile, but he'd *needed* me.

He didn't need me today. Hurt by hurt, he'd paved his way through the world, and while I'd been digging my hole deeper, he'd been climbing up to the sun. What would he think of me now? No, I couldn't read how well he was doing, what adventure he was planning, which art gallery was showing his new collection, what he and Fay had done over the weekend...

I preferred lying here, like this, in perfect communion with the darkness around me. Safe. Unmolested by the truth. Not everyone was built to fight. Some of us didn't have the stamina for it.

And there was nothing wrong with that. I'd leave the battles of love to the handsome, the young—the conquerors.

Chapter Four

Cameron shook his head, squinting at my computer screen. "You didn't save any of your files on your e-mail account or—"

"Can you believe how stupid I am?" I circled my desk. "I just…I can't understand why—"

"Give yourself a break, Allan. I've done worse things under the influence." He clicked and scrolled and clicked. It was making me insane.

"Can you retrieve them?" I rubbed my head, trying to keep from yelling at him. None of this was his fault. "This is my life's work. I thought I deleted only the working titles. I erased all of my short stories, half of my new—"

"Yeah, I can get them back."

"Oh, thank you, thank you." I kissed his ear and went to the window, looking out. It was a gray day. Sunday. I stared at the street below, seeing a ray of sunlight touch the pavement. "Did you make him French toast this morning?" I hadn't had the courage to ask about Cameron's night until now. I didn't look back at him. "Did you take Brian home last night?"

I noted Cameron's silence and could feel tension in the air. "Did you know he speaks Arabic?" he said, at last. "His dad is Lebanese."

"Wow," I sighed, leaning my forehead against the glass. I remembered how I'd felt when Elsie had begun seeing Dayton. Cameron never talked about his conquests seriously. I knew this was different— he hadn't given me his usual superficial comments. "Interesting" was all I found to say.

"Yeah, he went back to school last year." Cameron was still clicking away. "He works three nights a week and goes to trade school during the day. It's pretty amazing, I think. Takes a lot of guts to do that."

It sure did. So not only was Brian young and attractive, he was also determined and ambitious.

"I feel like maybe you're jealous?" Cameron asked that question under his breath, still typing.

"Why do you say that?"

"Because you're not talking."

I turned around. "I'm possessive of you, I think."

"I like him."

"I want you to like him. And I want him to love you. You know you deserve the best, right? Do you know that?"

He looked away, back at the screen. "I don't know, maybe."

"You've spent too much time with me and I've polluted you with my negative thinking." I went to him and spun his chair around, stooping to meet his eyes. He was so young still. "Look at me," I said. "I want you to forget everything I ever said about love. It isn't a lie and it's not dead. It happens, Cameron, do you understand? True love exists. Okay? It exists."

"You never said these things to me before."

"I know, and I should have. You looked up to me in some way, and I let you down. But listen, I know that love is real…because I lived it. I felt it. And if you open yourself up a little and are willing to take a risk, it can happen to you, too." I touched his pretty face. "I was like you once," I whispered, seeing myself—my younger self—in his eyes for a moment. "I fell in love and it was beautiful."

"But it hurt you."

"Yeah, it did." I stood. "And that's okay. It wasn't anybody's fault really."

"Are you saying…Allan, do you forgive yourself for what happened?" He rose as well, standing close to me.

"I'm saying I want to try."

"Open the letter."

I looked around, my heart pounding. "No, I can't."

"Allan, please."

"I don't know if I can—" My phone rang. I picked it up and my face flushed. "It's my sister."

"Really? Wow, it's been a while."

"Hey, how are you?" I answered her, pacing. "Is everything okay?"

"Is Fay there? Is she with you?"

I frowned at Cameron, stopping in my tracks. "What? What do you mean? No, she's not here. Why would she be here?"

Elsie yelled something out to Dayton and came back on the line. "Did she call you?"

"Okay, what's going on?"

She sighed sharply. "She left a note. We don't know when she left exactly. It must have been early this morning."

"Left? Left where?"

"For Toronto. For your house."

I had to sit down. "What?"

"Hold on." I heard her shuffling around papers. "The note says, 'Mom, I took the bus for TO and I'm gonna go see Uncle Allan. I don't know why he stayed away for so long and why he left, but I don't want you to tell me. I want him to explain what happened. Uncle Dav won't say anything, but I'm not stupid. I put it together after I saw Uncle Dav's new exhibit, the only one he didn't invite me to. It's called *La Maison D'eau*. And that means *the house of water*. Waterhouse.'" Elsie paused. "And then she tells me not to worry and that she loves me."

I was unable to speak. Cameron sat by me and queried me with a look. "What?" he mouthed.

Waterhouse.

"Allan? She's gonna come and she's gonna have questions, and you're gonna have to answer them."

"What do you want me to say?"

"The truth. All of it. She needs it. We all need it. It's time."

"She hates me. I mean, what should I expect?"

"Expect a nineteen-year-old woman looking for closure."

I nodded, taking Cameron's hand. "Okay, I get it."

"I want you to call me as soon as she gets there. And, Allan, don't fuck this up."

"Okay, I'll call you," I whispered and hung up.

"What is it?" Cameron looked absolutely panicked.

"Can you help me clean up this place and set up the guest room?"

"Who's coming?"

I stood and went to the window again. The past was coming.

"Allan?"

I stared at the end of the street, waiting for the past to turn the corner. "My niece," I said. "Fay."

❖

"Get rid of this," I said, tossing a few of his glossy porn magazines on the bed. "And don't put them in the recycling bin either."

Cameron grabbed the magazines and opened the guest room closet. "Can I just move my clothes to the right? How long will she be staying? I'm sure she's not gonna have all that much stuff—"

"I don't know. A few days, I suppose." I emptied the nightstand drawers. "Put these somewhere." I threw the lube tube and packaged rubbers on the bed. "I'm going to strip the bed. Can you get me the nice blue sheets out of the linen closet, please?"

"Yeah." Cameron paused in the doorway. "What's she like?"

"I'm not sure anymore." I moved fast, rushing from one thing to another, but my mind seemed to have come to a stop. I couldn't organize my thoughts.

"Hey, it'll be okay. I know this is tough for you, but it's kind of exciting, no?"

I didn't feel excited. I felt *trapped*. Maybe I wasn't ready for this. "I don't think I can do this," I said, sitting on the edge of the bed, the intense emotions finally dying out, leaving me with nothing but a light head and sweaty palms. "I don't know what she expects of me."

"Don't think of it that way," Cameron said, coming to me. "And it's not just her wanting something from you, okay? You have to be considered in this, too. I won't let her walk in here and crush you or something. No way."

"I'm really terrified."

"What you did, you did for her, for her mom. Don't let her tell you otherwise. If she wants the truth, she'll have to be willing to hear it first."

"It was hard leaving them. So hard."

"You'll tell her that. You'll tell her everything." He kissed my face. "I'll stay until she gets here, okay?"

"Thank you." I sighed, looking around. "This is it, I guess. I have no choice."

"It's a good gift for a fortieth birthday."

"Maybe." I rose and began pulling the sheets off the bed.

We worked together, in silence, getting everything ready. When we were done, I went to the washroom and cleaned up in there.

"I'll make coffee," Cameron yelled out from the kitchen.

I stepped out into the living room and looked around. This was good enough.

"Now we wait," Cameron said, meeting me. "Can you stand it?"

"I think so." I went to my bedroom and opened the nightstand drawer.

Cameron watched me from the doorway. "You're gonna do this now? Don't you think that maybe—"

"I need to be prepared. How can I be strong if I can't even face the words in this?" I held the letter.

"Do it, then." Cameron walked in. "Do it."

"Oh, fuck," I moaned, tearing the envelope carefully. "Oh, my God." I pulled the letter out. I unfolded it, but pressed it against my chest. "I can't."

"Give it to me."

"No, no, okay, wait, I can." I held the letter up and recognized Davinder's elegant handwriting. I read his words.

Dear Allan,

I will be showing my art at the DKV, in Toronto. The opening night will be November twenty-third. I took the liberty of putting your name on the guest list. But know this, even if you don't come, you're still going to be there.

In every drawing.

I've spent the last three years working on these portraits.

Some, I conjured up from memories of your face. Some, I had to dream up. And some are projections of what I hope you have become. In these portraits, you are as I see you in my mind, the only place you still really exist.

But if you came...if you moved through the borders of our secret lives, and if I saw your face again, not in my mind, but with my eyes...

I'd know that art can transcend life and love can survive it.

If not, if you choose to remain on the other side, if you decide to close the gates of our garden forever, I'll understand.

I'll even accept it.

But my beautiful man, my half, my heart, my soul...I will always miss you.

Davinder

I sat down, the letter shaking violently in my hand. I heard my heart beating inside my ears and for a moment, nothing felt right. I couldn't breathe.

"What? What did it say?"

Limply, I held out the letter to Cameron and he snatched it out of my hand.

November twenty-third. That was four days from today. I put my face in my hands.

"Oh, Allan," Cameron cried, grabbing my shoulders. "That's the most fucking romantic thing I ever read in my life!" He shook me. "Hey? Hello?"

I looked up at him. "He still loves me," I said, curling up on the bed. "That's impossible."

"Why is it impossible? You still love him, right?" Ten years had passed. I didn't look the same or even think the same. I was a different man than what he remembered. He loved the young man in his drawings. One look at me today, and he'd see it was best to remember me through his art.

"Listen to me," Cameron said, carefully. "You have to go there. You have to."

So much had happened.

"And you'll go with Fay."

He hadn't forgotten about me.

But my beautiful man, my half, my heart, my soul...

"Allan, no more fucking around. Life is giving you a second chance, and if you don't take it, then you're doomed for real this time."

"I have to think—" The doorbell rang.

CHAPTER FIVE

Though she tried to hide her graceful figure under a big bomber jacket, painted her eyes dark, and wore her bangs long, Fay couldn't disguise her striking features.

Here she was, sitting on my couch, her long legs folded under her, mumbling words to her mom on the phone. I didn't remember what being nineteen really felt like anymore.

Not quite grown up, I supposed.

"All right," she said, putting her phone back in her jacket. "She's fine."

I sat in the chair, holding my cup of coffee in my unsteady hands. When she'd shown up, we'd hugged awkwardly and exchanged a few words about her bus trip. She'd glared at Cameron and muttered a quick "Nice to meet you" before walking in to look around my living room. After Cameron left, I'd found myself explaining our friendship to her. She'd relaxed after she understood Cameron didn't live with me and wasn't my boyfriend.

"You look different," she said, staring at me from under the long fringe of her dark bangs. She'd shaven one side of her head. "From the pictures Mom showed me."

"So do you…You're very beautiful, if you don't mind me saying so."

She shrugged and rose, walking slowly to my bookshelves. "You have a lot of books." She skimmed her index along the novels piled up on the crowded shelves. "I guess it comes with being a writer."

"Yeah," I whispered.

"I remember I used to hear you type a lot when I slept over at your house." She had her back to me, still looking at my books. "Were you writing?"

"Yeah, I was."

"These?" She picked one of mine off the shelf and turned around.

The look in her eye pained me. She seemed so small and fragile all of sudden. "Fay, I'm sorry if I hurt you in any way—"

"Are you hungry?" She held my book close to her, standing still. "I've only had vending machine food since this morning."

"I'll make you something," I said, rising.

"Where do you usually go out to eat? I'd like to see the places you go. I'd like to see what your life is like."

"I don't go out much."

"Yeah, Mom told me." She looked around, sighing. "You don't have friends?"

"I do. I have friends, but I don't see them much anymore."

"Why?"

"Because I'm not very good at keeping in touch. I'm not very good at letting people close to me."

"I'm like that, too," she said, putting the book back. "Maybe I got that from you, huh?"

I stood and walked to her. "I want you to know something, Fay. Your mom told me that you came here for answers, and I should give them to you. And I want to. I will."

She frowned, chewing on her lip. I could see the emotion move over her features. But she held it in. "There's a lot of things I wanna know, Uncle Allan."

I hadn't heard her call me *uncle* for so long. A tidal wave of memories crashed into me. Our mornings together. Her rag dolls. Our afternoons at the pool. Tucking her into my bed. Our conversations on my balcony. The way she'd looked as she'd walked down the aisle, proud and bold, carrying her mother's bouquet. Where had time gone? How could we have missed out on ten years of our lives together?

"Fay," I said, reaching out to her, "come here." I held her against me and she was rigid for a moment, but then hugged me tightly.

"Why did you leave us?" she asked, holding me strongly.

I rocked her a little, not wanting to let her go. "I thought it was the best thing for us all at that time." I leaned back and looked at her. "I couldn't stay, Fay. I couldn't, I swear."

"Because of Uncle Dav."

I sat down again. Picked up my cup.

She hurried back to the couch and sat. "That's it, isn't? Please, Uncle Allan, tell me. Tell me right now. Not later, or tomorrow. Right now."

"What do you want to know?"

"Everything."

"Okay, but let me take you out for dinner."

She smiled. "Yes."

"You know, I thought you'd be angry and—"

"I thought so, too." She fiddled with her plastic bracelets. "The whole way here, I planned everything I was gonna tell you, and none of it was nice...But I don't know, when I saw your face, I just...I remembered how sweet you were to me, and how you took care of me when Mom was busy with her shop or Dayton...And how much I missed you."

"I missed you, too, baby." I grabbed her hand over the table. "I'm so glad you came and—"

"God, Mom is so annoying," she said, pulling her phone out of her pocket. She inhaled sharply. "Oh shit," she muttered.

"What?"

"I have to get this or he'll freak out." She answered her phone, settling back into the cushions, playing with a thread in her socks. "Hi," she said, "I thought you were up north, building—" She listened and nodded. "Oh, that was last week? Where are you now?"

This was probably the new boyfriend.

Her face turned red and she coughed. "You're in Toronto? Like, right now?"

"Everything okay?" I couldn't help asking.

She waved frantically and put a finger to her mouth, urging me to be quiet.

"No, I'm watching TV. Did you speak to my mom today?" She stared at me while she spoke. "Oh, no reason...So, what are you doing in Toronto anyway? Not that many acres of land here—" She listened, nodding, her cheeks still red. "I thought you were opening that exhibit in Montreal."

Opening?

"Well, that's really cool," she said, calmer now. "This Thursday? That's awesome."

She's on the phone with Davinder.

I perched on the edge of the seat, sweating.

"Me? I'm…I'm…Well, actually…Uncle Dav, can you hold on for a second?" She pressed her hand over the speaker and looked at me with panic on her face. "What the hell do I tell him?" she whispered.

"Tell him you're in Toronto, visiting a friend," I replied. "And tell him you're fine and that your mom knows."

"What if he asks me if I wanna meet up with him or something?"

"Then you will."

She told him what I'd suggested, and they talked for a few minutes before she hung up. "He bought it, I think," she said. "I had no idea he was going to be here."

"I did." I got up and went to my bedroom. If she wanted the truth, we'd have to start somewhere. I came back with the letter and dropped it on her lap. "He wrote me this two months ago."

"Uncle Dav did?" She looked down at the paper. When she was finished, she gently set the letter on the table, and for a moment, I wasn't sure what to expect. "He called you his soul," she said after a while. "So it's true, then. You and Uncle Davinder really did have a secret affair."

"Yes, we did."

"While he was married. For how long?"

"A little over a year."

"And you left because you were afraid everyone would find out?"

"I left because he couldn't be with me the way I wanted him to, and because I couldn't stand it."

She didn't say anything.

"Now do you understand what happened a little better? He was married and his kids were still very young, and we both knew there was no way to make it work."

"But he isn't married now. And his kids are all grown up." She looked at the letter again. "All those drawings, they're all of you. You should be the first to see them, right?"

"Let's go out to eat." I pulled her up. "Come on."

In the doorway, she stopped. "Now I know why I'm here. I'm gonna make you go to that exhibit."

I smiled a little. "I don't think so."

"Oh yes, I will," she said. "You'll see. That's why he loved me so much and took care of me like I was his own."

CHAPTER SIX

F ay slept on my couch, under the quilt I'd draped over her.
    It had been a long night for both of us, and it was now nearing two a.m. I needed sleep. Cameron had kept me on the phone for the last hour. He wanted to be the first one to wish me happy birthday, and he was curious about my evening with Fay.

Dinner had gone smoothly enough. I'd taken her to my favorite bistro and we'd shared a pitcher of beer and a plate of their best entrée. I'd been wary about the beer, but she promised she'd drank before and could handle a few glasses. She'd been uneven in her behavior throughout the evening in general. She'd tell me stories about her friends or go on a tirade about her favorite bands, but if I asked about her plans for the future or what she was interested in aside from music, she'd grow sullen and start moving food around her plate. She didn't know. Didn't want to talk about it. I was in no position to give her any kind of life advice, but as we began to relax around each other, I saw what Elsie meant when she'd warned me about Fay's obstinate nature. My niece had opinions on every single thing, most of them radical. She didn't think people were meant for monogamy. She didn't believe in having children. She thought the world was overpopulated enough. She would never vote and didn't aspire to own anything in her life. As I listened to her I'd heard the words of a scared child. She obviously didn't want to be attached to anything or anyone, and she certainly didn't want to be made to feel vulnerable.

It saddened me. If I'd been there, she'd have turned out so differently. Her father had left her as an infant, and I'd bailed as well.

But how could I make it up to her now? What could I give her? I had no wisdom, no true handle on life. And sometimes when she looked at me, I could see all of the expectations behind those hazel eyes.

Cameron had urged me to call Dayton tomorrow. Fay was, in so many ways, Dayton's daughter. Fay hadn't talked about her adoptive father much. I didn't know how she felt about the man who'd married her mother and given her a brother. There were so many things I didn't know about them all.

And it hurt.

The one thing I did know was I *needed* to be in Davinder's presence one more time. After Fay and I had come home, she'd asked me more questions. I'd answered as candidly as I could. She'd been shocked to find out that the last picture I'd seen of Davinder was one Elsie had sent me by mistake, four years ago. Fay had dragged me to my computer and pulled up Davinder's website.

Fay laughed. "If you only knew Uncle Dav the way I do," she'd said. "He's really not into the singles scene."

She'd clicked on his short bio, and when I caught sight of his face, I pulled up my chair and sat there, staring at the screen. It was a recent picture. A head shot. It was Davinder, exactly as I remembered him, only more beautiful. More beautiful because every new wrinkle on his handsome and intelligent face told a story. The fine lines I remembered around his mouth were deeper now, but his smile was so genuine and radiant that I couldn't see anything else. He seemed to be laughing at something. And I knew he'd finally solved that secret problem he'd been working on all those years ago.

He'd unmasked the demons that had tormented him. Unlike me, Davinder hadn't come out of this bitter. He'd come out of it whole and good. Today, I was forty years old.

Today, I was going to get my life back on track.

Today, I was going to change my ways.

And today, I was going to give myself another chance.

Chapter Seven

I shuffled back into the living room, barely awake.

Fay was at my computer, her hair hanging over one side of her face, her legs folded under her, and her fingers racing over the keyboard. She'd been on there for an hour. I hadn't even checked my e-mail yet. I also had some new ideas I wanted to write down, and everything was done on this computer she wouldn't let me have.

"So, what do you want to do today?" I looked over her shoulder at the screen. She was on Tumblr. "It's not so cold outside, so—"

"Hold on," she said, raising her hand. "I just need to post this."

I tried not to let my impatience show and walked back to the couch. I picked up my book—*The Social Contract* by Rousseau—and flipped it open. I'd read it a long time ago, but my love of philosophy had reemerged recently. One night I'd pulled out my old books on the subject and was in the process of reading them all once more.

I read for ten minutes and put the book down. "Fay? How long are you going to be on there?"

"I don't know, why?" She clicked and typed. "A few more minutes."

I stared at her for a long time, but she didn't turn around. "Well, I'm going to get cleaned up and—"

"Yeah, okay."

"Today's my birthday," I said, walking to my bedroom. I grabbed some clean clothes and a towel and started for the bathroom.

"Why didn't you tell me?" She stood in the living room, looking at me. "I didn't know."

"It's no big deal."

She hesitated and gave me a quick hug. "Happy birthday, Uncle Allan." She leaned back and looked around, blushing a little. "What are we doing, then?"

"It's up to you."

"Aren't you gonna have a party or something?"

I was—but she'd be gone by then. On Saturday, Cameron was organizing a small get-together at his place. "This weekend. So, let's see, do you want to—"

"That'll be great. I can't wait to meet your friends." She fell on the couch and stretched her legs out, reaching for the remote.

"The thing is Saturday. I mean, you'll be home by then."

She flicked the TV on. "No, I won't," she said, cheerfully, her eyes on the screen. "I'm gonna stay here for a while. With you."

"What do you mean?"

She looked over at me and smiled. "I don't wanna go home. I wanna stay here with you. I wanna make up for lost time." She held my eyes for a moment, then turned her attention back at the TV.

❖

"Take a breath," Cameron said. "What did she say exactly?"

I made sure my bedroom door was properly shut and spoke softly into the phone. "I told you, she wants to stay here with me." I paced around in my boxer shorts. "I can't live with my niece, you know what I mean? I just can't. I don't do well with—"

"With nineteen-year-old women?"

"Exactly." I sat on the edge of the bed. "I love her, but she's been here for a day and I'm already feeling a little suffocated. Oh man, Cameron, what am I supposed to do here?"

"You missed out on ten years of her life and you owe her a lot, but she's not your responsibility. She can't take you hostage like this."

"Am I being selfish? Be honest. Am I being a jerk?" Was I?

"No. Absolutely not. Listen to me, call her parents. Call her dad. They need to know."

Dayton…I hadn't spoken to him for so many years.

"I don't think he's going to want to talk to me."

"A lot of time has passed," Cameron said. "If you want to get your family back, you're going to have to start with him."

"I know." I took a deep breath, looking at my bedroom door. "I just call Dayton up? Just like that?"

"Yep. Just like that. His daughter is asking you to move in. He needs to know this."

He was right again. I ended our conversation, promising I'd get back to him soon, and yes, I'd be there Saturday, and yes...I was going to think about Thursday night. The exhibit.

But what Cameron didn't know was that I'd already made up my mind about it. I was going. I didn't know how I'd manage to muster the courage to see Davinder again, but the consequences of not seeing him were too dire to face.

After I hung up, I checked up on Fay. "We'll go see a movie," I said. "If you want to use the shower, go ahead. I have a few calls to make."

"Cool." She didn't move.

She'd feel betrayed when she'd find out I'd called her dad. The young Uncle Allan would have called Dayton with no hesitation. She couldn't run from her problems and I wouldn't be her enabler.

I shut myself up in my bedroom and searched my old contacts for Dayton's cell phone number. I found it and dialed. If I was lucky, he'd be at lunch and able to talk.

On the fourth ring, he picked up. "Fay?"

I froze. He'd seen my name on his caller ID and assumed it was her. "No...It's Allan."

The line went silent. Cold and silent.

"She's here with me—"

"Yeah, I know...How is she?"

Hearing his voice after all this time was more difficult than I'd expected.

"Well, that's the thing," I said. "She's been talking about staying here and I just wanted—"

"You mean with you?" I heard some voices and a door being shut. "Put her on the phone, please."

"Dayton, listen—"

"Put her on the phone, now."

"She doesn't know I'm talking to you."

He exhaled loudly. "What game are you playing?"

"Can we talk? Can we just talk for a second? Can you give me a chance here?"

He didn't say anything.

"Dayton, I know what you think of me, and I'm not going to try to change your mind, okay? But she came to me, and she's here, and in some way, she needs me. No matter what you say, she needs me. I'm her uncle. I was there for the first ten years of her life." My words came fast. Like a dam had been broken inside me. "I took care of those girls for nine years before you. I was there at Fay's birth. I put a roof over their heads, paid their bills, helped Elsie start her business, watched over Fay seven days a week—" I stopped, my voice breaking. I was on the edge of tears. "When you came into my sister's life, I opened my heart to you, right away, do you remember that? You said I could have made it hard on you, but I didn't. And I'm asking you, for my sister's sake, for your daughter's sake, I'm asking you, please, Dayton, can you see it my way for just one small minute?"

There was another long pause. "I know," he said at last. "I know you did good by the girls for a long time. I'm not saying you didn't."

I had to lean back on the wall. "I was in lo—" I stopped, too shaken and choked up to speak.

"You were in love with him. Is that what you were gonna say?"

I could only nod.

"Yeah, I know that, too."

I tried getting myself together. "I never meant for any of this to happen. I couldn't function without him, and I tried to resist it and—"

"It was a long time ago. I don't even know how I feel about it anymore."

"Do you...do you hate me?"

"I did for a while. I won't lie to you. But no, Allan, I don't *hate* you." He sighed deeply. "I really don't. Jesus, even Eileen forgave you. She's doing good, by the way, better than when she was with my brother. That's important to me. That everyone's doing good. How about you? How are you doing?"

"Not too hot," I said, laughing though I felt like crying.

"My brother with you?"

"What?" I stepped away from the wall. "No. Why would he be? I haven't seen your brother in ten years."

"You're shitting me...he's not with you? But he went to Toronto and—"

"We never kept in contact, never. He just wrote me two months ago to let me know that he'd be in town."

"You stayed away from him all this time?"

"Yeah, it was the right thing to do. For Eileen and the kids, and him."

Dayton was quiet again.

"You thought we were—"

"Yeah, I mean, in the last years, at least."

"No."

"You mean to tell me that everybody here went through hell and back because you two guys were in love, but you're both living alone and wandering around like two dumbasses—" He snorted. "Well, shit."

"Are you saying you wouldn't mind if—"

"Look, Allan, my brother's not getting any younger, and I don't want him up there alone. I don't get it. I really don't. This whole big mess for what?"

"What do you mean, 'up there alone'?"

"He didn't tell you...Look, never mind that. All I'm saying is, I want my brother to be happy, that's what I want. I'm sick of worrying about him and I'm sick of this story already. I figure, you're obviously the one he wants, so who am I to stand in the way. I just want peace, man."

Peace. I'd forgotten that word. Couldn't remember how it felt to wake up in the morning and face the day with serenity. Ever since I'd met Davinder, almost twelve years ago, I'd lived every day with turmoil in my gut.

"So what's this nonsense about Fay wanting to move in with you? Put her on the phone."

"Okay, here she is. But, Dayton, be cool."

"Yeah, I know." His voice sounded different. This felt good to him, too. "I'm gonna wire you some money for her bus ticket—"

"Please, no. Don't do that. I'll take care of it." I opened the door. Fay was still watching TV. "Here," I said, handing the phone to her.

"Who is it?"

"Your dad."

Her eyes hardened. She snatched the phone out of my hand.

I went back to grab my clothes and towel. I'd take a nice, long, hot shower, and she'd have to deal with her father.

Chapter Eight

Fay, Cameron, and I were crammed inside my small bedroom, looking down at the mount of clothes on the bed. "This one's nice," Cameron said, picking up my gray cardigan. "I like you in this one. Makes your eyes stand out."

"It's itchy." I grabbed my favorite black shirt instead. It would make me look thinner, at least. "This, with a white T-shirt underneath and maybe my—"

"No, not black. It'll make you look older."

Fay leaned back, sighing. "You guys are worse than me and my girlfriends on a Friday night."

"How about this?" Cameron spread out an outfit on the bed. It was my thin fitted Ralph Lauren long-sleeved blue shirt, matched with my oldest pair of blue jeans. "Yeah," he said, stepping back with an air of satisfaction. "Exactly right. You'll look like a writer out on the town."

"And what is that supposed to look like?" I stared at the outfit. It could work. *If* I still fit in this shirt. "All right, everybody out." I ushered them into the living room, threw the pile of rejected clothes into my closet, and slipped out of my T-shirt. I stood in front of the mirror. My chest was hairier than it had been. My stomach was round around the navel and definitely not as hard as it had been. I ran a hand through my hair. It was thinner than last year, but still blond. No gray hairs yet. I faked a smile and saw the lines form at the corner of my eyes and mouth. I had a few new wrinkles on my forehead as well.

"What are you doing in there?" Cameron walked in, not bothering to knock. "You're not even dressed. It's seven-forty-five." He tossed the shirt at me. "Let's go, move it."

"How did I get this old?" I let him button up my shirt. "Where did the decade go?" I pushed him away gently and pulled my pants off, slipping into my jeans. Good, everything still fit.

"You're forty, Allan. Not eighty. Get a grip." Cameron fussed with my belt. "Loosen it up a little or your belly will bulge."

"Thank you, really," I said, sarcastically, stepping to the mirror again. "How do I look?"

He walked up to me. "Do you remember when we met? Do you remember what state you were in?" He took my face into his small, warm hands. "And look at you now, Allan Waterhouse. You're back in the saddle again, my friend."

"I couldn't have done it without you."

"Come on, Fay's bored out there. It's time to go."

"I wish you could come with—"

"It's not my place, you know that. What's the poor guy gonna think if he sees you walking in with this hot little piece of ass at your side." He winked. "Now, enough stalling."

I took one final look at my reflection, and for a moment, I saw myself ten years ago.

"All right," I said.

❖

Fay and I stepped out of the cab onto the crowded, bustling sidewalk.

It'd been a long time since I'd been anywhere exciting. On the ride over, Fay'd been quiet—she'd been quiet for the last three days, ever since she'd spoken with Dayton. We'd had an argument, and I'd listened to her rage until late in the night. When she'd calmed down, I'd tucked her in as I'd done all those years ago, and she'd let me. She loved me, I believed it. And she certainly loved her Uncle Dav.

She was going to have to work it all out, and that would take time. I'd be here. I'd keep a close eye on her this time around. She'd be able to count on me, even if that meant I'd take a hit from her once in a while. We'd lost ten years, but we still had time to turn this thing around.

And we would.

"Is that it?" She pointed to the brightly lit windows of the gallery.

"That's it." I didn't move.

"Are you okay?"

People were walking in and out of the gallery. I hadn't been out in a crowd for too long. I had slipped into a sort of hermit way of life... Cameron was right after all.

"Uncle Allan?"

"Could you...could you go in there and..."

"No, you have to come." She grabbed my arm and pulled on me. "It's gonna be okay. He'll be happy to see you."

"Fay, I'm not going to see his face for the first time in ten years with a room full of strangers looking on. I don't know how we'll both react, okay?"

"So, what are you—"

"Go inside, tell him I'll be out here, standing over there." It was three doors away—a small enclosed courtyard between two buildings. I'd sat and read there many times before. "He'll understand."

"I'll tell him!" she yelled back before disappearing into the gallery.

I pulled my coat closed around my chin—it wasn't cold at all, but I was shaking—and walked to the courtyard. There was a wrought iron bench with a statue of a woman reading to her child molded into the seat. I stood with my back against the brick wall and waited. My anxiety seemed to be leveling down now. I watched the light of the antique street lamp create shadows on the statue's smooth surface. I took a few shallow breaths, stuffing my hands into my coat pocket. Five minutes passed. What would he say? What would he think of me?

I stared at the thin film of snow on the ground.

"Allan?"

I turned my head in his direction, seeing him walk up to me.

Davinder wore a long wool coat, tied at the waist—a sort of officer's coat. He was still long and elegant. His face looked exactly the way I'd remembered it, but something in his eyes had changed.

And I'd forgotten his walk—the cavalier manner about him.

Oh, but I remembered all of it now.

"Allan." He said my name again, and for a moment, I thought he'd kiss me or hug me, but his features twisted into an expression of utmost pain. "Oh, Allan," he said, covering his mouth with a fist, bursting into tears.

He crouched down and wept into his hands. "Allan," he said. "I can't believe it."

I stooped down by him. "Hey, it's all right...don't cry."

"I'm sorry," he said in a hoarse voice. "It's just the nerves." He rested his head back on the wall. "It's been a long week, and with this stupid exhibit, and you...I'm sorry." He wiped his eyes. "I'm sorry. Man, I thought I'd be cool and collected. Look at me, I'm a mess." He dug into his pocket and took out a tissue. He blew his nose. "Thank you for coming."

I stood up, unsure of what to say.

Davinder rose as well, meeting my eyes. "You got my letter, obviously. You read it? Well, of course you read it."

"Yeah, I read it last week," I said, unable to look away from his face. "It took me a long time before I could open it."

"Why?" Even his tone was different. There was a sweetness about him that was making me ache. "You didn't want to read it?"

"It's not that." I took a step closer to him. "I was scared, that's all. I didn't know what you were going to say to me."

"And are you scared now?" He was still shaking. "I know *I'm* terrified. I've never been so scared in my life. I've been wanting to get in touch with you for three years."

I moved closer to him. "Oh, Davinder, just come here." I pulled him close, holding him. "I missed you," I said in his ear. "I can't believe you're here, in my arms."

He didn't say anything.

"Dad?"

It was Noah.

"What is it?" Davinder moved out of my arms. "Do I have to go back in there already?"

"Yeah, and they won't let me have a drink if you don't tell 'em I can." Noah looked at me, his blue eyes roaming over my face. "Hi."

"Hello, Noah." Noah was as tall as Davinder, but more solid and imposing. He was a beautiful blond with chiseled features. "It's so good to see you."

"Aren't you gonna come see your drawings?" Noah asked.

"They're all of you, so I guess you should have the guts to come inside."

Davinder started. "Noah, hey—"

"Not tonight," I said. "It's a little too much for everybody, I think."

"Dad? Are you coming in or what?" Noah left without another word.

"I'm sorry, but he didn't tell me he was coming. He drove out here today. I think he knew we'd—"

"Don't worry about it, okay? It's—"

"He's an amazing man, my son. They both are."

"Oh, I know. I know that." I fought the urge to touch his hand. Comfort him. "You should go back inside. Tonight's your night and—"

"Allan, I'm leaving in the morning. I wasn't supposed to, but I have to go up north to check up on things. Man, I didn't think you'd show and—"

"So you're driving back tomorrow morning."

"I'm sorry. Had I known—"

"Fay told me you have some kind of van you've made into a five-bedroom apartment or something." I tried to laugh to convince myself I wasn't completely crushed. "You drive? Since when?"

"I've lived in my van from time to time, but it's really not as bad as it seems. It's actually pretty nice. I had an apartment, but in the last years, I've been living in a small room I rent from a wonderful old lady who used to know my dad. I've been saving my money, that's all. And yeah, I drive."

"Saving your money for what?"

"It's too early to be talking about that and—"

"Uncle Dav?" Fay stood at the entrance of the small courtyard. "Honestly, people are starting to think it's weird you're not in there."

"Ten years," Davinder said under his breath, "and I can't even get five minutes alone with you."

"It's my fault. I should have read that letter before." I stepped back.

"You got a card or something?" He was nervous again. "I read all your books, you know."

"Yeah?"

"They're good. Very good. You're still doing that, right?" He shook his head. "Wow, we have so much to talk about, it's making me crazy. I'll get in touch with you tonight, all right? As soon as I get back to the hotel. I'll call you and we can talk." He moved closer to me. "So what now? How do we say good-bye?"

I stood there.

"Or maybe we just don't," he said.

I gave him my card.

"I'll call you. The minute I walk in."

"Keep an eye on Fay for me and—"

"Of course. I'll drive her home."

"Thank you," I whispered.

"And, Allan, happy belated birthday."

When he'd finally turned the corner, I leaned the side of my head against the cool brick.

CHAPTER NINE

"You must be exhausted," I said, stifling a yawn. My ear hurt from the pressure of the phone. In the last hour, I'd emptied half a bottle of red wine. It was all hitting me now—the emotion, the alcohol, and Davinder's deep voice on the other end of the line.

He'd kept his promise, calling me the moment he'd stepped into his hotel lobby. Fay and Noah had gone back to Noah's hotel room to hang out. The *kids*, as he referred to them, would probably spend a few hours on YouTube and drink Arizona Iced Tea. No big deal.

"Well, we've been talking for a couple of hours, I think." Davinder sounded drowsy. "You want to go to bed, then?"

I should have, but I didn't want to hang up just yet. "No, not just now." And besides, we were finally getting to the part of his and Renaud's reconciliation and second affair. They'd resumed their relationship during his trip to Germany, and though their second affair had ended, I was still consumed with jealousy. Maybe it was because I'd never met Renaud or seen a picture of him. In my mind, he was perfect. He was the man I could never compete with. He'd done great things with his life, and what had I done aside from publishing a series of books?

"Do you still keep in touch with Remaud?"

"We're friends," Davinder said, "I mean—"

"I know that. It's great that you were able to fix your relationship with him."

"That part bothers you, doesn't it?"

"I don't know why it bothers me so much," I said.

"It bothers you because I never set the record straight with you. I never said what you really needed to hear. And that made you feel insecure."

"I'm not insecure," I lied. "I don't care about Renaud. It's the past."

"Allan, sometimes I feel like you're afraid of hearing the truth."

"From you, yes." I sat up.

"I think we've said enough for tonight," he said, to my surprise. "We don't have to cover everything in one conversation, right? There'll be plenty of time for that."

"Thank you for being so honest and—"

"Allan, honesty is all I have to win you back."

I sat up straight, seeing his beautiful dark eyes in my mind. "There's so much history between us, Davinder. A lot of pain. It just doesn't seem like we could ever—"

"I'm not asking you—" But there was a pause on the line. "I have another call. It's Noah. Hold on."

The line went dead and I chewed on my lip. Ten years had gone by, but nothing of him was lost to me. It was all there—even the hurt.

He came back on the line a few minutes later.

"What's going on? Is everything okay with the kids?"

"Listen…Don't panic or anything, but I need to go pick up Noah and Fay right now."

"What happened? What's going on?" I stood, moving for my coat and boots. "Davinder?"

"I don't know, I think she drank too much. Noah's a little overwhelmed and—"

"Where are they?" I opened the door. "Is she sick? What are they doing getting drunk?"

"I don't know, Allan. Noah couldn't talk to me…She was pulling on the phone and slapping him—"

"What?" I shut the door behind me and ran down the steps. "I'm taking a cab there, so give me an address." It was cold tonight. Damp and windy. I looked around—the streets were dead. I wouldn't get a cab so easily. I'd have to call one and wait. "It's gonna be a while before I can get a taxi here—"

"Allan, don't worry about it. I'm on way right now. I'll bring her home to you, okay?" I heard a door slam. "Just go inside and warm up. We'll be there soon."

❖

I'd washed the dishes in the sink, tidied up the living room, and prepped Fay's bed.

Leaning up against the kitchen counter, sober and nervous, I waited for the coffee to finish brewing. It was 2:26, but I was no longer tired. My second wind had kicked in. Davinder had called fifteen minutes ago to let me know they were on their way. I wasn't sure what to expect. He hadn't said much about Fay's state, but I figured she was drunk and in dire need of sleep. I could handle that. No problem.

I poured some fresh coffee into my cup and went to the living room. I drank, peering through the blinds at the deserted street.

I saw the headlights cut through the snowflakes and set my cup down on the coffee table.

I opened the front door and came face-to-face with Davinder and Noah, who were holding Fay up between them. I didn't say anything, just watched them carry her in.

"Bed?" Davinder asked, looking at me from over the tangled mess of Fay's hair. "In here," I said. When they passed into the room, I lifted Fay's head, holding her face in my hand. "Hey, kiddo, how are—"

"I'm sorry," she slurred, shaking her head. "I'm sorry. I'm sorry."

"It's okay." I brushed her hair back. "Don't worry about it."

"I'm sorry," she cried again. She moved out of Davinder's arms and stumbled to the bed, lying down over the blankets. "I'm so sorry." She was sobbing.

I looked over at Noah. "What happened? Why were you guys drinking?"

His clean blue eyes flickered with embarrassment. "She had one too many shots, that's all. She had a bottle of Sailor Jerry in her backpack." He looked away, his features softening. "She just...she was having a lot of fun and then we went outside to spray-paint the side of the building, but she tripped and fell, and it all went—"

"I wanna call my mom," Fay said, her voice muffled from the pillow. She was crying hard, her shoulders heaving. "I wanna call my mom." She sobbed louder. "I wanna call my mom. I want my mom."

Davinder hesitated for a moment, and sat on the edge of the bed, touching her shoulder gently. "Your mom's sleeping. You need to calm down, Fay. You need to sleep." He looked up at his son, who stood in the corner of the room, clearly ill at ease. "Get me a glass of water."

"I don't want water," Fay said, turning on her side, curling her knees under her. "I want my mom." Her hair hid her face and I could only see her mouth. She was still crying, holding herself. "She's the only one who's always been there for me." She turned her face into the pillow. "And I'm so mean to her all the time! But it's your fault because you left me and that messed me up!"

"Fay, come on now. You know why your uncle had to leave, and I thought you understood...Don't you see he did it for you and your mom?"

"Oh, Dad, that's a bunch of bullshit." Noah stirred in the corner. "You both want to stick to that story, but if you hadn't done what you did back then, none of this would have happened."

"Exactly!" Fay cried, sweeping the hair off her face. "Why didn't you think of us before—"

"Think?" Davinder said, his tone harsher now. "Don't you *think* we tried to stay away from it?" He turned his dark gaze to Noah. "I tortured myself day and night, and I know you don't want to hear it...I know that." He shook his head, clearly upset. "No matter what I say or do, I'm gonna be guilty and I'm gonna be wrong. But let me tell you something, both of you."

"No, I don't want to hear it," Noah said. "Because you have no idea what I'm going through. What Jude is going through—"

"Where is this coming from, Noah? I thought we'd worked this out a little."

"Well, maybe I lied. Maybe I was scared to lose you again...I don't know." Noah leaned back against the wall, his handsome face clouding over. "When did you know you were gay, huh? Did it happened before or after you married Mom?"

"Can we just all get some rest and try to talk about this tomo—"

"I want him to answer my question," Noah said. "Because I want to know if I'm gonna have a family and then wake up one day and realize I'm gay. Huh, Dad? Is that how it—"

"I'm not gay," Davinder snapped, rubbing his face. "I told you all this before, but no matter how I explain it, you just won't believe it. I was always bisexual, okay? Always. You want the truth, here it is again...I knew I liked men way before I married your mom, but I never stopped being attracted to women, and I loved your mother."

"Ah, that's clear."

"Noah," I said, softly. "Don't."

"Uncle Allan, why do you wanna interfere now?" Fay sat up, her makeup running down her cheeks. "You've been silent for ten years and—"

"And now maybe he wants to say something. Can he? Is he allowed?" Davinder looked back and forth from Fay to his son. "Or has he forsaken that right as well?"

"What right? He has no rights." Noah's face reddened. "What he had were responsibilities, though, and—"

"Yes!" Fay chimed in. "You both knew the consequences of your—"

"Yes, we knew," Davinder said, cutting her off. "We knew them all too well, but now that I look back on the last ten years of my life—" Abruptly, he stopped, standing up, staring at the floor.

"But what? Huh? Say it, Dad, come on."

Davinder raised his stare to his son. "The regret I feel about breaking up our family is terrible, yes. But now that it's broken, what I regret the most is—" He stopped again, his voice failing him. He was choked up and trying to hold back from crying.

Noah sighed. "I don't hate you, Dad." He seemed to want to move to his father, but couldn't. "I know it was hard for you."

"I tried, you know." Davinder quickly wiped a tear away. "In the last years, I tried to make up—"

"No, I know, I know that. And you did, and I'm—"

"How much more do you want me to suffer, Noah?"

"I don't know," Noah said, knocking the back off his head on the wall in exasperation. "I'm just so fucking sick of this mess."

"So am I," Fay said, lying down again. "I wanna be happy, but I'm so angry all the time."

"And you have every right to be." I knelt by the bed, looking at her. "I don't expect you to forgive me all at once…You're nineteen, Fay, and that means being angry sometimes, because that's part of growing up. You're seeing the world differently and it's going to piss you off sometimes, but if you can't keep using the past as a way to avoid your future—"

"What future?" She sniffled. "I don't even know what I'm doing, or what I want."

"Welcome to adulthood." I dared to touch her arm. "You'll figure it out, and I'd like to help you along the way, if you let me."

"Sometimes I'm scared of how quickly I'm forgiving you and what that says about me."

"I know what you mean. I understand. And I won't take advantage of that."

"I wanna fix things with Daddy Dayton, but—"

"Fay," Davinder said, his voice steady again, "there's nothing to fix. I know my brother, and all you need to do when you get home to make him the happiest man on earth is give him a great big hug and tell him you love him."

"He's been good to me. Good to my mom."

"Dad, when we get home, we need to sit down all three of us, me, you, and Jude, and talk. Really talk."

"I'd love nothing more that that."

"When are you moving up north?"

Davinder looked over at me, uneasy. "Um, I don't know yet, and—"

"You're moving?" A chill went up my spine. "Where?"

"I have a lot of things tell you, Allan."

"What's gonna happen now?" Noah asked "Are you two going—"

"Yeah, are you two going to get back together? We really want to know."

"We haven't gotten to that part yet," Davinder said, before I could answer. "And I don't think I want to be talking about this with you two anyway." He looked at his watch. "It's really late. We're driving back early."

"Can I go back with you tomorrow?" Fay asked in a little voice. "I think my mom would like that. I miss her anyway. Do you mind, Uncle Allan? I mean, I could come back and visit, right? It's not far and I'm getting my license this spring—"

"Don't worry about it. I think it's a good idea you go home tomorrow. Of course you could come visit. You can come whenever you like. But maybe it's my turn to come down there." I glanced over at Noah. "It's been a very long time. I'd like to see everybody there again."

"It's your home, and you shouldn't have to question your right to go home." Fay spoke these words with her eyes on Noah. "After all, why should you be blamed for all of this? You're not the one who was married."

"So my dad's the only guilty one, then?"

"Guys," Davinder interjected. "There's no need to get into this right now. Listen to me, you're both old enough to hear the uncensored truth about what really happened, and I don't know, maybe it'll make everything clearer for you."

"Finally," Noah said.

"Allan, do you mind?" Davinder asked me. "The last thing I want to do is make you feel uneasy in your own house."

"I'm a little past uneasy." I leaned back against the dresser, nervousness stirring in my stomach. "Tell them what you want."

"All right then." He focused his attention on Noah. "I knew I was bi from the time I was in my early teens, and I didn't mind it. I wasn't very confused about it either. It was just something I lived with. Another one of my dualities. I spent my life dealing with all of the contractions in my mind and spirit, so I guess bisexuality was just one of those things that came with the package. But in all honesty, I never fell in love with guys, and I really believed I was best suited for straight relationships. I wanted a family and I liked the idea of sharing my life with a woman. I had a period where I thought I was in love with a man in my early twenties, but that was something else altogether. Do you follow me so far?"

Noah shrugged.

"I just have a lot of different inclinations and I'm very curious by nature, and when I like someone, sometimes I take it to a higher level than maybe you would." Davinder paused, reorganizing his thoughts.

"After I left Paris...I didn't feel very good about myself and I sought out your mom because I remembered how good she made me feel, and really, that was my first mistake. I fell in love with her and she with me, for the wrong reasons. We both needed the other to fix us. But then we had kids together, and that was it for me...I'd always wanted to be a father, and she made that dream come true. For a while, that's what it was...a dream."

"You did love her," Fay said, gently. She was sobering up. "You were happy, then?"

"No, not really. Because there was always that longing inside me. Whenever things got tense between us, I'd shut down and start getting those cravings. Not for men specifically, but for freedom, adventure..."

"You felt trapped by us."

"Sometimes, yes."

"You weren't the marrying kind. Is that what you're saying?"

"No, Noah, I wasn't. That's the bottom line, isn't? I wasn't suited for it. My temperament...My nature, if you want to call it that way."

"And fatherhood? Were you suited for that?" Noah's tone was icy.

"I think I would have been a better father if I'd listened to myself and been honest with your mom from the first time I started doubting my ability to be faithful to her."

"I don't understand you."

"I know it's complicated."

"It really isn't. Either you love someone or you don't. You do right by them, or you don't."

"Maybe you're right." Davinder shot me a glance, and looked back at his son. "As a matter of fact, I know you're right."

"So you didn't love Mom, then."

"I cared for her." Davinder's breath was short. "I cared for your mom," he said. "And she remains one of the people I admire and respect the most. I believe she feels the same way about me, but there are things she hasn't told you about her part in this...things you should probably know. She, too, had her reasons for being with me. And she, too, hung on for much too long."

"So you're saying she knew."

"She knew who she married, that's all I can tell you. I cared about your mother profoundly, all right? But the way I feel about Allan…"

"I think we've said enough for tonight." I couldn't hear this with Fay and Noah staring at me. "I'm sorry, guys, but I'm exhausted and I can't…I really can't."

"My father ended his marriage for you. And what did you—"

"Noah, don't even—"

"It's okay," I said, a little too weakly, turning to Noah. "You want to know what I did?"

"Allan, you don't have to stand accused here and—"

"No, let him talk, Uncle Davinder." Fay threw her finger up at Noah. "And you, you better listen to him."

"Why should I?"

"Because he's the man I love," Davinder said, his voice rising. "And you're my son and if there's going to be some kind of peace between us one day, it has to start tonight. It has to start with you trying to see this man through my eyes a little. And not like the enemy."

"Maybe there can never be peace." I stepped back to the door. "Maybe it's hopeless…this whole thing…"

"No. No way." Davinder was angry now. "I'm not gonna let you sacrifice another minute of your life, Allan!" He gestured at Noah. "Do you understand that? I'm not gonna let him crawl back into his cave because you're too immature and selfish—"

"Selfish? You're gonna tell me I'm selfish?" Noah took a step toward his dad. "Really?"

"Stop it!" Fay screamed, throwing her arms over her face. "I can't stand this shit anymore."

"God forbid you ever make a mistake, Noah." Davinder's voice sank. "I hope you show yourself more mercy if you ever do."

"I'm going to bed," I said. My head throbbed. "I'm sorry, Noah, I don't know what to tell you anymore."

"If you loved my dad, then why did you leave? Why didn't you come back after he got his divorce?"

"Would you stop it?" Davinder stepped up to Noah, staring him in the eye. "It's enough."

"No, I want to know how he was able to let you suffer through all that if he loved you so."

"Because we're not all the same! Okay?" I shouted those words. "Because I was afraid to try. Have you ever been afraid to try, Noah?"

"My dad needed you."

My eyes found Davinder's. "And I needed him," I whispered. Davinder reached out to Noah. "Let's just take it one small step at a time here."

"It's not hopeless," Fay said to me as Noah and Davinder spoke quietly in the corner.

I walked to the bed and sat by her. "I don't know what to do. I really don't. I'm so afraid of making another mistake."

"Do you still love him?" She almost mouthed the words. "Do you?"

I didn't—*couldn't*—answer her.

"I think you do," she said, pulling the blankets over her body. "You don't have to tell me. I see it when you look at him. I don't think I've ever seen two people look at each other the way you two do. Not even my mom and Dayton."

I rose. "You need to sleep. And so do I."

"We're gonna go," Davinder said, breaking away from Noah. "You're gonna be okay, Fay?"

She was already dozing off. "Don't come too early, please."

Davinder snorted softly. His face was paler and he looked very tired. He was leaving. And I wanted him to stay. How I needed to strip him of all of his clothes and lay him down in my bed. "What time do you think you'll pick her up?"

"I'll call you around eight."

Noah was fidgeting by the doorway. "I'm not the jerk that you might think."

"Noah, I don't think you're a jerk at all."

"You know I don't hate you, right?" He bit down on his lip. "I'd like to try to get to know you maybe."

"That's good enough for me."

"Maybe I'll write you a letter or something."

I thought of that box. That box full of unanswered letters. But this would be different. As I walked them to the front door, I began to feel better. More together. Maybe even a little hopeful.

Noah slipped his coat on. "I read your books," he said, uneasily. "Not my cup of tea, but you're a good writer anyway."

"Thank you. Your dad told me that you're studying languages."

"I'm going to be a linguist." He wrapped his scarf around his neck and gave me his first smile of the night. "In seven years, give or take."

"Impressive for a boy who couldn't string three words together, huh?" Davinder squeezed his son's shoulder, pride in his eyes.

Noah stepped out and Davinder turned his attention back to me. "Are you okay?"

"Quite a night."

"If I could have stayed tonight...would you have let me?"

I couldn't lie to him "Yes...I would have."

"Thank you for saying it."

"We have to take it really slow."

"I live six hours away from here. You don't get any slower than that."

"But you're moving even farther?"

"Let's not talk about that tonight." He moved in closer. "Not just yet."

"Are you playing a game with me?"

"No, God, no." He touched my face. "No games. But please don't worry about me moving, okay?"

I couldn't stop my finger from tracing the lines around his mouth. "Maybe your face has changed a little, but your eyes are the same."

"Yours are different." He took the final step to me, pressing his chest against mine. "You look sad."

"I am," I said. "I'm always sad." I skimmed my lips against his mouth. "Always."

"I'm gonna change that," he murmured.

I pulled away, a little light-headed. "You have to go," I said. "Call me tomorrow morning."

"And then I'll call you the day after that."

I pushed on him a little and shut the door halfway. "Sleep well."

Halfway down the steps, he stopped and turned around. "You were cute when I met you, but to me, you're even better-looking now, Allan."

"Really?" I asked.

"The weight looks good on you." A flash of the younger Davinder illuminated his face. "I've got a thing for bulky thighs and meaty asses."

I tried not to laugh. "Go home. Good night."

I checked up on Fay and went straight to my bedroom, falling atop the bed with my clothes on. I lay there, looking up at my ceiling, recalling everything Davinder had said to me. He'd told me about the first months after I'd left Montreal and the major depression he'd survived. He'd recounted his descent into hell, and how he'd found truth and motivation in his art again. He'd given me details about his trip to Berlin, his affair with Renaud, the people he'd met and how they'd changed him forever. Since his return to Montreal, he'd been involved with various benevolence organizations around the city. How did he manage to make a living? When he and Eileen had sold the condo on the Plateau, they'd made a killing, and he'd used the money to fund his art. He chose to live small and focusing on his passion for community service and visual arts, combining the two, helping the groups he worked with. His two most cherished causes were mental health and environmental issues. I was drifting in and out of sleep. When my phone buzzed somewhere in the apartment, I shot up out of bed. I found it on the coffee table.

It was Davinder.

"Hi," I answered in a breath. "Everything okay?"

"Yeah, yeah," he said, softly. "Noah's safe in his hotel room."

"Did you guys talk a little on the way?"

"We did."

"And?"

"Things are better, but I needed to hear your voice one last time before I went to sleep."

I crept back to my bedroom and lay down. "What do you want to talk about?"

"Nothing. I just want to listen to you breathe and know that you're not too far away."

"Okay…sure." I shut my eyes, making myself comfortable in the pillows. "I won't hang up until you fall asleep."

"You don't have to."

"I want to, Davinder."

He'd been lonely for too long. I didn't want him to be lonely anymore.

Not ever again.

CHAPTER TEN

There were twenty or more people in Cameron's one-bedroom apartment.

I had to give it to him—he knew how to make someone feel important. Though half of the guests possibly didn't know who I was, or that the party was actually for my birthday, it was nice to be here anyway.

Since Davinder and Noah had left the day before and taken Fay with them, I'd been doing nothing. Absolutely *nothing*. I'd find myself sitting up in bed with a book, not reading, and later, staring at the television screen. I hadn't even touched my computer. I missed Davinder more than I could stand. I was no longer in control of anything. My body and soul wanted Davinder.

"Are you having fun?"

I looked up from my glass to find Cameron staring down at me. He looked fantastic tonight—positively radiant. Brian had to be good for him. I'd been watching the two of them, and if only Cameron could relax and trust himself, they could make a go at it.

"Thanks for doing this for me," I said over the loud music. I took his hand in mine. I'd missed him this week. "And are you happy?"

"You're acting so weird tonight," Cameron replied. "You have this crazy expression on your face. Thinking of him, huh?"

I twirled my glass in my fingers. "I can't help it."

"Come on, let's go to my bedroom." Cam walked off. I followed him, stopping a few times to say hello to friends. I'd managed to build a life here. Bit by bit, and without knowing it. I had *survived* Davinder.

Cameron pulled me into his room and shut the door behind us. "Are you and Davinder all caught up?"

I'd told Cameron about my late-night phone conversations with Davinder and how we'd basically covered everything important in the last forty-eight hours. "Yes, pretty much. Davinder's been really honest with me and—"

"He still loves you, then?"

"He says he never stopped."

Cameron's eyes searched my face again. "Are you sure? I mean, you believe him? You trust him?"

"Are you worried about me?"

"I don't want you to get hurt, *but* I also know this is something I can't really understand."

"You will."

"No, Allan, I probably never will. What you and Davinder have is exceptional."

"I've come to a point where living without him is not an option anymore."

"Good, that's what I wanted to hear." He coughed, his voice catching in his throat. "Listen…I…Well, I need to tell you something… Last night, I had a few drinks and looked him up…And I called him."

"What? What do you mean? You talked with Davinder? What'd you say? What did you guys—"

"Relax, I didn't say we'd slept together or anything."

"I wasn't worried about that."

"Oh." Cameron smiled, embarrassed. "I thought…anyway, we talked a while. And it was nice…he's nice, okay? He obviously feels the same way about you. Shit, it was like hearing you speak. It was quite nauseating."

I laughed. "Did he ask you why you were calling him? He must have thought it was a little—"

"Actually, no, he didn't think anything of it. After I told him you and me were tight, he encouraged me to ask him whatever I wanted. So yeah, I started out looking for things I didn't like about him, but in the end, I was opening up to him like I was at confession or something."

"He has a way, doesn't he?"

"Sure does."

I kicked Cameron's foot. "I can't believe you called him," I said. "Now, let's get out of your bedroom before Brian starts getting jealous."

"Wait, Allan, that's not what I wanted to tell you." Cameron was flustered, grabbing my arm. "I don't know what you'll think of this and—"

There was a knock on the door and Brian's face appeared in the wedge. "Sorry to disturb you two, but there's a guy here for—"

"We'll be right out," Cameron said, pushing on the door gently. "Give him a drink and show him around or something."

Brian frowned, looking at Cameron strangely. "But—"

"Baby, we'll be right out."

"What's going on?" Davinder showed his handsome face in the door. "Where's the birthday boy?" He was grinning.

"Dav, oh my God."

"Surprise," Cameron said, opening the door wide. He gestured for Davinder to step inside. "Come on in."

"What are you doing here?" I reached my hand out, but didn't touch him. "When did you get in the city?"

"I came for you. I drove straight through from the Laurentians." Davinder took my hand, pulling me closer. "How are you?"

"You came all the way here for me?"

Davinder whispered, "Yes, but, Allan, the plan is to get you to come back with me."

CHAPTER ELEVEN

I came back to the living room with a glass of water. "You sure you're not hungry? I could make some—"

"Come here." Davinder patted the empty space beside him on the couch. "I want to say a few things to you."

"What is it?" I asked, innocently enough. I sat at his side, but turned to face him, our knees touching now.

How long would we play this game?

"Allan." He stopped my hands, holding them firmly. "When you left me—" But then he stopped, holding something back from me.

"What is it?" I moved closer to him still.

"No," he said quietly, "I don't want to discuss the past, okay? That's not the point, but I need to let you know that if you...if we—"

I interrupted him with a kiss. "I know what you want to say, and I understand."

"Do you?" He leaned back, gently resisting me. "I've made my peace about why you left me and what it did to me, to my mind. I'm willing to never bring that part up. I'm willing to forgive you for not even giving me a few months to come clean to my wife, for bailing on me when I needed you the most, and hell, I'm even willing to forgive you for not even trying to make contact with me after my divorce."

"Oh and you did?" I scowled at him, my fever cooling fast. "And why did I leave exactly, Davinder? Huh? Because—"

"Oh, don't give me that...Okay, fine. I'm not gonna go there with you."

"No, you're already there. It'll never stop, see? There's always gonna be this… *blame* between us. We're always going to cut each other down, Davinder. Because even though you try to show me different, you're still very hurt or even angry about what—"

"That's not true." He bit his lip, looking away.

"Yes, it is. And you're right. Maybe I should have stayed and waited it out."

"Yeah? But maybe you just didn't *love* me enough." The sharpness of his words surprised me. Was that what he thought? He was on the brink of crying, holding everything down. "I needed four, five months maybe. Five months, Allan. We could have made something out of our lives."

"Dav," I said, holding his knees, "my sister asked me to leave. Do you understand? She threatened to tell your brother about us." I spoke these words as gently as I could, seeing his expression change from hurt to incredulity. "Elsie was scared she'd lose her family. The family she'd hoped for all of her life. And there was Fay to consider in this. I knew we'd be discovered eventually. It was a question of time, so when my sister told me you were still sleeping with Eileen and patching things up with her, I just—"

"You left because of Elsie and Fay?"

"No, I used that as an excuse." I looked down at my hands. So then, that was *my* truth, the very thing I'd tried to escape all these years—I'd convinced myself I'd left Montreal to spare my sister the pain and to protect my niece from the ugliness of a family scandal, but I'd been *running away*. "It was easier for me to tell myself it was out of sacrifice," I said. "When really, I was just too scared to love you and be loved by you. I have so many regrets."

"No, Allan, you can't think like that. Everything that happened, happened for a reason, and even in my darkest hours, I believed it. I needed to go through those years alone. I had to touch the bottom to kick back up."

"I wish I could have been with you through it all."

"You were, in some way, you were always there. In my thoughts, my dreams, my art. I used to swim my laps, pushing myself to do two more, hearing you in my mind."

"You're a different man," I said, touching his face. "But you're a better man."

He leaned his forehead on mine, as he used to do, and shivered. "You gotta tell me now…Do you still love me? And if you do, is your love as strong as it was?"

"Yes, Davinder."

"Allan, on my life, I'll never let anything or anyone get between us again."

Somehow I believed him fully. And with his promise came a new optimism I'd never allowed myself to entertain. It was a sense of *What if?* "So what happens now?"

"Now? Well, I don't know." I saw lust in his eyes. "Any ideas?"

I wanted to lie in bed naked with him. I wanted no sheets, no inhibitions, no secrets to come between my skin and his. I wanted to make love with him for as long as we could stand it.

I remembered our touches of long ago, and knew it would never be like it was between us.

"How I've longed for this," he said into my ear, pulling me close by the nape of my neck.

I was crazy for him.

No, it wouldn't be the same.

But it would be better.

❖

I opened my eyes and squinted, my face bathed in morning sunlight. I knew it must be past eleven. I glimpsed the digital clock on the nightstand—it was nearing noon.

I turned to my side and watched Davinder sleep. He was naked to the waist and I lay there enjoying the view. If I should look as good as he did at fifty-two years old, I'd never complain again.

Frowning, Davinder stirred a little and sighed. I flipped to my back and stared up at the ceiling.

Last night, we hadn't made love after all. We'd ended up lying next to each other in the dark, talking again. He was adamant about getting it right after all these years apart.

Of course, I'd lain there, slightly annoyed. I'd come to understand just how fantastic it would be to be with a man who knew who he was and what he wanted.

A man who could not be persuaded to compromise on things that were important to him.

I looked over at him again.

It all came back to me. I remembered everything: the first time I'd caught sight of his dark eyes, his know-it-all smile, our first time alone together, our long, heated talks, our secret meetings, the first time we'd touched each other, the pain and joy I felt around him then.

I remembered the night I'd watched him turn the corner of my street and the cold that seeped into me after he'd left me for good. That chill had stayed within my heart and soul for the last decade.

The sun filtered through my bedroom window, warming me, melting away the hurt and fear.

I turned to my side and gently touched a finger to Davinder's lips, feeling his breath on my fingertip. The years were gone—we'd never been apart. We were here, together, bound by something greater than I could explain, and when I leaned in to kiss his mouth, my heart pounded. I caressed his hair and kissed his chin, his neck, moving down to his collarbone, my hands gliding across his chest, my whole being calling him out of sleep.

I'd make love to him and bring him back from the place he'd been hiding. Or maybe I'd be the one to step inside that place and make it my home. That place I'd seen in his eyes from the very first instant we'd met—that secret life he lived in his mind. That garden I'd only glimpsed through ivy-laced gates.

"Davinder," I whispered, my fingers reaching his swollen dick, my heart ready to blow inside my chest, "wake up." *Wake up from the dream and experience it.* I stroked him, kissing his chest, the salt of his skin slowly intoxicating me. "You're mine." My lips burned on his stomach, lingering on the soft golden down below his navel. I held his hands in mine, across his thighs, and he groaned as he lifted his hips to my mouth. I looked down at his beautiful engorged dick, and as I took it all inside my mouth, deeply and slowly, he whispered my name, squeezing my hands, his thighs tightening under my chest, his hold on me becoming stronger and stronger. I climbed on top of him, fusing our bodies. My hands found his again, and I leaned over him, rocking my hips. As we fucked, his stare penetrated me deeper than his body ever could. There was a sweet pain searing through me, but I knew the pleasure would come if I let it. I leaned back, let go of his hands and remained still, barely moving at all. Davinder's eyes clouded with pleasure as he caressed my thighs and dick, stroking me now, watching me tense with the coming orgasm—it was coming, yes, and I rocked him faster, losing my breath, my self-control. I fought it but wanted it all at once.

"Baby," Davinder groaned, his whole body jerking under me. I shuddered, ejaculating on his stomach with a long shiver that stole a cry out of me.

I didn't move, but stayed, straddling him, with his softening dick still inside me. I stared down at the beautiful mess we'd made of each other, and the sun was on his face and in his eyes. When he smiled, I laughed. "That wasn't so bad, huh?"

Davinder playfully slapped my ass. "Stop it," he said, chuckling. "But I'll tell you this, Allan Waterhouse, forty definitely looks good on you."

"I'm gonna move now."

"Oh," he moaned as I did. "So soon?"

I wrapped the sheet around my waist. I needed a shower. But in the bedroom doorway, I stopped and turned back to look at him. "Will you tell me your plans now?"

"Yes."

"All right," I said, laughing again for no particular reason. "They better be good."

As I walked away, I heard him say, half to himself, "They are, but only if you say yes."

CHAPTER TWELVE

It was Sunday evening and Davinder was gone.

He'd left two hours ago, shortly after dinner. Tomorrow morning, he had to attend a meeting with the managing board of the crisis center he volunteered for. They were going to have to replace him shortly, and he was in charge of interviewing and training new volunteers on the help line.

I sat in the kitchen, looking at the sink full of dishes, the phone in my hand. I wanted to call my sister, but hadn't mustered the courage yet.

Davinder would have to be replaced at the crisis center. He'd be closing his art studio on Greene Street in the next few weeks, because he'd be leaving Montreal.

Forever.

I looked around my kitchen, seeing a room I'd never ever made my own. I'd bought this three-unit apartment building after I'd sold my duplex in Montreal, and moved into the third floor, renting out the two apartments below to students. This place was just a second income. I had no emotional attachment to it. I didn't particularly like it. It was my office during the day and a hotel at night. I slept here and worked here, period.

I'd lived in Toronto for ten years, but had yet to visit it really. I went from one place to the next, always taking the shortest possible route between A and B. The friends I'd made were all work related—editors, proofers, people I'd met during book signings or writer's conferences.

They knew Allan Waterhouse, the author, but they didn't know who I was as a man. I'd never let anyone close enough for that.

I had nothing here.

I took a deep breath and dialed Elsie's number.

"Allan?" she answered. "That's so weird, I was just thinking about calling you."

"How are you? How's Fay?"

"We're okay. We're all doing much better. I don't know, but when she came back from visiting you, she seemed calmer, happier, I think."

"We had a few good talks."

"Yeah, she told me." She paused. "I wanted to thank you for that, I've been meaning to call you."

"Don't thank me. I'm really glad Fay showed up here and it was very cathartic for all of us. I saw Noah again and...I just feel like maybe—"

"Everybody's been asking about you here."

"Yeah?" My heart fluttered a little. "And what do they say? Do you think maybe they'd be willing to see me again?"

"Yes, I think so."

"Dayton, too?"

"He's not angry with you anymore, Allan. I'm not sure he ever was. It was just such a confusing time for everybody."

"I miss everyone down there. Especially you, Elsie. And the kids."

"I've been telling Finn about you lately, showing him pictures... like maybe I knew you were coming home soon. Are you? Is that what—"

"No, I mean, yes, I want to come home for a visit and I want—"

"You're welcome to." She sounded like she was crying. Was she? "Anytime. I really do miss you, Allan."

I stared at the floor.

"So, how was your weekend with Davinder?" she asked.

I jumped a little. "Um, it was nice. Really nice."

"He called Dayton that day, before he drove out to Toronto. He wanted to ask for Dayton's forgiveness for the hurt he'd caused him. They were on the phone for a long time, and it did Dayton a lot of good.

He never really talked about it, but I think that Davinder not being open with him all their lives cut him deeper than he could admit."

"I can see that, yes."

God, I missed Davinder already. Talking about him only made it worse.

"Anyway, Dayton and him seem to be on the right track...He also asked Dayton for something else. Davinder wanted his blessing. Needed to know if you and he started a new life together, that he could still count on Dayton's love."

"Yeah?" I couldn't say anything else.

"And Dayton said he didn't need to ask for his blessing. That he'd paid his dues a long time ago and that he was proud of Davinder for what he'd done with his life. He told him it was about time he got out there and got some happy now."

"What do you think?" I whispered.

"I think my husband is a wise man with a heart of gold."

"Davinder and I are in love."

"I know."

"And I want to be with him."

"I know."

"I want you to be happy for me."

"Allan, I am."

"I don't blame you for asking me to end it ten years ago. You were right. He was married. It was impossible."

"That's the past. That's over now."

"He's built a solar house."

"I know, with his engineer friends from Germany."

"It's finished, and he's got a contract with the municipality to handle their educational and environmental marketing campaigns."

"It's very remote, Allan. Cut off from everything. An hour drive from a town of two thousand people, all around."

"He's got a permit to fish the river there and he's been teaching himself how to smoke meat and—"

"But it's so far," she said, her voice rising. "You'll both be working from the house, cooped up in that place for months and months, alone, with not a soul in sight. It'll be like a prison."

"No, *this* place is my prison. And what you're describing to me now sounds like heaven. Elsie, Davinder and I spent ten years apart... we've got a lot of catching up to do." I smiled, thinking of Davinder's eyes when he'd enthusiastically explained his plans for us this morning. After his divorce, he'd wisely kept his share of the funds from selling the house in the bank.

"What if something goes wrong up there?"

"It'll be fine, Elsie. It'll be beautiful." Davinder had schooled himself on solar power, plants, herbs, cooking and preserving goods, and he'd read every book he could find on alternative living. This idea had kept him sane and focused, and when he'd finally decided he would make it happen—he would live independently and self-sufficiently— he'd crushed out his last cigarette.

"And he wants to live there with you? He's a hundred percent sure?"

"Yes."

"And you want to live there with him?"

When he'd explained all this to me, I'd laughed a little. Did he really think he could show up again and convince me to leave my house, my friends, my whole life just because he believed it was "what we were meant to do"?

But Davinder had looked at me with those intelligent dark eyes of his and had said, simply, "Yes, Allan. We'll be so happy there."

We'll be so happy. There was nothing I wouldn't do for him. Yes, I'd pack my things and go off with him in some shack in the woods. Whatever. I had nothing to lose. I couldn't help laughing.

"What is it?" Elsie asked. "Why are you laughing?"

I'd write the very best book I could, and I'd do it there, in our little solar house, with nothing around me but trees—when was the last time I'd been surrounded by *trees* anyway?—and I'd probably look up at the window once in a while, catching sight of Davinder chopping wood, and I'd most probably shake my head as I was doing right now, laughing to myself.

But in the dead of the night, when he crawled into bed with me, and the only sound we heard was the wind rattling the leaves, or the rain tapping our roof, then, oh yes then, I'd know we were where we belonged.

"I'm gonna go up there with him, Elsie."

"Yeah, I thought you'd say that." There was a smile in her voice. "All right, I'm not gonna try to convince you otherwise, but can you at least stop by Montreal on your way there?"

I nodded, standing, looking around my kitchen again. I'd miss nothing of this. Nothing. "I'm gonna call him right now and see what the plan is."

She chuckled softly. "Now, can I tell *you* something?"

"What?"

"Dayton and I are expecting another baby."

"What? Oh, Elsie—"

"I know. I'm forty-three. It'll be twins, I'm sure of it. Big, blond twins. Boys, too. I can feel it."

"That's fantastic news," I said. "What does Dayton say?"

"First, he went very pale and didn't talk about it for two days, but now he's ecstatic and he says it's going to bring our family closer." I heard Finn's voice in the background. "I gotta go," Elsie said. "But we'll see each other soon, right?"

"I promise."

When we hung up, I stood in the middle of the kitchen. I didn't want to be here anymore. If I could have left tonight, I would have. But I needed to get a grip—there was still a lot to do and organize.

And there was Cameron.

I'd have to break this news to him gently.

CHAPTER THIRTEEN

Cameron lay in my arms, his face cradled in my neck.

It was Monday afternoon, and I'd invited him over to talk. When I'd first told him my plans to move, he'd reacted fairly well. But as the truth of it had sunk into him, he'd turned on me. Soon enough, he was crying and throwing couch pillows at me.

When I'd reached out to hug him, he'd run for my bedroom and slammed the door. I'd sat on the edge of the bed. He'd pulled on my clothes and kissed me.

I'd kissed him, finally calming him down, and now we were lying together, waiting for the tide to recede.

"You're the only man that I've ever freakin' loved." Cameron sniffled. "I mean, I didn't think that I loved you, really loved you, until now."

"Do you trust me?" I stroked his hair. "Do you believe in me?"

"Yeah, Allan, all the time."

"Okay, so listen to me now. It'll pass…this thing you feel for me, it'll pass. It's not what you think it is. It's you needing someone to care about you, care that you're alive, that you exist."

"You're saying I need a father figure, and you're so wrong."

"I'm saying you need attention and affection."

"That's love."

"No, Cameron. That's not love. Love is different than that. I can't explain it to you. But you'll get it." I kissed his forehead. "You'll get it."

"I don't want to be with Brian."

"Then don't be with him."

"Who's gonna make sure I do things right and not fuck up?"

"You will."

Cameron shook his head against me. "I don't want to be a waiter all my life."

"Then don't be." I made him look at me. "Do you understand what I'm saying to you? Just because your parents stopped caring doesn't make you unworthy of their love. And you don't have to be a child for the rest of your life. You can—"

"I don't want to talk about it."

"You know," I said, "you're lucky. You're still so young, so very young."

"You're only forty."

"No, I feel much older than that, Cam. But that's okay. We've all got our path to travel, and I've traveled down mine alone for a long time. What I mean is, you've got so much ahead of you, and if you choose to survive your past, no matter how much hurt is buried there, you can break free."

Finally, he glanced up at me. "I don't want to lose you, Allan. Ever. I don't want you to become another ghost in my life."

"Never. Do you hear me? Never. I'll keep you close. Always."

"When are you leaving? You have to sell this place and—"

"Davinder got me an agent and it'll be done while I'm gone."

"But your stuff and—"

"He said I only need my clothes, my books, and a typewriter."

"You won't have a computer?"

"No, not for a while. He's working on Internet access." I pinched his arm. "It's a little crazy, huh?"

"A little?"

"But it feels so right, Cam. So right."

He sat up, tousling his hair. "Damn, there's nothing I can say to keep you here."

"I don't think you really want to anyway."

"To keep you here?" He seemed to think about that for a moment. "I guess you're right."

I took his hand in mine and squeezed it tight. "I'm going to

Montreal to visit my sister the day after tomorrow, and staying there
for a few days."

"And then?"

"I don't know…It's up to Davinder. He's up north, tying up the
loose ends, getting everything ready."

"He's quite the man," Cameron said without a trace of bitterness.
"I'm glad you opened that letter."

I smiled. "Shit, yeah."

"You're gonna write another book?"

"Yes, I think so."

"What will it be about? I think you should write yours and
Davinder's story."

No, our story couldn't be written. It had only just begun.

"I'm not sure yet," I said. "But once I'm up there, I'm going to
have a lot of time to think."

He laughed. "Well, make sure you don't grow a beard and carry
an axe." Cameron would be all right. Besides, I'd always make sure
he was. This time around, I wouldn't abandon anyone to save my own
skin.

"Are you nervous about seeing your sister and Dayton?"

"Yeah, a little."

Cameron's eyes widened and he clapped his hands. "I got an
idea." He climbed out of bed and went to my closet. "I saw this on
a show once…see, all these letters, they're keeping you attached to
those mistakes you feel you made. They're reminding you of it and it's
almost like…Well, remember when we met? I could see those letters on
you. Do you know what I mean?"

"I guess so, yeah."

He pulled the box out and opened it. "You should burn them,
Allan. Every one of them." He picked a pile up. "All these words…
what do they really mean now?"

I knew all of them by heart. I rose and stooped by the box, looking
into it. "I held on to them for a long time, didn't I?"

"Burn them." Cameron grabbed the box and left the room. "On the
balcony. We'll make a little bonfire. I'll get the scotch and soda."

And we did. We sat around a pasta pot, watching the flames turn
those letters to embers. Wrapped in a blanket, drinking our scotch, we

waited until the ashes cooled, and as the sun began to set, Cameron got up and collected the pot. "There," he said, "you've been cleansed." He looked down at me, the blanket hanging off his shoulders, the wind blowing through his hair, his eyes reddened by the cold, and threw some of the ashes on me. "Go, my child, the demons are no more." Ceremoniously, he turned away, swinging the blanket over his shoulder like a cloak, and called out to me. "Come inside and make me something to eat!"

We had dinner together. When we were done, I watched him walk down my front stairs and then down my street.

Would I see him again?

Yes, I would. And when I did come across his lovely face once more, he would be a different man.

Chapter Fourteen

F inn gently set his clarinet down and shrugged. "That's all I have." He'd played *Furioso* for me. He was still struggling with the instrument, Elsie said, but he'd only been playing for four months. "That's really good." I'd only been in my sister's house for an hour, and I was still uneasy. As soon as I'd arrived, Finn had been eager to tell me all about his school projects and had taken me to his bedroom to show me his Smurf collection. I'd been pleasantly surprised at his enthusiasm. He was nothing like his big sister Fay. He was outgoing and trusting, always smiling. He was tall and lean, with a head full of strawberry-blond hair. He was a good-looking kid.

"Would you like another cup?" Elsie picked up my coffee. "Or maybe—"

The door opened and Fay came running in. "You're here!" She hugged me before I could even get up. "That's so cool."

"Hey, how are you?" I was looking at her with amazement. She'd cut her bangs and dyed her hair back to her natural color. She had little or no makeup on. "Look at you. Where you coming in from?"

"She had an information session." Elsie pulled on Fay's ponytail. "At Dawson Cegep."

"I see."

"Don't get too excited," Fay said, falling into the couch. "I'm only checking my options for the spring semester, that's all."

Elsie winked at me. Dayton walked in, and I froze. I knew he'd be home soon and was preparing for it, but hearing his voice brought a rush of memories. I didn't feel up to turning around.

"Allan, hi."

I could almost see him looking down at me from my sister's balcony all those years ago. I rose and turned around. He looked great. Married life had treated him exceedingly well. Perhaps what they said about married men living healthier lives was true. I held out my hand to him and smiled nervously. "Dayton, wow, hi," I muttered, shaking his hand. His grip tightened around my fingers. He pumped my hand vigorously.

"It's good to see you," he said, grabbing my wrist with his free hand, shaking me all over.

"Dad," Finn was pulling on Dayton's arm, "did you get it?" He was already snooping around in his dad's coat pockets. "Did you?"

"Yeah, yeah, of course I got it." Dayton reached into his back pocket and produced a small plastic square, which sent Finn into near hysterics. As the boy jumped up and down with excitement, Dayton was all smiles. "He's wanted this for a while."

"I can see that."

Finn shot up the stairs. "I'm gonna go play with it now!"

There was a bit of an uncomfortable silence, but Elsie and Fay struck up a conversation about one of Fay's friends whom Elsie had seen at the mall, and while they discussed the girl's latest provocative attire, Dayton and I listened. Elsie and Fay were quite something when they were worked up. They were both hilarious and seemed to feed off each other. Mother and daughter shared the same warped sense of humor.

"Once they get started on that poor girl," Dayton said, sitting back, "they never stop."

I'd returned to my seat. The house had changed, the kids had grown, Dayton and Elsie were expecting another baby.

Was this the point in my life where the tracks would meet? Fay got up and gestured for me to follow her.

"Where are you guys going?" Elsie asked.

"I wanna show Uncle Allan something."

"Allan, you're staying for supper, right?" Elsie looked over at Dayton, and I detected a slight tremor in her features. They hadn't discussed this prior to my arrival?

"No, I'm meeting a friend," I lied. "I haven't seen her in a while and I promised—"

"That's too bad," Dayton said. "I thought the plan was for you to stay for dinner."

"Yeah, Uncle Allan," Fay chimed in, "call this girl and reschedule."

"Yeah, I could that. I mean, if I'm not—"

"Good. I'll get on supper right now." Dayton rose out of his chair. I could see that he was tired. The man worked hard every day.

"I'd love to help with supper."

"Yeah?" Dayton stopped short in his tracks. He rubbed his hair, looking at me. "All right, yeah, sure, why not."

I smiled. "I'll be right there," I said as Fay pulled me up the stairs, clutching my arm. We passed Finn's room. He sat on his bed, his little fingers racing over a portable game console.

Fay led me to her room and cracked the door open. "It's a little messy, but I've been busy."

We stepped into what looked liked the bottom of a Pepto-Bismol bottle. I couldn't have guessed a person could love pink this much. Aside from some posters, the rest of the bedroom could have been that of a four-year-old pageant queen. There was even a tiara on one of the plushy golden bears sitting atop her bed.

"Wow," I said, trying not to laugh. "It's very—"

"Yeah, I know." She sighed, looking around the room dejectedly. "I've been meaning to perk it up."

"Perk it up?" This time, I laughed. "This room is one perk away from a heart attack."

Fay squinted at me.

"What did you want to show me?"

She spun around and went rummaging through her top drawer. "It's nothing spectacular or anything, just a little something I wanted to give you." She pulled something out and stood there with the object hidden behind her back. "I figured you didn't have one of these."

What could she possibly mean?

"Remember Mom's wedding? Well, she let Noah and me run around and snap pictures with her digital camera, and last week, I came across the old files on her computer, and guess what I found?" She handed me the framed picture before I could answer.

I looked down at it and saw me and Davinder sitting at the bar together. We'd put our heads close together, not close enough to attract attention, and his arm was halfway wrapped around my shoulder, but in such a way that we seemed to be goofing around. Two brothers-in-law posing for a picture.

I stared at the picture, remembering that night, my sister and Dayton's wedding reception, Fay and Noah chasing fireflies...and Davinder's confession in the courtyard.

How I'd believed we would be together from that night on.

"It's yours if you want it." Fay touched my hand. "Are you okay?"

I tore my eyes away from our young faces and looked up at her. "Thank you," I whispered. "Not just for the picture. But for being you. For being so wonderful. For still loving me."

"Oh, Uncle Allan," she cried, throwing her arms around my shoulders, "I do love you and I've been doing a lot of thinking lately, remembering how you took care of me and Mom and all of the things you did for me."

"So we're okay, then?" I pulled back. "Can we start again, you and me?"

"Yes, right now. Today." She laughed and swung my arm as she used to do as a little girl. "After dinner, I wanna show you my dance recitals. From when I was twelve up to last year." She pulled me out of her room and shut the door. "And after that, I wanna show you my grad book."

As we went down the stairs, she added more and more activities to the evening's agenda.

I wasn't going anywhere, and that was fine with me.

Davinder was at "our house," as we now referred to it, and wouldn't be coming into Montreal until the end of the week.

I missed him.

I went to the entrance and found my coat. I looked at the framed picture in my hand again and touched a fingertip to Davinder's face.

From behind the kitchen swinging doors, and over the sound of clanking pots and pans, I heard Elsie and Dayton. They'd started on dinner.

I looked around their living room.

Maybe this wasn't all that unfamiliar. Maybe in some way I'd been with them all along. And maybe this was exactly where I was supposed to be today, in this very spot, in this very moment.

I slipped the picture into my coat pocket.

Whatever lay in front of me now, whatever other dreams would come, I'd chase and live them with Davinder. In our home, in our own secret garden he'd built for us, we'd savor every moment and enjoy each second.

It was ours now, all of it, and we'd walk through those gates and never look back.

I went to the window and peered through the blinds, seeing the first signs of spring. I could feel it all the way down into my bones—a change was coming.

I'd embrace it this time.

And maybe, just maybe, up there, lost somewhere in those woods, with nothing but our will and love to sustain us, Davinder and I would be always and forever...

Young.

EPILOGUE

The firewood was slowly dying in the fireplace, and with effort, I set my red pen and latest manuscript down beside me and rose from my chair. I picked up a log and tried to pry open the fire screen. The thing was old and stubborn, so I jiggled it hard, holding on to the log with the other hand.

"What are you doing? Let me do that." Davinder grabbed the log out of my hand. "And it's hot in here. We don't need more heat."

"I'm freezing my ass off."

"Where's your blanket?"

"Hanging outside for two days. It's still wet."

"Because it's been raining."

"And you said you'd take it in."

"All right." Swiftly, he pried open the screen and placed the log in the flames.

How did he manage to do everything with such ease, when I had arthritis in every one of my joints and found it difficult to move around in here?

Davinder said it was in one's head. This age thing. Every morning, I watched him climb out of bed and tie up his running shoes, and then off he went for his daily walk. Yet lately, he'd returned from those walks more and more winded.

"Are you done for the night?" he asked me, looking down at my manuscript.

I wasn't, but I knew he hoped I was. In the last thirty years, we'd never gone to bed alone, no matter what preoccupations one of us might have. It was one of our golden rules. "I'll finish up tomorrow," I said, flicking off the reading lamp. "You're tired, huh?"

He'd spent the day hacking off some of the bothersome shrubs along our property and closing up the garden. Fall was just around the corner and it was time to prepare for winter.

I wasn't very enthused about spending another winter here. Every year, it got more and more difficult for us to get through it, even with our family's help. Our grandkids loved spending time up here with us, and all of them brought us a touch of magic and youth every time they visited, but aside from that, we were still very alone, and I was afraid for Davinder. He pushed himself too much. He'd had chest pains this year, had spent a week in the hospital, but he was as stubborn as that damn fire screen and still had a one-track mind. He refused to let anyone cut our wood, and if any of our town friends offered to help with anything, he'd always smile and accept, but then when they came driving up to our property, he'd pretend he couldn't remember mentioning any such thing.

"We got Miranda's wedding invitation."

Miranda was Fay's oldest daughter.

"Yes, I saw that." I walked off to the bedroom, my back sore and stiff from sitting in that awful chair for too long. "It's next month. Noah said he'd drive us."

"Why would he do that?" Davinder followed me into our bedroom and helped me with the buttons on my sweater. "I'm perfectly capable of driving down to Montreal. Snow won't come for another six weeks—"

"Old man, you need a wake-up call."

"Old man?" He smiled, rubbing my bald spot. "Hey, at least I still got all my hair." He pulled the sweater over my head and gently set it on the dresser. Davinder had built that dresser, ten—no, *twenty* years ago. On my fiftieth birthday. This whole bedroom set. Oak. Solid as he was. "Beside, Noah's busy."

Noah didn't come up here often. He'd recently gone through a nasty divorce and was in the midst of a custody battle.

"Or Cameron could come up. He and Marco were thinking of taking a little holiday and—"

"No, Allan, I'm driving us there or we're not going at all."

"You'd miss your own grandchild's wedding because of your pride?" I tried to make eye contact with him, but he was dodging my stare. "Davinder, what's eating you lately?"

He grumbled something I didn't catch and began stripping back the blankets and sheets.

I went to him and touched his arm. "Are you angry with me?"

When he turned to look at me, I saw his eyes were wet.

"What's wrong? Don't you feel right? Do you want me to call the doctor?"

"I'm fine," he said, softly, sitting on the edge of the bed, looking at the floor. "I just don't want anyone to drive us to the wedding, that's all."

I sat by him and took his hand in mine. I'd held that hand for thirty years, but tonight, in this moment, it felt quite new to me. His skin was soft, and his fingers, still very straight and elegant. How could he do everything he'd done around this place and keep his hands so young? I looked at his profile, his chin, nose, dismissing the creases in his neck, the dark speckles on his cheeks and forehead, his thinning hair. I saw only his mouth—the mouth I'd kissed a million times or more, and his eyes, those dark eyes that had seduced me all those years ago.

I kissed his cheek, very close to his lips, softly, so softly.

He turned his face to mine, surprised.

Desire stirred deep inside me and I kissed him again, this time on that supple mouth of his, and moved closer to him, holding his neck in my trembling hand. "Okay, Davinder," I whispered, still kissing him, "you'll drive us there if that's what you want."

He touched my face, leaning his forehead on mine. I looked into his eyes, my heart beating hard and steady in my weathered body, my mind playing me back the first time he'd kissed me, in his kitchen, when both of us had been young and hungry men.

"We've had a good run," Davinder said, his forehead still pressed against mine. "But we're not finished."

"No, Davinder, we're not finished."

He released me and stretched out. "Come on. Come lie down with me." He seemed so tired tonight.

I turned the light off at my side and pulled the blankets over us.

"Good night," I said, reaching for his hand under the sheet. "I love you."

"I love you, too." He turned to his side, wrapping my arm around him.

Outside, the rain tapped our roof and I closed my eyes, listening to the familiar sounds that had made up my nights for the last thirty years. The rain or wind, and always, Davinder breathing slowly and deeply next to me.

That night, I dreamt I was lost, wandering through our woods, fearing I'd never get out. No matter which way I took, I always ended up at the very same place, but just when I began to despair, the moon shone through the black trees, showing me the silhouette of a man, his face hidden in the shadows.

I called out to him, and with a hand gesture, the man beckoned me forth.

I made my way to him through the darkness.

As I came upon him, he stepped out of the shadows and smiled. It was Davinder. Young and handsome, his dark hair slicked back and his eyes glimmering with humor. "You're here," he said, taking my hand.

I looked down at our hands and couldn't recognize my own. It was strong and smooth.

"Where are we?"

Davinder pushed on the gates, and I realized it was daytime now…I hadn't seen those gates in the darkness. The sun beamed down on us, lacing Davinder's hair with amber.

"Am I dreaming?"

Davinder turned around, holding out his hand to me. The sun was in his eyes and I struggled to see his expression.

"Where are we going?" I asked, staying back, unable to move. I couldn't follow him. Not where he was going. Something held me back.

I stood, frozen, watching him walk farther and farther away from me. "Davinder, wait," I screamed out, panic thundering through me. "Don't go on without me!"

A flock of birds fitted across the sky and I looked up to see them zoom through the blue horizon. When I looked back at the gates,

Davinder had reached the far end of the road, and I called out to him again. "Baby, wait for me!"

For a moment, he stood still, watching me. I took a step forward, but heard him say, "No, Allan."

"Davinder!" I shouted until my voice broke. "Davinder, wait, my love!"

But he only smiled again and blew me a kiss.

About the Author

Mel Bossa is the author of many novels and short stories. She lives in Montreal with her partner and their three children. She volunteers for a crisis center, where she learns about herself and others every time she answers the help line. She wrote her first story through a Ouija board in an attempt to convince her friends spirits exist, and since then, she has never been able to put those voices to rest. She still believes books, especially books about queer men and women, can change our world.

Books Available From Bold Strokes Books

In His Secret Life by Mel Bossa. The only man Allan wants is the one he can't have. (978-1-60282-875-9)

The Moon's Deep Circle by David Holly. Tip Trencher wants to find out what happened to his long-lost brothers, but what he finds is a sizzling circle of gay sex and pagan ritual. (978-1-60282-870-4)

Straight Boy Roommate by Kevin Troughton. Tom isn't expecting much from his first term at University, but a chance encounter with straight boy Dan catapults him into an extraordinary, wild weekend of sex and self-discovery, which turns his life upside down, and leads him into his first love affair. (978-1-60282-782-0)

Raising Hell: Demonic Gay Erotica, edited by Todd Gregory. Hot stories of gay erotica featuring demons. (978-1-60282-768-4)

Pursued by Joel Gomez-Dossi. Openly gay college student Jamie Bradford becomes romantically involved with two men at the same time, and his hell begins when one of his boyfriends becomes intent on killing him. (978-1-60282-769-1)

Timothy by Greg Herren. Timothy is a romantic suspense thriller from award-winning mystery writer Greg Herren set in the fabulous Hamptons. (978-1-60282-760-8)

In Stone by Jeremy Jordan King. A young New Yorker is rescued from a hate crime by a mysterious someone who turns out to be more of a something. (978-1-60282-761-5)

The Jesus Injection by Eric Andrews-Katz. Murderous statues, demented drag queens, political bombings, ex-gay ministries, espionage, and romance are all in a day's work for a top secret agent. But the gloves are off when Agent Buck 98 comes up against the Jesus Injection. (978-1-60282-762-2)

Combustion by Daniel W. Kelly. Bearish detective Deck Waxer comes to the city of Kremfort Cove to investigate why the hottest men in town are bursting into flames in broad daylight. (978-1-60282-763-9)

Night Shadows: Queer Horror edited by Greg Herren and J.M. Redmann. *Night Shadows* features delightfully wicked stories by some of the biggest names in queer publishing. (978-1-60282-751-6)

Wyatt: Doc Holliday's Account of an Intimate Friendship by Dale Chase. Erotica writer Dale Chase takes the remarkable friendship between Wyatt Earp, upright lawman, and Doc Holliday, Southern gentlemen turned gambler and killer, to an entirely new level: hot! (978-1-60282-755-4)

Secret Societies by William Holden. An outcast hustler, his unlikely "mother," his faithless lovers, and his religious persecutors—all in 1726. (978-1-60282-752-3)

The Jetsetters by David-Matthew Barnes. As rock band the Jetsetters skyrocket from obscurity to superstardom, Justin Holt, a lonely barista, and Diego Delgado, the band's guitarist, fight with everything they have to stay together, despite the chaos and fame. (978-1-60282-745-5)

Strange Bedfellows by Rob Byrnes. Partners in life and crime, Grant Lambert and Chase LaMarca are hired to make a politician's compromising photo disappear, but what should be an easy job quickly spins out of control. (978-1-60282-746-2)

Fontana by Joshua Martino. Fame, obsession, and vengeance collide in a novel that asks: What if America's greatest hero was gay? (978-1-60282-675-5)

The Dirty Diner: Gay Erotica on the Menu, edited by Jerry L. Wheeler. Gay erotica set in restaurants, featuring food, sex, and men—could you really ask for anything more? (978-1-60282-677-9)

Sweat: Gay Jock Erotica by Todd Gregory. Sizzling tales of smoking-hot sex with the athletic studs everyone fantasizes about. (978-1-60282-669-4)

The Marrying Kind by Ken O'Neill. Just when successful wedding planner Adam More decides to protest inequality by quitting the business and boycotting marriage entirely, his only sibling announces her engagement. (978-1-60282-670-0)excited year-round. (978-1-60282-665-6)